A LIFE IMAGINED

Sydney Rutherford

Published by Black Hat Publications

ISBN: 978-1-0670159-4-7

For The Three.
Sorry and thank you.

1

Aldéric Pierre's estate was located deep in the southern French countryside, about a half hour's drive from the city of Avignon. The château itself was set back from the road, down a long driveway lined with pencil pines. It stood an imposing three stories tall, and each of the fourteen windows on the building's facade was flanked by mint-green shutters. The man's father, Aldéric Pierre Sr., was a well-regarded collector of historic European artifacts. He'd also recently keeled over at the ripe old age of ninety-six. His family's loss was an artful dealer's gain.

Elise gave a low whistle from the passenger seat as Mathias pulled the car up outside the entrance to the château. A man in a black suit and white gloves pushed open one of the large wooden doors and made his way over to greet them as they emerged from the car.

"Welcome to the Pierre estate," he said with a short bow. "Monsieur Pierre will meet you in the east wing." He gestured for them to follow him inside.

"Eighteenth century," Elise marveled as they walked up the stone steps, through an archway carved with cherubs, and into the cavernous entrance hall. The butler led them along a corridor paneled in rich-brown oak and dotted with decorative sconces. "You can tell by the gold leaf gilding."

It had been about eighteen months since Mathias had poached Elise Dumont from the Louvre's curatorial staff to work as his appraiser. Short and slight, with a shock of bright-blond hair cut close to her head, she had an enthusiasm for the job that knew no bounds. She pushed her wire-rimmed glasses farther up her nose and moved closer to inspect the details of a bronze-framed painting at the end of the corridor.

Mathias was less impressed. He found elaborate displays of wealth tacky, a crude attempt at exhibiting status that belonged to another era. And he was tired. This was their final stop on a weeklong tour of high-profile auctions across the country, and he was itching to get back to Calais.

They passed into another vestibule that split off to several closed rooms. They were met by a harried-looking man with salt-and-pepper hair, wearing an expensive cashmere cardigan. Mathias assumed this was Monsieur Pierre.

"Thank you for coming." Pierre's voice was soft and breathy, and his fingers fiddled with a stack of papers he held against his chest. "The classical paintings can be found in the ballroom across the hall, but we've assembled the more eclectic pieces from my father's collection in here." He gestured toward one of the closed doors and turned to Mathias. "As I mentioned over the phone, he had a... unique taste in antiques." Pierre's eyes darted to Mathias's face. He handed Mathias an itemized list of numbers corresponding to a series of different pieces. "You're welcome to mark down the ones you'd like to bid on. The auction will take place this afternoon at three."

The butler pulled open the door to the room Pierre had indicated, and Mathias and Elise stepped inside. The sizable sitting room had been converted into a makeshift exhibition area, but that wasn't the first thing Mathias noticed. Instead, he found his attention drawn to the large swastika banner draped across the back wall. Several display tables were laid out with an array of Third Reich paraphernalia—silverware, cigar boxes, and even comic books featuring a sprightly blond boy with a red armband.

Beside him, Elise gave a snort. "Any clients on the books with a penchant for Nazi memorabilia?"

Mathias picked up a framed photo of the führer himself, frowned, and placed it back down. *Can't swing a cat in Europe without hitting some old man's Nazi collection.*

"Maybe we'll find a Luger in all this junk." Elise began hunting through the pieces strewn across the tables.

Mathias's gaze fell on the spine of a red hardback book partly buried beneath a stack of propaganda pamphlets. He picked it up, recognizing the title. The paperback version appeared periodically on Rayan's nightstand, its page corners folded down in different places as he dipped in and out of the story. Rayan often read several books at once, and their presence around the house was a strange comfort, confirmation that all was well in the man's world. Mathias opened the cover to see the book bore its original 1942 publication date.

"Well, that's ironic," Elise commented, appearing at his side and peering at the title. "Published during the occupation. I'm pretty sure Camus was a bit of a hero in anti-Nazi circles. Must've made it in here by mistake."

Mathias closed the book with a snap. "We're done here," he instructed Elise and turned toward the door, his appraiser at his heels.

Monsieur Pierre seemed surprised to see them back in the vestibule so soon. "I was told you had somewhat of a particular clientele," he protested.

"Not that particular," Mathias countered.

He wasn't in the habit of profiting off the regime of a racist dictator, no matter how lucrative the market might be. That was the beauty of this business—he could pick and choose what he wanted to buy and whom he wanted to sell it to. Even then, he often withdrew an offer or withheld a much-anticipated piece from a bothersome client just because he could. These aristocratic elites, with more money than they could shake a stick at, weren't accustomed to being told no. So Mathias made it a point to give them an education.

"But I will take this," he said, holding out the book.

"You'll have to register your interest at the auction this afternoon."

"Or I can take it now for eight hundred euros."

Pierre's mouth turned down in a look of dissatisfaction. "That's not really how this works."

"Isn't it?" Mathias asked, arching an eyebrow. "In addition to his impressive shrine to Hitler, I heard your old man also collected his fair share of debts. You're going to have to shift a lot of fascist cutlery to make a dent in that."

Pierre flushed red. "Now, hold on—"

"Good luck." Mathias shoved the book into Pierre's hands and continued back along the corridor the way they'd come.

Once outside, he walked over to the car and pulled out his cigarettes. He lit one and took a much-needed drag. A few minutes later, he heard the approaching click of Elise's heels as she descended the stone steps to join him. She held out the book, and he took it with a smirk, offering the pack to her in exchange.

"You owe me eight hundred euros," she said, taking it from him and tapping out a smoke.

"You couldn't even bring him down?" Mathias scoffed. "Some use you are."

"Hey, I'm just here to establish provenance. Negotiation is your forte." Elise placed the cigarette between her teeth and handed him back the pack. Mathias retrieved the lighter from his pocket and reached over to light it for her. "I wanted to see the paintings," she complained.

"I've seen enough fucking paintings," Mathias grumbled, tapping his ash and watching as it fluttered down to the cobblestones beneath their feet.

"I don't know if anyone's told you this, but you come off as a little intimidating," Elise said, squinting against the midday sun as she sucked on her cigarette.

"I can't imagine why."

She gave a short laugh. "Your call, Chief. Shall we head home, then? I miss my own bed."

Mathias took another pull and let the smoke curl from the corner of his mouth. His mind reached back to the white brick house and the sun-drenched warmth of the upstairs bedroom. He didn't miss his own bed so much as who he'd find in it.

Rayan stared at the open book in his hand. The mesh curtains drawn across the open window in the bedroom stirred in the late-afternoon breeze. Beyond the window was the glittering blue gateway to the North Sea. He went over the passage he'd read moments before, and it made even less sense. Flipping back to the previous page, he skimmed the text only to find that none of it registered. He gave a frustrated sigh and leaned back against the headboard. Beside him, the bed remained undisturbed, as it had for the past week.

Mathias was traveling through Southern France for several days on a procurement trip. It wasn't uncommon—he often flew to places like Vienna and Madrid to make acquisitions or consult with clients looking to obtain a specific piece. Travel came with the territory, but that didn't make Mathias's absence any more tolerable.

The house loomed large without him, a silence filling the hallways and empty rooms. Rayan hadn't realized how much he'd come to rely on Mathias's daily presence in his life. His touch like an electric charge. Without it, Rayan hummed with unmet desire, making him aimless and easily distracted.

He'd done well, considering. He kept himself busy working at the center and out in the camp. The situation in Calais had worsened, and the growing needs of the seemingly endless stream of refugees arriving in the city had resulted in local officials withdrawing their support. It made charitable organizations like the Calais Center for New Migrants even more necessary as they found themselves on the front lines of a crisis the establishment no longer wanted any part of.

Rayan tossed the book aside and reached beneath the waistband of his sweats. He didn't have to mope—he was quite capable of meeting his own needs. He'd just found that, with Mathias around, he rarely had to.

Rayan closed his eyes and eased into the warm wave of building pleasure—gradual, familiar—and his cock responded accordingly. He knew whose hand he'd prefer in place of his own. Mathias liked to palm the head of Rayan's cock while squeezing the root, pushing him forward and pulling him back. He'd press his mouth to Rayan's ear, speaking in a measured voice, as he stripped away Rayan's composure one languid stroke at a time: "You want me to fuck you, don't you? That's what you're lying here thinking about. Say it. I can't hear you."

Rayan loved when snatches of the man's sadistic side flickered through. Mathias knew when he flexed his particular brand of control, Rayan was putty in his hands.

He heard the floorboards creak on the landing, and he froze, his eyes flying open. Mathias stood in the doorway to the bedroom, a smirk pulling at his lips as he stared down at Rayan on the bed. He wasn't due back until the next day.

"Don't stop on my account." Mathias dropped his bag to the floor and walked into the room. He lowered himself into the chair across from the bed, arms draped leisurely over the armrests, his eyes glittering. "Go on."

Rayan's stomach lurched, and a flush of embarrassment rose to his cheeks, but it was swallowed by an even more powerful surge of arousal. He began to move his hand again, deliberate, slow, lowering his gaze to avoid the imposing sight of Mathias as he watched him.

"Look at me," Mathias instructed sharply—his voice from before, that other life.

Rayan's eyes snapped to his, and he groaned as his desire leapt forward, his cock straining in his fist, fighting for release.

"Good boy."

Mathias's face betrayed nothing as Rayan began to fall apart beneath his gaze, desperate to look away and at the same time not wanting to miss a second. Mathias's eyes fixed him to the spot, exposing him, Rayan's pleasure bared for all to see. Rayan felt the crest of his release, a crackle of lightning that curled his toes, and gave a short grunt as he pulled up his T-shirt and shot across his bare stomach.

Breathing hard, he waited for the spots to leave his vision before using the hem of his shirt to swipe away the mess. He rolled off the bed, somewhat unsteady, moved toward Mathias, and knelt before him. Those piercing gray eyes lowered to Rayan's face. He slid his palms along Mathias's thighs to his belt, which he unbuckled then moved to unzip his slacks, the fabric stretched against the thick swell of his cock. Rayan took him into his hand, and a shiver ran down his spine. Mathias was rock-hard.

"Welcome home," Rayan said.

Mathias's lips parted, the lust filling his pupils, before Rayan blessedly took the man into his mouth.

2

"And this?" Mathias lifted Rayan's fingers from his lips and pressed them to his neck.

"*Raqaba.*"

"How about this?" Mathias guided his hand beneath the bedcovers.

Rayan smirked. "My mother only used a diminutive."

"There's nothing diminutive about it."

"That's true," Rayan murmured appreciatively, ducking his head to kiss the line of Mathias's jaw. "But she had two boys and was painfully modest, so we never used the proper word."

His Arabic had vastly improved over the past year and a half. Strange how much of the language was set in context. Rayan had known how to speak it within the confines of conversations he'd had at home with his mother, only to discover that his understanding of the world was limited to a child's vocabulary. In some ways, he was learning the language all over again, and he felt a quiet pride in reclaiming it.

They were languishing in bed the morning after Mathias had arrived home, catching up on each other. Rayan had begun to see a curve to the man's hard edges. Mathias took a reluctant pleasure in their shared intimacy and seemed content to simply lie there with him, limbs intertwined beneath the sheets. It filled a need that existed between the physicality of sex and the vulnerability of giving voice to his feelings.

A thin streak of sunlight from the gap in the curtains appeared on Mathias's cheek, and Rayan realized how late it was. "I have to go," Rayan said, disentangling himself from Mathias's warmth and getting up from bed. "I'm helping at the camp today."

"I don't see the urgency," Mathias grumbled, splaying his arms across the empty bed as Rayan dressed quickly. "It's not like they're going anywhere."

"We barely get to half the people who come by each day, and the service office's short on staff," Rayan said, pulling a sweater over his head. "Not everyone makes their own hours."

"You could if you wanted to. You just choose to let that insufferable couple dictate your schedule. Come work for me. I'll make up a job for you, pay you whatever you want. You only need to show up when you feel like it."

Rayan laughed. "Tempting." He reached over to grab his phone and wallet from the nightstand. "Why do you care what I do with my time?" The thought sent a flood of happiness through him.

Mathias caught his wrist and pulled Rayan down onto the bed. "I don't like to share." He kissed Rayan deeply, leaving him lightheaded when they finally broke apart. Mathias patted Rayan's cheek with his palm and pushed him away. "Fuck off, then. I've got things to do."

Rayan got to his feet with a grin. He lingered in the doorway, savoring the image of Mathias stretched out on the bed, before heading downstairs to catch the bus. Mathias had tried to strong-arm him into getting a car, but Rayan had little use for one, and he much preferred to walk. There were only a handful of places in the city he frequented, and those could all be accessed on foot or by public transport.

The camp itself, the largest migrant encampment in the area, was located on the site of a former landfill east of the Port of Calais. To get there, Rayan caught the bus to the ferry terminal and walked the remainder of the way. Aptly named the Jungle by locals and residents alike, the camp consisted of a sea of tents and makeshift shelters interspersed with the odd commercial venture. There were barbers, food stalls, and even a restaurant. Residents and aid workers had helped establish a library, a church, and several mosques—attempts to foster a sense of normalcy in a situation of extremes. Still, the place was sorely lacking in basic amenities, and there weren't nearly enough drinking water outlets and sanitary facilities for the sheer number of people living there.

Thousands of refugees had flocked to the Jungle within the past year, many of them attempting to cross into the United Kingdom, or waiting for their French asylum claims to be processed. They came from a myriad of places—Syria, Eritrea, Somalia, Iraq—and most had made the perilous journey to Europe across the Mediterranean Sea. While the stories were different, they were all linked by the common hope that leaving was safer than staying.

It had become apparent to Asmarina Moreau and her husband, Laurent—who ran the Calais Center for New Migrants—that to be of most use to the growing number of displaced people in the city, the organization needed to go to them. So they'd reduced the services available at the center and set up a portable generator-powered cabin within the camp itself. The service office, as they called it, provided a place for residents to access legal and immigration aid, charge their phones, and queue for food bundles and personal-hygiene packs that the local churches put together for them to distribute. Rayan still occasionally taught language courses at the center in town, but more often than not, he was stationed out in the Jungle.

When he arrived at the service office that morning, a line had already formed at the entrance to the cabin and snaked several meters through the camp. Asmarina was seated at one of the tables inside, helping a woman with one child strapped to her back and another playing at her feet to fill out a series of forms in French.

The center was Asmarina's brainchild. Her family had emigrated to France from Eritrea when she was in middle school, and she'd spent the better part of her life navigating the divide between two different worlds. When she wasn't working, she spent every free moment coming up with ways to improve the situation of the people in the camp, many of whom were her fellow countrymen.

"There was another incident last night," she informed Rayan after he'd plucked his blue vest from the hook on the wall. The city had started requiring aid workers to wear them so they weren't unintentionally targeted by police. Which said a lot about how the authorities were handling things.

"The police were here this morning," Asmarina went on, adjusting the patterned scarf that held back her wavy dark hair. She turned away from the woman and lowered her voice. "A young girl was attacked. The bigger this place gets, the more dangerous it becomes."

The French government had initially tolerated the camp and arranged for a series of shipping containers to be placed on the northeastern side of the site to be used as temporary shelters. But it was clear that sentiment had begun to shift. There was a growing police presence around the camp, and they were becoming more hostile, lobbing cans of tear gas down from the nearby highway and carrying out impromptu raids. Rayan had heard rumors that these were intimidation tactics meant to deter people from coming. The government was afraid Calais would become a permanent magnet for migrants—a prospect shared by many local residents, who considered the Jungle both a safety hazard and a blight on the city's image as a quaint seaside holiday destination.

Rayan watched the child on the floor roll a fallen pencil back and forth across the threadbare carpet. "This isn't good enough. We need safer housing."

Asmarina's expression brightened. "On that, Laurent has something he wants to talk to you about. He's in the back."

At the far end of the cabin was a small storage room that Laurent used for an office. Inside, Rayan found the man flipping excitedly through a stack of papers with Karl Hakanen, a project coordinator for the national NGO, Groupe d'action, which had established itself in Calais in recent years. Laurent and Karl were good friends, often trading information and supplies while sharing an exasperation with the lackluster efforts of the city council.

Karl, a frequent face at the service office, greeted Rayan with a wide grin. "Rayan, have you grown?" he teased, stepping forward to grip Rayan's hand in his.

Karl was Finnish and stood at least a foot taller than him. He was missing two fingers on his right hand, an injury he'd told Rayan he sustained in a training slipup during his compulsory military service. Not one to be deterred, he'd completed his conscription then joined the Red Cross and bounced around Europe for a few years before settling with Groupe d'action. Calais had become home to a range of aid groups, local and international, larger organizations brushing shoulders with the likes of homegrown initiatives like theirs.

Laurent beckoned him over. "Come have a look. I just got the renderings back."

Rayan leaned over and picked up the top sheet from a pile of drawings on the desk. Months before, he and Laurent had been tossing around ideas, frustrated with the lack of progress as officials handed the problem back and forth like a hot potato. They'd discussed the feasibility of building a targeted housing facility to prioritize the most vulnerable refugees—women, children, and young families. The complex could then be converted into private residences should Calais ever find itself on the other side of this crisis. Laurent had suggested they reach out to other aid groups for funding, and he'd asked an architect friend to draft something they could take around with their proposal.

Rayan scanned the drawing in his hand. Here it was—everything they'd discussed. He smiled ruefully. The project was ambitious, far beyond the realm of their collective expertise, but Laurent wasn't easily deterred. He'd quit his job as a computer programmer to open the center at his wife's insistence after Asmarina had declared she could no longer stand around doing nothing.

"You're seriously thinking of giving this a shot?" Rayan asked.

Laurent grinned and combed his fingers through his graying beard. "I've already had Karl shop this around his team, and there's also been interest from a Belgian NGO that's looking to make use of some targeted government funding."

"What about Durand?" Rayan asked, addressing the elephant in the room.

Claude Durand had been mayor of Calais for almost two decades, and it was no secret he harbored little sympathy for the plight of his illegitimate constituents. He was politically conservative and well-liked by those in the city who cared more about property prices than the people who washed up on their pristine beaches.

"We've talked before about the importance of local buy-in," Karl cautioned. "Even if we do manage to secure financial backing, a project like this doesn't come cheap, and the city will need to help make up the difference. We'll have to get Durand involved one way or another."

"Karl wants us to present at the Groupe d'action offices next week," Laurent said. "To submit an official proposal for funding. I wanted to know if you'd consider coming along. This idea's as much yours as it is ours, and I think the board would benefit from hearing about the importance of the project, based on your experience."

Rayan doubted his perspective would have any influence on the decision, but with things as they stood, he was willing to try. "If you think it will help."

When Rayan returned to the cabin, he found Amer waiting at the front of the line. Amer was a regular at the service office. Cordial and well-spoken, he always greeted Rayan as though they were neighbors meeting on the street. He lived in a small shelter with his daughter and three grandchildren who had traveled together from Misrata.

From their brief conversations, Rayan had discovered Amer was a schoolteacher. The Jungle was full of skilled professionals from all manner of backgrounds—engineers, academics, mechanics. When he spoke with the people in the camp, he kept that at the front of his mind. Rayan knew what it was like to feel as if his intelligence and his personhood had vanished behind the face of poverty.

Amer approached him with a smile and inquired about his health, a question Rayan politely returned. The older man asked if there were any hygiene packs available, and Rayan took two down from the shelf and gathered a few additional toiletries, which he placed inside Amer's frayed fabric bag.

"Let me carry it for you, *sayyid*."

"No, no. Many thanks, young man," Amer said, threading the bag over his arm. "What a beautiful day we have been given. Wouldn't you agree?" He gestured toward the window at the cloudless blue sky that filled the pane, sunlight streaming through the glass.

It was a beautiful day. Rayan had failed to notice it, being preoccupied, as he always was when he came to the Jungle—unable to shake the feeling that the camp and its occupants lay in the path of an encroaching storm.

Mathias sat in the café across the street from the warehouse and placed a thick envelope of cash on the table before Charles Aubert. The man took it with an obliging nod and slipped it into his jacket without opening the seal. He knew Mathias well enough by now to know he wasn't a cheat.

"That couple in Brooklyn wouldn't stop raving about the painting. You should have seen their place—wall-to-wall art, bunch of yuppie collectors. They sent me on my way with a nice little tip." Charles took a swig from his cup of coffee, and his prominent Adam's apple bobbed as he swallowed. "One of my contacts in New York sent me back with a set of Roman Imperial coins. Do you do collectables at all? They've been promised to a dealer in Berlin, but I'm sure he'd be willing to entertain a better offer." He handed Mathias a sheet of paper with a series of thumbnail photographs.

Mathias was occasionally contacted by clients in North America who were after a particular piece. Charles operated an ad hoc cross-Atlantic delivery service that Mathias employed when the need arose. Of course, there was a reason Charles insisted on being paid in cash—Mathias knew an opportunist when he saw one.

It hadn't taken him long to exhaust the client list he'd inherited from the previous owner. He'd purchased the business from Renaud Caillouet, a longstanding member of the Calais upper crust who'd run it as a passion project after finding himself the sole beneficiary of an enormous family fortune. When a series of recessions saw interest in high-value art dry up, passion alone couldn't sustain the enterprise. Neither could the man's tendency to prop up dwindling profits with large sums of his own money. By the time Mathias bought the business, Caillouet had been trying to get rid of it for years.

There were several things he changed from the outset—the name, for one. He'd opted for an ironic nod to his Quebec origins: Importations Fleurdelisé. Then Mathias had gutted the old warehouse he'd convinced Caillouet to include in the sale and had it completely refurbished. After that, he'd set about aggressively culling the client list, many of whom were friends of the former owner and had only bought pieces out of a sense of obligation.

While Caillouet had operated exclusively in continental Europe, Mathias didn't see the sense in limiting himself logistically. He followed the money instead.

And it was amusing what Americans would pay for a thing simply because it was sourced in Europe.

"Funny thing, actually," Charles continued as Mathias passed him back the photos of ancient coins. "While I was stateside, I made a trip up north to shift something for a friend. You know how it is."

He gave a conspiratorial laugh. Mathias knew it wasn't just art and collectables that he was shifting. Charles clearly had his hand in other, more lucrative ventures.

"I was surprised to discover you two are acquainted. Small world, isn't it? He, uh, sends his regards." Charles licked his lips nervously and reached into his jacket to remove a postcard, which he slid across the table toward Mathias.

It bore an image of the Montreal Olympic stadium on the front with the words *Wish you were here* arched across the sky. Mathias flipped it over. Scrawled on the back were the initials FDL and a phone number.

Mathias gave Charles a hard look. "Now you're a carrier pigeon?" He crumpled the postcard in his fist. "Don't make a habit of discussing my business with your friends up north. We clear?"

Charles gave him a series of rapid nods, more reverent than before. "Crystal. Forget I said anything."

Mathias dropped a handful of notes on the table and rose to leave. Charles held the sheet aloft. "What about the coins?"

"I don't want them."

"Don't be like that, Mathias," Charles wheedled as he strode out of the café.

Mathias tossed the crumpled postcard into the trash bin outside and crossed the street to the warehouse. He knew the person behind the initials: Filippo De Luca. The Narcotics head had supply lines that crossed the Atlantic and an army of contacts in Europe who moved product for him—but Mathias hadn't known Charles was one of them.

He shook his head wryly. *Small fucking world, indeed.*

The warehouse was the last in a row of buildings located by the entrance to the marina. Behind it was a gravel parking lot and, beyond that, the harbor. It wasn't much to look at from the outside—a giant steel shed with a set of roller doors that opened into the parking lot for deliveries, with a smaller staff entrance out front.

When Mathias walked into the main storage hangar, he found Elise counseling an irate freight driver, who was slapping a piece of paper with the side of his hand.

Elise gave a relieved grimace when she saw Mathias approach. "Thank God. Vicente is out on lunch, and the driver won't help unload."

"Why?"

"Union rules," the driver answered. "Recipient's responsible for offloading. It's in the contract." He held up the piece of paper he'd been gesturing at, as if Mathias had any interest in reading the small print.

Mathias sighed and reached into his pocket to pull a hundred-euro note from his wallet. He handed it to the driver. "I'm sure the union can make an exception."

The man's agitation transformed into eagerness, and he hurried away. Moments later, he returned, hauling a large crate on a moving dolly, and placed the crate on the floor in the middle of the warehouse.

"I don't know what he expected me to do," Elise complained after the driver had left. "Move it myself?" She bent to remove the packing slip.

"Tell Vicente he's not in Mallorca anymore. If he wants more than a half hour for lunch, he can find another job," Mathias said. "And on the subject of useless saps, I need you to find another contractor for our American outbounds."

Elise looked up from scanning the sheet of paper in her hand. "I thought we liked Charles."

"Not anymore." Mathias moved to retrieve the crowbar leaning against the wall.

"It's the Majapahit earthenware figures!" Elise exclaimed, holding up the packing slip with a bright smile. "I've been waiting weeks for these."

They'd purchased the series from a dealer in Indonesia. Mathias hadn't been thrilled about straying from their usual avenues of procurement, but Elise had proven insistent, enamored by the old man and his emporium of ancient sculptures. She'd authenticated the pieces remotely and vouched for them herself. Still not convinced, Mathias figured it was a good opportunity to take her down a peg or two. Elise benefited from the occasional hard knock, and he enjoyed the brief peace that followed a tumble.

Using the crowbar, he levered open the lid of the crate and pushed it to the floor. He reached in, pulled out one of the figurines, and removed the protective wrapping. Mathias turned it over in his hand and frowned. Something was off. He inspected the seam down the side of the clay to find it uneven. He brushed his fingers along the bottom of the crate, and they came away with the lightest dusting of white residue. *Shit.*

"Wait—they don't look like the ones he showed me." Elise stepped over to examine the crate's contents, and her face went white. "I... I think they're replicas." She glanced at him with a horrified expression. "I should have flown out to inspect them in person."

"That's the least of our worries." Mathias picked up the discarded crowbar and smashed it into the head of one of the figures.

"Jesus!" Elise cried. "How are we supposed to send them back—" She stopped abruptly when the plastic-wrapped chunks of white powder tumbled from the broken statue. "Is that...?"

Mathias picked up one of the packets and weighed it in his hand. "Someone's using us to import their stash."

It was a familiar tactic. The seller employed an unsuspecting middleman to bring the drugs into the country, and then an eager buyer magically appeared on the other side, providing a solution to their unfortunate predicament. Both the seller and the buyer were in on it, leaving the importer to shoulder all the risk. With the amount of money the importer had dropped on the shipment—and no chance of recovering it—of course they'd jump at an offer to take the counterfeit pieces off their hands.

Elise stood chewing on her lower lip. "What should we do?"

Mathias did a quick tally in his head, the number of bags multiplied by the number of clay figures. It wasn't a trivial amount, that was for sure. This wasn't some two-bit operation. They were dealing with a big player—a group familiar with moving significant volume through the European market.

"Hold off on axing Charles," Mathias said, dropping the packet and lifting the crowbar. "We're going to need him a little while longer."

3

Rayan came home to find the house empty, which was odd as it was almost eight. When Mathias worked late, the man forgot to eat, and then he returned home irritable and impossible to deal with.

Rayan flicked on the light in the kitchen and took out cured ham and cheese from the fridge. There was bread left over from breakfast, which he cut into slices and used to assemble two simple sandwiches. He ate one standing at the counter and placed the other into a small paper bag. In the hallway, he pulled on his jacket and shoes and headed back out in the direction of the warehouse.

It was a fifteen-minute walk from the house, and as Rayan drew closer to the building, he saw the lights were on inside. He made his way to the staff entrance and was about to turn the handle when the door swung open and Elise appeared, her face drawn and shoulders sagging. She let out a yelp and clutched her bag tightly against her chest, her car keys gripped between the fingers of her other hand. He hadn't expected her to be there. Most days she was gone by five.

"Rayan," Elise said, quickly masking her terror. "Sorry. I'm always a little jumpy after dark."

"I didn't mean to frighten you."

She pocketed her keys and held open the door then followed him back inside. "Oh no, don't worry," she said, returning to her usual buoyant tone, which he knew set Mathias's teeth on edge. "He's in the office." She led the way as if Rayan had never been there before.

He'd only spoken with Elise a handful of times since Mathias had brought her on as his appraiser. They'd first met after he'd shown up at the warehouse unannounced one afternoon. Elise was consulting an auction catalogue with Mathias at his desk when Rayan walked in. He'd expected Mathias to be annoyed, but he simply looked up and said, "Rayan, this is Elise Dumont." She'd stepped over to eagerly shake his hand, and that was the extent of their introduction. It was Mathias in a nutshell—he didn't feel he owed anyone an explanation.

Since their move to France, Rayan had found himself navigating uncharted territory. There was an openness about their living situation, though they maintained a shroud of caution that had followed them from Montreal. They were still careful around each other in public, but for the first time in Rayan's life, the prospect of being seen didn't carry with it a heavy sense of dread. Whether that was true for Mathias, he couldn't be sure. In either case, the caution remained. He only visited Mathias at the warehouse in the evenings, sometimes in an effort to lure him home but more often to see his most recent acquisitions.

While Mathias had little interest in the pieces he collected for his clients, Rayan found them fascinating. One would think—considering the man's line of work—their house would resemble a gallery. But Mathias almost never brought anything home, and if he did, it was for purely practical purposes. An August Endell coatrack stood by the door because the house didn't have a closet in the entranceway. A set of Carolean dining chairs—so intricately carved they could have belonged in a museum—were used to prop up Mathias's feet when he read the paper at the kitchen table. It was a riddle, attempting to figure out why a particular item had caught Mathias's interest.

One day, a silver frame decorated with tiny ornamental vines had appeared on the living room bookshelf. Rayan knew without asking that it was absurdly expensive and might have once belonged to a Bavarian prince or Swiss countess. Yet the frame, despite its obvious value, was rendered insignificant by what had been placed inside: the photo of Rayan with his brother and their mother. It was the photo Rayan had kept for years inside the book she'd given him. At moments when her face had grown blurry in his memory, the features no longer clear, he would take the photo out and study it carefully, angry at himself for forgetting. He couldn't remember the last time he'd done that, so he hadn't been sure when the photo had been spirited from the pages of Saint-Exupéry's memoir to a frame in their living room. But he had no doubt who'd done it.

Fortunately for Rayan, that evening Elise seemed distracted enough to carry the conversation on her own. "We've been trying to make a dent in cataloguing the pieces from this latest trip. You should see some of the stuff we found. The deliveries are starting to trickle in, and the paperwork's all over the place. You know how it is with estate sales and small-town dealers—things always seem to get misplaced."

He didn't know the first thing about estate sales or small-town dealers, but that didn't seem to matter much to Elise.

"And then there's the Louvre next week. They're selling a small collection of pottery shards from the Cour Napoleon excavations, and one of my old colleagues has promised us a preview before everything goes to auction. Some of the shards date back to the thirteenth century."

The office was located at the far end of the warehouse, and the route there took them past a series of large shelving units. Mathias kept the more delicate pieces in a separate climate-controlled section installed to one side of the main hangar. As they neared the door to the office, Rayan spotted an open crate of smashed clay figurines. It looked like someone had taken to them with a baseball bat. He wondered what lay behind that ominous sight.

"They found all sorts of things when they dug up the area during construction of the new museum. It's like a time capsule of life in Paris. I've always loved that collection." Elise spoke quickly when she got excited. "The French decorative arts is another favorite of mine. What about you?"

"Sorry?"

"Do you have a favorite collection at the Louvre?"

"I've never been."

Elise stopped to look at him, cocking her head. "Oh." Then she strode over to the office, gave a sharp rap on the door, and swung it open. "Rayan has never been to the Louvre," she announced in lieu of a greeting.

Seated at his desk in the corner, Mathias didn't look up from the papers in his hand. "And...?"

"He should come with us to Paris. I can give him the full tour."

Mathias gave a disapproving grunt and glanced up at Rayan standing in the doorway. Rayan raised his eyebrows, and Mathias turned pointedly to his appraiser. "Weren't you leaving?"

Elise held up her hands defensively. "Okay, but think about it. The place is a national treasure, part of our collective cultural education."

"Go home, Dumont."

She clasped her hands together and flashed Rayan a smile before bidding them both good night and taking her leave.

"She's concerned about my cultural education?" Rayan asked when Elise had gone.

Mathias snickered. "You're a hick from the colonies, remember? She considers it her patriotic duty." He leaned back in his chair. "The price I pay for employing the only qualified appraiser willing to work in this town."

"Guess there's no harm in being eager." Rayan stepped over and placed the paper bag on the desk. "Thought you might be hungry."

Mathias glanced down at his watch as though only having realized the time. Then he picked up the bag and took out the sandwich. "Look at this—full service."

While Mathias ate, Rayan looked around the office. Behind Mathias's desk were a metal filing cabinet and several shelves heaving with document boxes. On the other side of the room, Elise's desk was scattered with strange objects affixed with white tags. A labeled display of what appeared to be marble fragments was mounted to the wall.

"It's not that I don't want to see it," Rayan said absently. Naturally, the prospect of exploring one of the country's most prestigious museums appealed to him. And he'd certainly heard enough about it.

"Ignore her breathless fervor. The Louvre is mildly interesting."

"But you'd prefer I didn't come?"

"You're perfectly capable of making your own decisions." Mathias tossed the empty paper bag into the trash and got up from his chair. "Come on. I want to show you something."

"The crate of broken figures?" Rayan replied, catching the way Mathias's expression darkened. "What happened there?"

Mathias pulled open the office door. "Someone made a bad call."

He tilted his head for Rayan to follow, and they stepped back into the warehouse. Mathias led him down an aisle between two shelving units crammed with merchandise in marked crates and boxes. Rayan stopped in front of a powder-white sculpture of a woman holding a child to her breast. Behind her head spanned a sort of halo, and the dress that draped her body had been carved to resemble the gentle fall of fabric.

"That's ivory, late Gothic," Mathias said from the end of the aisle.

"It's beautiful."

"It's worth a mint. Some of this shit, you wouldn't believe."

Mathias reached a section of shelving that housed a clear container of books and opened the lid to remove one of the titles from the box. He handed the book to Rayan. Its red clothbound cover was slightly faded, and the corners were scuffed to reveal glimpses of the binder's board beneath.

"You'll be pleased to know I rescued it from a fascist treasure trove."

It was an early copy of Albert Camus's *L'Étranger*. Rayan couldn't recall the number of times he'd read it. Someone had stamped the name D. Montecot in the top left-hand corner of the inside cover. Below that, the publishing house and the year it was printed were listed neatly in black type.

"It's a first edition," Rayan marveled.

"It's yours."

Rayan closed the book. "I can't take this."

"What am I going to use it for, a paperweight?"

"Thank you." Rayan smiled and leaned in to kiss him. Mathias's hand found the back of his neck, and Rayan opened his mouth against the press of his lips. He felt his mind go blank as Mathias slipped his other hand beneath his chin and tilted his head back.

When Rayan broke away—a difficult prospect, like extracting himself from a powerful force field—he could only manage a mumbled "Let's go" before taking hold of Mathias's arm and pulling him toward the warehouse door.

At the house, Mathias lay back on the bed as he watched Rayan lower his mouth to his cock, evoking a familiar shudder. He liked the way the heat rose to Rayan's cheeks as the man stroked himself with one hand, aroused by Mathias's arousal. Rayan moved to the base of Mathias's cock, grazing his balls with his teeth. He trailed his mouth lower still, and Mathias stiffened. Rayan had tried before, gauging his reaction then backing off. Mathias's resistance hit against something he couldn't quite place. *Denial? Submission?* But the sensation was extraordinary, Mathias's own inhibition heightening it further. Mathias shifted his legs, allowing him access.

Too quickly, he found himself dangerously close to the edge, Rayan's hair bunched in his fist, his teeth grinding. It was almost a relief when Rayan came up for air. Mathias was untethered, wound taut, fearful of the depths he would fall if allowed to continue.

"You're halfway gone," he teased as Rayan straddled him—though it was as true for himself as it was for Rayan.

Rayan's cock strained against his stomach, the head already slick. Mathias brushed his fingers against Rayan's mouth, and the man parted his lips. Rayan took one finger into his mouth and bit down. Mathias felt a pull shoot through him.

"You liked that." Mathias could still feel the heady linger of Rayan's tongue.

"Almost as much as you," Rayan murmured.

Mathias rolled Rayan over and pinned him beneath him. He brought his mouth to the dimpled scar on Rayan's shoulder then moved to the firm buds of his nipples and down to the taut skin of his stomach, each flick of his tongue eliciting a shiver of desire from the man.

"Thought after last night you'd be all tapped out," Mathias said. To say he'd enjoyed Rayan's little display, upon returning home, would be an understatement. They'd gone several rounds after that.

"I'm making up for lost time."

"You can't manage without me."

Something flickered in Rayan's eyes. He knew Rayan hated how completely Mathias saw his need.

"You're confident," Rayan shot back, jerking as Mathias slipped a hand between his thighs.

Mathias stroked the pad of his thumb along Rayan's taint, and a soft moan slid from the man's parted lips. "I know you," Mathias said.

"I love you." It came out in a whispered burst, and Rayan blinked as if caught off guard.

Mathias envied the way Rayan's honesty was a force beyond his control. A warmth flooded his chest, tight and prickling. He bent his head and brushed his lips against the curve of Rayan's mouth. Rayan wrapped his arms around Mathias's neck and pulled him close. As he kissed him, Mathias marveled at the hold Rayan's words had on him. He couldn't remember ever wanting this, yet here he was, at the mercy of their communion.

Mathias ground his cock against Rayan's erection, and the man inhaled sharply, breaking the kiss only to return a moment later, ravenous. Rayan reached for where Mathias's thumb still lingered and moved his hand lower. Mathias needed no further encouragement. He pressed Rayan's knees apart and brought a slick finger to the hot clench of his opening. He felt the flutter of Rayan's eyelashes against his cheek, and then his finger found its target, and Rayan let out an involuntary groan. Rayan's breath quickened, short and shallow, as Mathias eased his fingers in and out, stretching him. Rayan arched his back, fighting impatience, wanting more, but Mathias would not be rushed.

"Enough, fuck—" Rayan pulled away and reached for the small clear bottle beside him on the bed. He pushed it into Mathias's hand. "Stop playing with me."

Mathias chuckled. "You're getting mouthy."

He ran a palmful of lube down the length of Rayan's shaft then slid an arm beneath his waist and lifted Rayan's hips to guide the head of his cock between the man's legs. Rayan's tongue darted across his lips, and his forehead furrowed as he relinquished each inch. When Mathias was in to the hilt, Rayan hooked his ankles around the back of Mathias's thighs and held him still. It was clear without words that, after the previous evening's frantic fucking, he wanted it slow.

Mathias gently rocked his hips, and Rayan pressed his mouth to his ear. "I don't like it when you're gone."

Mathias still wasn't sure how it had happened—how he, staunchly solitary and adamantly self-reliant, had come to depend so much on this man. He'd once found the very idea of sharing his bed offensive, only to become reliant on Rayan's nightly presence—the exchange of those final tired murmurings before sleep—and then waking to find himself enveloped in Rayan's warmth and simply lying there, in no hurry to leave it. He'd reworked the fabric of his life to find Rayan woven into every part.

"I don't like being gone." Mathias tilted Rayan's chin to capture his lips and kissed him as the rock became a thrust—even, tempered, entirely in control. When there was no more resistance, Mathias raised himself onto his knees and drew all the way out before driving forward.

Rayan threw his head to the side, his eyes closing. "Fuck... yes... there..."

Mathias loved when Rayan gave himself over to sensation. He upped the pace, his own desire building, and he felt Rayan's nails dig into the flesh of his forearms. When he saw the telltale signs—the way the muscles in Rayan's neck tightened, his teeth biting down hard on his lower lip—Mathias stopped.

Rayan's eyes flew open, his expression a mixture of surprise and frustration. But Mathias was already pulling out and rolling him onto his side, using a knee to stack Rayan's legs as he slid down lower on the mattress. Mathias wrapped an arm around Rayan's waist and pressed him to his chest before easing back in from behind. As Mathias began to thrust, he lowered his other hand between Rayan's thighs and teased the man's cock through his fist. Rayan raised his hips for more contact, but Mathias loosened his grip, keeping him wanting.

On his side, he had the benefit of stamina and could edge Rayan until he broke. Mathias took his time coring him, drawing his hand up and down Rayan's shaft, squeezing and releasing. Rayan pressed his face into the mattress, stifling the ragged sounds of his pleasure.

Mathias couldn't look away. He swallowed a groan and attempted to rein in the surge of lust that threatened to overwhelm him. He kissed the back of Rayan's neck then brought his teeth to the soft flesh of his earlobe and bit down. Rayan shuddered, and his hand shot out to grip Mathias's wrist, yanking it in quick, tight jerks along his cock.

"I'm going to..." he panted in a strangled whisper. "Harder... don't fucking stop—"

No longer restrained, Mathias began to slam against the man, hard and furious. Rayan's body stiffened, and he clenched around Mathias with an open-throated growl. Mathias felt the muscles in his thighs tense, and a coil of pleasure rose from his toes to the base of his spine. He tightened his grip around Rayan as he came, the world contracting to a single point—a hot, blinding dissolution.

When his breath returned, Mathias eased himself out yet remained pressed against Rayan's back, his face buried in his hair, blissfully content. He was about to drift off when Rayan spoke, his voice husky.

"I'd like to come."

"You just did."

Rayan turned to shoot Mathias a look, unable to hide his grin. "To Paris, to see the Louvre."

"Suit yourself." Mathias peeled away and reached down to the floor for his jacket. He pulled out his cigarettes. "But don't say I didn't warn you about Dumont. She will talk your ear off if you let her."

Rayan's expression grew thoughtful. "Earlier tonight, she seemed off somehow."

It hadn't escaped Mathias either. She'd been bent out of shape about the shipment, which was to be expected, but there was something else. He'd noticed it on occasion—the way she sometimes fell silent, staring into space or anxiously picking at her cuticles. She constantly referenced her old job at the museum and reminisced about her time there with a glowing nostalgia.

So why did she leave it to come and work for me? His offer had been generous enough, but Elise had never struck him as the kind to be swayed by money.

Mathias tapped the pack and pulled out a smoke. "You couldn't pay me to get in that girl's head."

Rayan gave him a knowing smile. "You like her, though. She wouldn't have stayed this long if you didn't."

Like was a strong word. He could appreciate Elise's expansive knowledge and her passion for the task. She shared his cynicism of the world, and he'd observed a familiar wariness in her—the knowledge that not everything was as it seemed.

"And she likes you," Rayan continued, looking at him archly.

Mathias smirked. "Does that intimidate you?"

Rayan gave a quiet laugh. "Not in the slightest. I know what you like, and she can't give it to you."

22

"Is that so?" Mathias tossed the unlit cigarette to the floor and moved so he was above Rayan on the bed. He wrapped a hand around Rayan's throat, and the man's breath hitched. "Isn't that lucky, then?"

4

Rayan stared out at the crowds gathered around the Grand Bassin Rond with a look of barely concealed awe. "Never thought I'd walk through the Tuileries."

Beside him, Mathias lit a cigarette and masked his smile. So far, there wasn't much about Paris that didn't impress Rayan. They'd left the car at the hotel and headed out on foot at Rayan's insistence. Elise had gone on ahead to catch up with her former colleague and would meet them at the Louvre in time for their appointment.

While the capital was only a three-hour drive away, this was the first time Rayan had left Calais since they'd arrived in France. It hadn't occurred to Mathias that the man would want to see the places he traveled for business. Rayan had seemed content with his routine and the responsibilities that tied him to his work. And jetting off on a whim wasn't part of his programming. Rayan's world had shrunk early on, and over the years, he'd become conditioned to it. But that didn't mean he wasn't hungry for more. And Mathias had never thought to ask. For once, Elise's interfering had proven useful.

"A sight nicer than what you're used to."

"Right. The camp doesn't have a fountain," Rayan said wryly.

Mathias took in the stores that lined the surrounding streets and the well-dressed people dining on outdoor terraces. A whimsical veneer. One only needed to step away from the main tourist thoroughfares to discover sidewalks piled with trash that stank of piss. Nothing had changed there.

He didn't have many fond memories of Paris, or France for that matter. He'd accompanied his mother to the city several times as a child, but she would leave him at the hotel while she made social calls. Then there were the years he'd spent living here while attending Université PSL.

He remembered arriving, newly liberated from the clutches of Montreal, determined not to be seen as some wide-eyed country bumpkin. He'd wasted no time in using the city to further his education, more outside the classroom than in.

Student life didn't suit him, so he quickly determined what was needed to obtain his degree and skated by on the bare minimum. Dumb, eager kids wanting to join the family were a dime a dozen. He figured his time at university would give him some credibility and help him stand out when he returned to Canada. As it turned out, he hadn't needed any more reasons to stand out. The disgrace of his origin had been more than enough.

Mathias viewed his time in Paris as a temporary detour on the way to his real life. For three years, he'd left it all behind—the baggage he'd been saddled with at birth and the drive to reclaim what was stolen from him. He always knew he would return to the plan he'd designed, but he also relished the taste of freedom. And in the space it created, he went looking for what he'd denied himself since the desire had first crawled, unwelcome, into his thoughts.

For him, it was purely about sex—the faces and names nothing but inconsequential details. He'd been possessed by an overwhelming need for physical sensation, something to quell the gnawing hunger of a man starved. He would return to his apartment afterward and marvel at the fact that he'd once believed he could go through life without this—only to be reminded that for the rest of his life, he would have to. The pleasure he'd sought from men was not transferable to the future that had awaited him in Montreal.

In the gardens, Mathias sucked on his cigarette as the midday sun beat down overhead. Rayan shrugged off his jacket and rolled up the sleeves of his pale-blue shirt, revealing the lean lines of his forearms. Mathias was well-acquainted with the feel of those muscles beneath his grip—the way they tensed and released. If he'd found it difficult to reconcile the heady drive that had plagued his youth, he'd been entirely unprepared for the combination of that same desire with the disarming power of affection. With Rayan, everything he'd once considered inconsequential had become captivating.

"Where do you like to go in the city?" Rayan asked.

Mathias exhaled a stream of smoke through his nostrils. "If you want an exhaustive guide to Paris, Elise will be more than willing to oblige."

"Not landmarks, just places. Where would you go now, for example?"

"Somewhere I can get a drink."

"On second thought, I will ask Elise."

As they were talking, Mathias noticed a man standing several feet away, staring at them. He wore an oversized trench coat, despite the heat, and a baseball cap pulled down low over his face. They locked eyes, and the man headed toward him, calling out something in broken French. Mathias saw him reach into his coat, and then Rayan was between them in an instant. Rayan grabbed the man's arm, and as he yanked it back, a folded sleeve of postcards slipped to the ground at their feet. The man yelped and broke free of Rayan's grip then bent to retrieve his fallen merchandise, mumbling incoherently. Rayan's expression flickered from anger to confusion. He gave Mathias a tight smile that didn't reach his eyes.

He had put himself in front of Mathias as he'd always done, an enduring sense of duty he couldn't seem to shake. But Mathias wasn't his capo anymore. He'd been woken several times by Rayan yanking back the covers to scour Mathias's body in a half-awake panic. Rayan was cagey about his dreams, but after the third instance—groggy and annoyed—Mathias had demanded he tell him what it was about.

"Believe me, if I was shot, I'd be the one waking you," Mathias muttered after hearing Rayan's reluctant recounting of a phantom job gone wrong. While Mathias's tone was sharp, his hands were gentle, and he drew Rayan to him and pulled the covers back up. "According to your subconscious, I'm a pushover."

"It's me," Rayan had said, his voice hollow. "I can't get to you on time."

They continued walking through the gardens, but a tenseness had descended that hadn't been there before. Mathias flicked his cigarette to the ground.

"That's a first. I'm not usually mistaken for a tourist."

"You forget you're with me," Rayan said darkly.

Mathias gave him a sidelong look. He had a point. Once, back in Calais, an old man passing on the street had confused Rayan with someone from the camp. Mathias had seen the way Rayan stiffened at the slur that followed, hurled like a knife at his back.

They reached the outer edge of the gardens and emerged onto the street across from the Louvre. At the entrance to the museum, they bypassed the line of tourists and walked through the blue priority queue, where a security guard consulted a clipboard and waved them on to the staff elevator.

Elise was waiting for them in the lobby. She gave Mathias a dazzling smile. "Hope you don't mind—I've already had a quick peek." She indicated that he and Rayan should follow her through a door with a sign that read Curatorial Staff: No Entry. "You're going to love the selection."

He doubted that. If thirteenth-century pottery shards had the power to stir anything in him, it could only be boredom. She led them through a maze of corridors until they arrived at a small conference room. A glass display case rested on the table in the center, and a man with a shoulder-length ponytail rose from his chair to greet them. He and Elise began chatting excitedly.

Mathias stepped over to look inside the case, and Rayan sidled up beside him. He couldn't tell whether Rayan was curious or indifferent. Knowing the man's inexhaustible interest in most things, he assumed it was the former.

It was unusual for the Louvre to sell to private collectors. However, on occasion, less-significant items were auctioned off to fund new acquisitions. Elise had told him that the museum was looking to acquire three Egyptian papyri and had decided the excavated fragments might assist their fundraising. Mathias had a client who was a Parisian history buff and had amassed a large collection of artifacts from various periods in the city's development. He'd reached out to Mathias to see if there was any chance of getting his hands on a few of the pieces, and Elise had used her connections to secure them a private viewing—plus first dibs on the items up for sale.

"Sometime today, Dumont," he prodded.

Caught in mid-sentence, she snapped her head up as though emerging from a trance, eyes blinking behind her wire frames. "Right, yes."

Elise walked him through the pieces in the display, and it was clear she'd done her homework. On the spot, he signed off on the six items she'd selected. Then the man with the ponytail disappeared and returned several minutes later with a folder of documents for Mathias to fill out.

"We'll get these sealed up, and once the funds clear, they'll be dispatched to you shortly," Elise's former colleague announced after the paperwork was complete.

On their way back from the conference room, Mathias listened as Elise told Rayan about her plan to cover all three wings of the museum that afternoon. He almost felt sorry for Rayan. The man had no idea what he'd signed up for. When they reached the lobby, Mathias hit the button on the wall to call the staff elevator.

"Wait, you're not joining us?" Elise protested.

He gave his appraiser a scornful look. "In what world...?" Besides, there was something he had to take care of. "I'll meet you back at the hotel." He caught Rayan's eye for the briefest of moments before moving to leave.

Once outside, Mathias checked his watch and walked to the main road, where he hailed a taxi. He gave the driver the address and sat back as the car sped through streets that were both strange and familiar.

"We'll skip the Denon Wing for now. The crowds should start thinning out by late afternoon. *The Raft of the Medusa* is what you really want to see there, as well as some of the Italian Renaissance paintings, but let's leave that for last." Elise led

Rayan into the main lobby of the museum, which was teeming with people. "I thought we'd start with Near Eastern and Egyptian Antiquities then head upstairs to the decorative art galleries."

Rayan looked up at the giant glass pyramid that rose above their heads, each pane a perfect diamond.

"Does that sound good, or is there something specific you'd like to see?" she asked.

"That sounds fine."

"Great." Elise turned to him with a smile. "It's so wonderful you could come."

Rayan returned the smile with half the woman's enthusiasm, and even that felt forced. "How long did you work here?"

Elise's eyes sparkled. "Six years. I started right after finishing my PhD. I spent some time interning and then managed to elbow my way into a paid position. Working here was always a dream of mine." She directed him toward the entrance to the Richelieu Wing. "How about you?"

Rayan looked at her quizzically.

"What was your childhood dream?" she asked. "The thing you always wanted to do?"

She said it so flippantly, as though one's purpose was cultivated from childhood. He'd had vague fantasies of future vocations when he was younger, usually tied to whatever he was obsessed with at the time—planes, languages, ancient civilizations. Those all disappeared when simple necessities in his life became fantasies of their own—a house to live in, food to eat.

"I didn't really have one," he said.

"No? But you must have been interested in something."

"Not particularly."

They made their way into an ornate gallery filled with glass cases displaying a collection of pots and statues and stone tablets.

"This is the Galerie d'Angoulême," Elise explained, lowering her voice so it didn't carry in the hushed space. "The pieces here are all oriental antiquities, mostly from Mesopotamia and the Levant. Some of the works in this collection are among the oldest in the museum."

Rayan walked over to a white limestone slab standing in the middle of the room.

"That's a stela depicting Baal, the storm god," Elisa said. "It was found in the ancient city of Ugarit, which is modern-day Syria."

It was hard to believe the weathered etchings had existed centuries ago. Compared to that, the span of a human life was a blip. Rayan moved to a display featuring a series of unglazed water jugs.

"So, are you in finance?" she asked.

He glanced at Elise. "What?"

"Mathias mentioned something about working in private lending back in Canada."

Right. Private lending.

"Did you two work together?"

"Something like that."

"How did you get into it?"

Rayan attempted an indifferent shrug. "Just one of those things you fall into. Practical, pays the bills."

"It's hard to imagine Mathias in a job like that. Customer service isn't exactly his strong suit. He once refused a client's request because she asked too many questions."

Now, that sounds familiar.

They continued through the gallery, the click of Elise's heels on the patterned marble tiles echoing around the room.

"Is that what you do now?" she asked.

"Not anymore. I work at the center for new migrants."

Elise's eyebrows shot up. "Really? Do you have anything to do with the camp?"

"We run a service office out there."

She shook her head. "It's a disgrace, the way the government's handled things. I can't even imagine what it's like, leaving your homeland, everything you know. And then to end up in a place like that."

They stopped by a carved stone relief mounted to the wall. In the center of the band, a regal figure stood in a chariot pulled by three servants.

"Do you miss it? Canada?" Elise asked.

"Hmm," he replied noncommittally. "Tell me about this one."

As Elise launched into an explanation charting the reign of King Xerxes the Great, Rayan's mind returned to Quebec. There were things he missed about Montreal—the familiarity of it more than anything. In France, things still had a way of surprising him—customs or words that seemed alien. Montreal tied him to memories of his brother and mother. Being away meant those memories had started to fade, and a part of him was afraid that one day, he'd lose the link completely.

They left the gallery and crossed to the neighboring wing, where the Egyptian antiquities were laid out across multiple rooms.

"It's strange to be back, if I'm honest," Elise said as they walked past a row of upright sarcophagi. "I always imagined being on the museum acquisition committee one day, making decisions about funding for exhibits and which pieces to procure. But if I think about it, the chances were so slim. My old colleague, who showed us the shards earlier, he started three years before me, and he's still in the same department with the same job. Meanwhile, in the eighteen months I've worked for Mathias, I've selected and purchased more pieces than I did during my entire time here."

In the corner of the room, a clay burial casket lay open inside a glass cabinet. The outside of the coffin was adorned with rows of stacked hieroglyphs, a story told in tiny sketches of gods, people, and animals.

Rayan stepped closer to peer at the sequence of panels. "You're happy you took the job, then?"

"It wasn't my first choice, but I think moving to Calais turned out to be a good thing for me. It was a relief to get away from Paris."

"Why?"

A deep blush bloomed across her cheeks. "It's actually incredibly embarrassing," she said hurriedly. "I'd rather not to talk about it."

So, there's something even she won't talk about.

"What about you? Are you happy you made the move to France?"

He took in her expectant expression. "I guess."

"But your family—don't you miss them?"

Rayan felt a familiar clench in his stomach. *Every day.*

"There's no one to miss."

Elise's forehead furrowed. "I'm sorry. Your parents have passed?"

It was theoretically true. His father might as well be dead, for all he cared. Rayan had almost forgotten they still inhabited the same world, breathed the same air. Rayan had been horrified when he found out Mathias had gone to see him. That broken house, the old man's trembling hands, those terrible memories. He'd never wanted Mathias to witness the extent of his shame.

Elise seemed to interpret his silence as assent. "Were they from Quebec?"

"Only my father."

"And your mother?"

"Lebanon."

She nodded as if that somehow clarified things. "Is that why you help out at the center?"

"Because I inherited a sense of displacement?"

Elise flushed again. "No, I didn't mean—"

There were parallels, to be sure. It was part of why he'd been drawn to the work. He couldn't ignore the call of recognition and the hope that he might be able to help someone else's story end differently.

"How did your mother end up in Canada?" she asked.

He'd been too young to remember the specifics, though she had told him a carefully crafted version, shrouded in romance. His father, a better man, a hero even—a former soldier turned peacekeeper who'd fallen in love with an orphaned girl in a foreign land and spirited her away to a better life. As an adult, Rayan held a far more cynical view of his father's intentions. Perhaps the man had thought a broken horse would be easier to tame. But who knew? Maybe he'd loved her once— and she him. Maybe he had been a hero—until he returned home to find himself nothing but an ordinary man, and the drink had taken whatever was left.

Suddenly, Rayan was tired of looking at the remnants of cultures long past. "You said the decorative arts collection was a favorite of yours. I'd like to go there."

Elise's face brightened. "Of course. Let's head upstairs."

5

The apartment was on the top floor of an old Haussmann-style building a short walk from the Bonne Nouvelle metro station. Not that the woman would be caught dead taking the metro. Mathias had been here several times and hadn't mentioned anything to Rayan. It felt like something that was better left separate, an unnecessary imposition to burden the man with. After all, that was how Mathias had always viewed her—as an unnecessary imposition.

He knocked on the door and, within moments, heard the purposeful clip of heeled footsteps. He smelled her first, the waft of perfume that conjured a lifetime of splintered memories. She'd worn the same scent since he was a child.

Marguerite smiled when she opened the door, as though expecting him. Which couldn't be the case, because he never told her when he'd be in the city.

"Mathias," she said, holding the door open. "Come in."

Six months after he'd left Montreal, his mother had reached out to him in France. He'd given her a number in case she ever needed to make contact—a number he had hoped she would never use. She'd been distraught over the phone and told him there was nothing left for her in Canada. After forty years, she wanted to come home.

The move had been simple enough to arrange. He'd used a company to relocate her things and found her an apartment in her old neighborhood in Paris. When she arrived, he went—albeit reluctantly—to collect her from the airport. There was something humbling about her when she stepped out into the arrivals area of the terminal. It was one of the few times he'd seen his mother truly disheveled. She appeared panicked until she spotted him and then reached for his hand and squeezed it tightly, the closest thing to an embrace Mathias could remember.

After that, he'd come to see her a handful of times when business brought him to the city. She'd returned to her polished ways, but the humbleness hadn't left her. It was as if his leaving had shattered her and she was attempting to put herself together anew.

"The humidity has been horrendous." She stood at the sink, filling up the kettle under the tap. "I'd forgotten how hot it can get in early autumn."

Mathias flipped through the newspaper she'd left out on the kitchen table. "Hmm."

"How's the work?" she asked as the kettle boiled. *The work* was code for whatever he did that allowed money to appear in her bank account each month—the nature of which was not up for discussion. "Business is good?"

She wrung her hands in this new way of hers—this altered version of his mother, who asked questions and listened attentively and always seemed to be watching him. The sudden interest was jarring. Mathias wasn't sure he liked it any better than her self-absorbed prattling.

"Same as always."

"I have some of those pastries you liked." She withdrew several spiral-shaped Danishes from a brown paper bag and placed them on a plate, which she ferried over to the table. "When you were little and we came here, you'd pick out the same ones in every bakery we visited."

Mathias stared at them. They didn't look familiar. He couldn't recall ever having liked pastries, or sweets for that matter. Then again, there was so much from those ill-fated trips that he'd blocked out.

His mother stood, looking on expectantly.

"I've eaten," he said.

They sat and drank their coffee, and his mother spoke of reconnecting with old friends and visiting places from her childhood. She seemed more at ease than when he'd first arrived, the flutter of panic receding. When he was done, she walked him to the door and stopped, reaching up to brush a stray piece of lint from the shoulder of his jacket. Mathias's first instinct was to recoil, a deep-rooted reaction that he had to rein in carefully. The gesture of familiarity was alien, like she was playing the part of the doting mother and he the obliging son—although neither of them knew much about that particular performance.

"Who is she?" his mother said with a knowing smile, her blue eyes catching his. "The girl that's brought this out in you? I've never seen you so..." She trailed off, the word floating in the air.

Happy? Mathias thought ruefully. *Has she ever seen it in me so as to recognize it now?*

"Goodbye, Mother." He turned to leave, and all the things that remained unspoken stretched between them.

Mathias hailed a taxi from outside his mother's apartment. It was late afternoon, and knowing Elise, they wouldn't be done until the museum closed for the day. He had the driver drop him off at a bar several streets from the hotel and went inside for a drink.

The city had gotten under his skin. He was irritated, unsettled. His mother's comment was lodged in his mind, and he kept returning to it, unsure why it rankled. These days, it felt more and more like he'd become someone else entirely.

By the time he left the bar, it was early evening, and the streets were backed up with cars. Not wanting to sit in traffic, he decided to walk the remainder of the way to the hotel. As Mathias approached the hotel entrance, he saw Elise and Rayan standing on the sidewalk with a young man who was pacing restlessly. Mathias didn't recognize him. He was thin and wore all black, his hair dyed silver at the tips. His face was screwed up in a caricature of fury, and he kept jabbing a finger at Elise.

Then the man stepped forward and shoved Rayan in the chest. Mathias felt the sharp edge of anger and quickened his pace toward them. He watched Rayan's face harden. He'd seen the expression earlier when the souvenir peddler had approached him in the gardens, and Mathias knew what came next.

"Theo, back off!" Elise cried, stepping between them.

Theo's eyes swung to Mathias, who'd arrived on the sidewalk beside her. "And who is this?"

"The better question is, who the fuck are you?" Mathias stood over Theo, a good head taller than him, but the man didn't back down.

"Oh," Theo scoffed, turning to Elise. "So you've got two going at the same time? I mean, I knew you were easy, but this is just pathetic."

"Oh my God," Elise whispered, her hands clenching at her sides.

Mathias felt the dull thud of an encroaching headache. He despised the inane flavor of human drama. This dumb kid had his wires crossed, and Mathias refused to waste another moment on their moronic interaction. There was an easy way to clear this up.

"Come, *chéri*," Mathias said, looping a possessive arm around Rayan's shoulders.

Elise's mouth went slack, and the hostility on Theo's face stalled, his eyes narrowing in confusion as Mathias angled Rayan toward the hotel's revolving door.

"Take care of this, or I will," he said to Elise as he passed.

They walked to the front desk, and Mathias got a room, not bothering with two—they were done with that fucking charade. Stepping into the elevator,

Mathias hit the button for their floor. He and Rayan stood in silence as the doors closed and the elevator lurched upward.

"*Chéri?*" Rayan said finally, his eyes fixed straight ahead.

Mathias snickered. "You're far too easy to please."

He leaned over and pressed his lips chastely against Rayan's. The man grabbed the back of Mathias's jacket and pushed against him, the kiss becoming anything but chaste. Mathias soon had him against the back of the elevator, one hand on the wall above Rayan's head, the other slipping beneath his shirt. The elevator came to a stop, letting out a melodic ping, and Mathias straightened so that they once again stood side by side.

The doors opened, and an elderly couple walked in smiling politely. "*Bonne soirée.*"

Mathias returned the greeting while Rayan tugged at the hem of his shirt where it had come untucked. Mathias took a secret pleasure in his flustered appearance. Rayan had never been as practiced as Mathias at remaining composed.

When they got to the room, Rayan sat down on the sofa across from the bed and kicked off his shoes. "Who was that?"

Mathias dropped the keys onto the table by the door. "No doubt another of Elise's mistakes."

"I was about to knock his teeth in."

Mathias tutted. "So violent..." He walked over to the sofa, and when Rayan looked up at him, Mathias felt the air shift.

"You've never called me that."

Mathias slid his shoe into the space between Rayan's feet on the carpet and pushed them apart, spreading the man's legs. He knew now why his mother's observation had bothered him—it was disarmingly apt and, at the same time, entirely misplaced, seeing and not seeing. It had dislodged a feeling of rebellion he didn't fully understand.

Rayan began to rise, but Mathias put a hand on his shoulder and pushed him back against the sofa. He reached down to unbutton Rayan's shirt and splayed it open to reveal the smooth plane of his chest. Then Mathias knelt between his legs and tugged Rayan's pants below his hips, the man's cock springing free. Rayan made a noise in his throat.

"Like me on my knees, don't you?" Mathias drew his mouth across Rayan's bare chest and brought his teeth down on his left nipple.

Rayan gave a slight jerk and a murmur of pleasure, and Mathias traced his mouth lower to the feathering of hair below his navel. He smelled of soap and the lingering scent of Mathias's cologne where it had rubbed against Rayan's skin as though marking him. The thought sent a surge of blood to his cock, and Mathias reached down to free it from his pants. Rayan moved to slip the jacket from his shoulders, but Mathias pushed his hand away, concerned only with the man's arousal, which curved ardently toward his stomach.

Kneeling in a Brioni suit. I have well and truly lost my mind.

Mathias brought his mouth to Rayan's cock, a fist gripped at the base as he teased the beading head with his tongue. He was rewarded with a low moan as Rayan wound his fingers through Mathias's hair and clenched tight. Mathias's own cock strained between his legs, and he lowered his other hand to stroke it, moving in tandem as he took Rayan deeper into his throat.

"Christ... Mathias..." Rayan choked out, his chest heaving, and Mathias pulled back, keeping him on the edge. Rayan released the grip on his hair and guided Mathias up to kiss him, lips parting for their tongues to meet. Mathias nipped his bottom lip, and Rayan groaned against his mouth.

Breaking away, Mathias bent to take the man's cock once again, matching his movements to the urgency of the noises escaping Rayan's clenched teeth. He quickened the jerk of his own hand and found it hard to stay focused as desire corrupted his restraint.

Rayan reached out to graze Mathias's cheek with his thumb and let out a shaky breath. "Close..."

Something about bringing Rayan to the city, having him here, felt like the merging of two selves—one leaving Paris, determined to deny this part of him, the other returning to embrace it.

Rayan's hips lurched, and he gave a strangled cry before spilling into Mathias's mouth with a violent shudder. A white-hot burst of pleasure traveled through Mathias, and he clamped down on the base of his cock, holding back. He swallowed, waiting for the tension to leave Rayan's thighs, then drew away. He rose to his feet and stood over Rayan, his own cock agonizingly hard in his fist. He brought his hand along the length of it—quick, short strokes that narrowed his mind to a single focus.

Rayan stared up at him, lips parted, skin flushed. "Fuck..." he panted. "Look at you..."

His expression was so hungry, so reverent, that Mathias couldn't fucking stand it. He let out a growl and shot across the man's chest.

Rayan leaned forward and brought his mouth to the tip of Mathias's spent cock, his tongue flicking across the head, before pushing it past his lips. Releasing him, Rayan raised his chin, and Mathias moved to kiss him, soft and tender.

After he'd returned himself to his pants, Mathias picked up a towel from the bed and wiped the slick from Rayan's skin. Then he eased onto the sofa, and Rayan lay back to rest his head in Mathias's lap.

"So, was it everything you'd hoped?" Mathias asked, pushing Rayan's hair back from his forehead with his fingers.

"We are talking about the tour?"

"Careful."

Rayan's eyes danced with amusement. Mathias wasn't in the habit of fishing for feedback.

"It was exhausting. Like being interrogated while plied with information at the same time."

"I did warn you."

"Where were you earlier?" Rayan asked after a moment.

Mathias considered lying, but what would that accomplish? "I went to see my mother."

Rayan sat up with a jolt. "Your mother's in Paris?"

"She is."

"You asked her to come?"

"Please, you should know that the farther I am from my mother, the better." He stared at the last slivers of daylight as they stretched across the carpet from an opening in the blinds. "After all this time, she decided to move back."

"And you helped her?"

"I did."

Rayan smiled. "You're a good son."

Mathias gave a snort of laughter.

"You are," Rayan repeated, insistent. He looked at Mathias, his brown eyes serious. "She's lucky to have you."

Mathias shifted as if to brush aside the sentiment.

"She grew up in Paris, didn't she?" Rayan asked.

"Up until her mother left, and then she moved back with her father to his family home."

"Where was that?"

Mathias paused. "Calais."

Rayan's eyebrows shot up. "You never told me that. Did you use to go there to visit?"

"We only went once, that I can remember. I must have been nine or ten. She wasn't on good terms with her father. When she left school and ran away to Canada, he cut her off. She thought returning to France with his only grandchild might put her back in his good books—make sure she didn't lose out on her inheritance."

His recollection of that visit was hazy. It had been strange to witness his mother deferential and pleading. His grandfather was a large, imposing man with a shock of white hair and a weary face. He didn't smile once the whole time they were there. It had been Mathias's first encounter with a grandparent, and he felt—yet again— he'd been set up for disappointment. Guillaume Beauvais was not the doting type.

"He thought even less of me than he did of her. Said it was an embarrassment for a bastard boy to carry the family name. He came from a long line of wealthy paper merchants and owned a house in town that had been in the Beauvais family since the Revolution. Guess I was a blight on the legacy." Mathias had liked the house, though, with its grand staircase and sweeping views of the ocean. "The man never changed his mind. When he died twenty years later, my mother got nothing. He left everything to a local conservation group. So, when they put the house up for sale, I bought it."

"The house... That's your family home?"

"His, not mine."

"But you reclaimed your inheritance."

"No," Mathias said tightly, still raw after all these years. "I succeeded in spiting an old man."

From outside, there came the faint sound of an emergency siren. Rayan leaned back against the sofa cushions. "Well, it's yours now," he said into the silence that followed. "Whether he likes it or not."

It was his. The closest Mathias had to a part of family history, a connection to a lineage that went back generations. Even if it still felt like a false claim.

6

Too lazy to leave the hotel room, they ordered room service, and after eating, Rayan found his second wind. Mathias proved no match for his persistence. "Your days are numbered, kid," Mathias remarked, equal parts scornful and impressed, when they collapsed onto the bed afterward. Not for the first time, he'd made use of Rayan's remarkable turnaround time. "Those bounce backs won't last."

"Yours are pretty impressive for someone closing in on middle age."

Middle age? "Watch your fucking mouth."

Rayan laughed softly and lifted a hand to Mathias's cheek. "Believe me, age has nothing on you."

He kissed him then curved against Mathias and fell asleep almost immediately. While Rayan was a restless sleeper, he also possessed the uncanny ability to black out in seconds, especially once certain other needs had been met.

Mathias, on the other hand, found himself unusually wired. He got out of bed and pulled the covers over Rayan's shoulders then headed, naked, to the shower. When he returned to the room, he dressed and patted down his pockets for his cigarettes only to find the pack empty. He'd planned to stop at a superette on his way back to the hotel but had been sidetracked by the scene unfolding out front.

Mathias pocketed the room key and took the elevator down to the lobby. As he walked past the restaurant toward to the hotel entrance, he caught sight of Elise sitting alone at the bar. He slowed to a stop, silently cursing himself, then turned back and strode into the restaurant.

"Scotch, neat. Make it a double," Mathias instructed the bartender as he pulled up a seat beside Elise.

His appraiser straightened and blinked at him, visibly tipsy. "Chief?"

"You look a sight."

"I won't deny that." She knocked back the remainder of her drink. "But you'll be happy to know I got rid of him."

"The mouthy little shit?"

Elise's lips quivered. "That was Theo. He does this—turns up out of the blue. He must have found out I was in Paris. We've been broken up two years. After I ended things, he started showing up where I was, waiting outside my apartment."

That explained the jumpiness, the anxious silences. *She certainly knows how to pick them.*

"I used to get my coworkers to screen my calls at the museum because he'd phone, asking to see me," she said with a grimace. "I don't know how he does it. He reads all this stuff online, about location pinging or something. I've changed my number twice, but then it happens again. Like today."

Mathias's drink arrived, and beside him, Elise tapped her glass for a refill. The bartender took her empty glass and retrieved a bottle of gin from the selection lined up on the shelf behind him.

"When your contact first approached me, I only agreed to meet with him because I was desperate," she said.

Shortly after Mathias had taken over the business, he'd reached out to an old contact in Paris who moved in museum circles to see if he knew of any qualified appraisers who might be persuaded to make the move to Calais. Everything else, he could manage, but Mathias didn't know the difference between a Rembrandt and a Renoir.

"Don't take this the wrong way, but I accepted the offer because of Theo. I couldn't stay in Paris anymore." Elise thanked the bartender as he placed her drink on the coaster in front of her. "I'd already been looking elsewhere, but the chances of finding a similar position outside the city, where I could actually do what I've been trained to do, were practically nonexistent."

"You'd think I asked for your undying loyalty." Mathias took a swig of scotch, aware of the irony. He'd expected nothing less from his subordinates in the past. "I don't care why you took the job. I just needed it filled. Ideally by someone quieter."

Elise gave a short laugh. "You know, you're the first person who didn't tell me to go to the police."

"What are the cops going to do?"

"Exactly!" she cried, triumphant. "Nothing—that's what. I did go, by the way, and they looked at me like I was an idiot." Elise sighed and removed her glasses to clean the lenses with the hem of her blouse. "Anyway, I'm glad I did. Take the job, that is. Despite your sunny personality, it's been a real trip. Going out on my own, picking out pieces. At the museum, I barely had any say in what I was assigned to, whereas you just hand over the money and leave the rest to me. Honestly, sometimes it seems like you don't even care about the work."

"That's because I don't."

Elise snorted and raised her glass to take a sip. When she put it back down, she turned to him, suddenly serious. "The worst thing is, I know he's crazy and controlling and a complete asshole, but every time I see him, it just serves as a reminder that there's no one else, you know?"

Mathias recognized the pained glint in her eye. It was strange to have grown so accustomed to the loneliness that only when it was gone could he see how much space it had taken up.

"What does that mean? Is that the best I get?" She exhaled through her lips. "At least he cares, right?"

"I'm sure that's what everyone will think when you turn up dead in a dumpster."

Elise glowered at him.

"Have some self-respect," Mathias admonished her. "The man clearly has a screw loose. Where does he live? I'll talk some sense into him."

"No, no." She shook her head adamantly, and her cheeks reddened. "I think I got through to him today. I made it very clear. He said he's not going to bother me again."

Mathias eyed her skeptically and took another swig from his glass.

Elise fiddled with the coaster under her drink. "Thank you, by the way. For before." Her eyes darted down to the counter. "I know you did that for me. I didn't want to assume because I figured you're not... well..." She stopped, appearing to grasp for the right words. "You're a very private person."

Mathias almost laughed. She was more perceptive than his own mother. "I don't give a shit what you assumed."

She glanced at him. "Rayan..."

"What about him?"

"You're lucky."

That's new. He'd always thought himself skilled and determined, but never lucky. Everything he'd gained in his life, he'd worked hard to get, except for the one thing that meant more than the rest of it. That had fallen clean into his lap—a credit to Rayan's formidable tenacity. Perhaps the woman had something there.

"I've had enough bad to know a good one when I see it," she said quietly.

"What do you want from me, Dumont? You're not going to get advice or sympathy. As far as I'm concerned, the less your personal life encroaches on mine, the better."

She smiled and leaned over to clink her glass against his. "Amen, Chief. Just listening's fine."

"If I see that smug fuck again, I'm all done listening."

They downed the last of their drinks, and Elise flagged down the bartender for another refill, but Mathias put a hand over her glass and signaled for the bill.

"Please," she protested. "I'll take care of it."

"Don't insult me." He dropped a handful of notes on the bar, and she got down from her stool, wobbling slightly.

She must have registered his misgivings because she reached out to pat his arm. "I'm fine, really." Then she lurched unsteadily toward the hotel elevator.

Mathias left the restaurant and walked to the superette at the end of the street. He bought his cigarettes but no longer felt like smoking. Instead, he returned to the hotel room, undressed, and slipped beneath the covers beside Rayan's sleeping form.

The man roused slightly and stiffened. "Where are we?" he murmured.

Mathias wrapped an arm around his waist and buried his face into Rayan's neck. "The hotel. Go back to sleep."

Rayan let out a breath, and his body once again went slack. In moments like these, the words rose fully formed in Mathias's mind, and still, even with Rayan asleep, they failed to make it past the threshold of his lips. But they lingered on his tongue, evoking a tenderness that was both fierce and sweet.

When Elise arrived at the hotel restaurant for breakfast, she looked decidedly less perky. There were dark circles beneath her eyes, and her hair was pulled back from her face in a simple ponytail.

"May I?" she asked, placing a hand on the chair across from Rayan.

"Of course."

She sat and poured herself a glass of water from the pitcher in the middle of the table. "Good morning, by the way. I hope you slept well."

He'd slept like the dead. Rayan often had trouble sleeping in unfamiliar places, but he'd woken that morning feeling alarmingly refreshed.

"I did. And you?"

"Not exactly. I might have had one too many before bed last night." She made a grimace and waved down a passing waiter for coffee. When the waiter returned with her drink, Elise reached for the small jug of milk and poured a generous serving into her cup. "How's the buffet?" she asked, gesturing at his plate of bread and fruit.

"Decent."

Elise took a scalding sip of coffee and cleared her throat. "I wanted to apologize for yesterday. I put you in a difficult position."

Rayan had thought at length about the events of the previous evening. Beneath the shock of disbelief, he'd felt an overwhelming swell of elation at how Mathias had claimed him—the rightness of his arm around Rayan's shoulders, coupled with the knowledge of just how far out of his comfort zone Mathias had ventured. The man had never been demonstrative. It wasn't in his nature.

Rayan still remembered how careful they'd been in Montreal—an unspoken agreement sustained by little more than eye contact. When had that agreement changed? It was impossible to deny that things had shifted. The threat of danger that had overshadowed their relationship from the beginning had faded and something else had taken its place—a growing acceptance of what they were to each other.

"No," Rayan said with a shrug. "Your friend was mistaken, that's all."

"He's not a friend," she said brusquely. "But I'm hoping that's the end of it."

Elise's reluctance to talk about her reasons for leaving Paris, back at the museum, made more sense after yesterday's unexpected confrontation. He recalled how she'd gripped his arm when Theo had approached them on the sidewalk outside the hotel. "I'm so sorry, Rayan," she'd whispered in a panicked voice. Nothing about Theo had given Rayan cause for concern, yet his appearance had clearly frightened Elise.

"You're hoping?" he asked.

"I know," she corrected with a conviction that rang false.

But it wasn't Rayan's place to press. The woman's life was none of his business.

"Do you want anything else while I'm up?" Elise asked, getting to her feet.

"No, thank you," he said, and she continued to the buffet table.

While she was gone, Mathias appeared at the entrance to the restaurant. Rayan had left him sleeping in the room and had come downstairs to find something to eat. Mathias had never been much of a breakfast person. He walked over to the table and eyed Elise's coffee cup before pulling out the chair to Rayan's right and taking a seat.

"Interrupting something?" His tone was surly, and Rayan knew he'd have preferred another hour in bed.

Rayan shook his head, with a smile, and Mathias set about ordering coffee.

When Elise returned, she placed her plate down and greeted Mathias airily. "Don't usually see you this early."

"You look tired, Dumont," Mathias baited. "Rough night?"

She busied herself with buttering a piece of bread, attempting to appear nonchalant. The waiter brought Mathias his coffee.

"So," Elise said, setting down her knife. "When did you two—"

"No," Mathias interjected, putting an end to the line of questioning before it began. He was much better at it than Rayan, who'd found himself outmaneuvered at the museum. She was skilled—he'd give her that.

"Okay, okay." Elise picked up her fork to spear a slice of fruit on her plate. "I thought we could stop by the Sacré-Cœur on our way out of town," she announced between bites of melon. "It has one of the best views in the city."

"You do like to push," Mathias said. "This isn't a vacation. We're here on business. And now that it's done, we go home."

"We've had this discussion before." Elise glanced at Rayan. "He doesn't see the glitter of Paris, only the grime. He's immune to her charms."

"And you're too susceptible to them," Mathias retorted.

"I've never been to Montreal, but I guarantee whatever charms it has could fit into a single neighborhood in Paris."

She wasn't wrong. From what Rayan had seen so far, the city was a marvel. There was something new to be found around every corner. He'd heard little about the time Mathias had spent here while at university, but he knew the man didn't hold Paris in any special regard.

"I'd like to go," Rayan said. He'd read about the Basilica in a book about the Paris Commune and was curious to see it in person.

Elise turned to Mathias. "You could wait in the car," she offered, scooping up a forkful of eggs and bringing it to her mouth.

"Like your chauffeur?"

"It'll be fun," Elise said, some of the color returning to her cheeks.

"Fun," Mathias muttered and picked up his coffee.

They checked out of the hotel and drove to Montmartre, a cobblestoned neighborhood full of charming old buildings. The Sacré-Cœur Basilica was perched on the hilltop overlooking the district. Mathias parked on a street nearby, and together, they made their way up a steep set of steps that led to the famous landmark.

It was late morning, and already, a crowd had gathered on the forecourt in front of the church, taking in the iconic view of the city below. Elise walked beside Rayan and regaled him with tales of the surrounding area and the building's history.

Mathias hung back, uninterested, the smoke from his cigarette rising above his head.

"There was a lot of opposition during construction, which continued after it was built," Elise said as they headed toward the carved wooden doors at the entrance. "Around the time the Statue of Liberty was transported to America, opponents even proposed installing a full-size copy of the statue on top of Montmartre, directly in front of the Basilica."

Rayan stared up at the towering white structure. "Clearly, that never came to pass."

Elise laughed. "No, thank God."

Mathias opted against joining them, and Rayan and Elise went inside alone. The church was dimly lit, and the ceiling curved upward in a series of cavernous domes.

"This is the most notable work inside." Elise pointed to the giant mosaic of Christ looming above them. *Le Triomphe du Sacré-Cœur de Jésus.* It took three artists to create and is made up of over twenty thousand pieces."

Rayan stepped forward to inspect the depiction of the man clothed in white, a golden heart shining from his chest. The image was intricate but disquieting, and as they continued through the interior of the Basilica, the glittering eyes of Christ seemed to follow him.

They emerged from the building, and Elise spotted an old woman at a small booth in the plaza outside the church. She was sitting on a foldout chair beside a painted sign of an open hand.

"I promise I won't be long. I've always wanted to get my palm read." Elise reached into her purse for her wallet and headed toward the woman.

Rayan found Mathias standing by the railing at the far end of the plaza. He was looking out at the city stretching into the distance, a cigarette between his fingers.

"You can't say it's not beautiful," Rayan said.

A smile pulled at the corners of Mathias's lips. "I can say whatever I want."

Rayan rested his elbows on the stone ledge of the railing and watched the people milling about in the park below. "What was it like when you lived here?"

"Like crossing something off a list."

"Must have been freeing, though. Being away from everything."

"Hmm."

"Do you ever wonder what would've happened if you'd never returned to Montreal?"

Their eyes met, and Mathias's face darkened. "I was always going back. I was always going to join. I had it planned out since I was a kid."

"To be like your father?"

"To eclipse him," Mathias said in a hard voice. His gaze returned to the view, and he took one last drag before flicking his cigarette to the ground at his feet. "Go and tell our tour guide enough with the distractions. I want to get back on the road."

Rayan walked over to where Elise sat across from the palm reader. Their heads were bowed together, and her hand was in the old woman's lap. The woman released her hand when he approached, and Elise raised her sleeve to swipe at her eyes.

"We're heading out," he said.

Elise nodded. "Right, okay." Her voice quivered. She stood and began to gather her things.

Rayan felt a pinch on his arm. He turned to find the old woman staring up at him, her milky eyes studying his face.

"You're an interesting one." She captured his wrist and pulled back his fingers to peer into his palm. "Two large islands on your lifeline. Things have not been easy," she murmured. "But your heart line runs deep." Rayan jerked his hand away, and the woman let out a cackle. "That one's for free."

He backed away and followed Elise down the stairs to the street. Mathias was ahead of them, already at the car.

"Did she tell you something?" Elise asked, glancing back up the steps. "She was scary accurate."

"No," Rayan said, unnerved by the eerie encounter. "She just wanted money."

7

When Mathias arrived at the warehouse the following morning, a woman was seated in the chair across from his desk, talking to Elise. He stopped outside the door to the office and studied her through the glass panel. Elise caught his eye and excused herself.

She slipped out of the office and closed the door behind her, speaking to him in a low whisper. "She showed up a few minutes ago and asked to speak with you. I wasn't sure when you'd be in."

"I'm never in before ten," Mathias said, shrugging off his coat and draping it over his arm.

"I know, but she insisted on waiting. She seems important. This could be a big commission." Elise adjusted her glasses, unable to hide her excitement. "She mentioned she was interested in Asian antiquities."

Mathias narrowed his eyes. "Did she?" He reached into his pocket, pulled out several bills, and handed them to his appraiser. "Why don't you head across the road and get us some coffee?"

Once Elise had left, he stepped into the office, and the woman turned to look at him curiously. "Monsieur Beauvais?"

There was no getting around it—she was beautiful. Her angled features and sinewy limbs looked like they belonged on the pages of a fashion magazine. She wore a tight-fitting black dress and Louboutin pumps that she tucked demurely to one side of her chair. Her blond hair was styled to frame her perfectly made-up face, accentuated by large green eyes and too-plump lips, hinting at money meticulously spent. She exuded an opulent glamour, and by the time she lifted her manicured hand to shake his, Mathias had seen right through her.

"That would be me." He released her hand and moved to hang his coat on one of the hooks along the back wall.

"I hope you don't mind if we continue in English. My French is not very good, I'm afraid."

Mathias took a seat at his desk. "I'm sure I can manage," he replied, switching to English.

The woman's lips tweaked into a smile. "Impressive. I don't detect an accent."

The same couldn't be said for her. By the sound of it, Mathias guessed she was from the Balkans—maybe Bosnia or Bulgaria, but his money was on Albania.

"Have you spent time abroad?" she asked.

"Some."

The smile widened. "You're not what I was expecting, Mr. Beauvais."

"What were you expecting?"

The woman recrossed her legs, and the hem of her dress slid higher up her smooth thigh. She made no move to adjust it. "An old man with a bow tie who likes to collect junk. You, on the other hand, are quite a treat."

Their eyes locked, and it was written all over her face—so overt it was almost cheap, despite her polished appearance.

"My associate tells me you're looking for Asian antiquities," Mathias said flatly.

"Apologies—how rude of me. My name is Marsela Asllani, and I represent a small group of investors looking to purchase high-value oriental art. They have a particular interest in Javanese Buddhist idols."

"What a coincidence," he remarked. "We just received a shipment of earthenware figures from Indonesia."

"I'd love to see them."

"Unfortunately, they were damaged in transit. Shipping companies aren't what they used to be. We're in the process of lodging an insurance claim so we're not left entirely out of pocket."

"That is unfortunate." The lightness of the woman's tone had disappeared.

"I'm on good terms with the dealer. If your group is interested in something similar, we can source it directly."

"Is there any chance I could have a look at the pieces you received so I can get a sense of the quality if we were to order something else?"

"By all means." Mathias stood and held open the door to the office. They made their way through the warehouse, Marsela's heels clicking briskly on the concrete floor.

The woman appeared uninterested as they walked past shelves crammed with unique pieces. She certainly didn't give off the air of an enthusiastic art procurer. But then, neither did he.

Mathias stopped by the open crate Vicente had shifted to the back of the warehouse. His store hand had placed a square of black plastic over top to cover the contents. Mathias lifted the plastic and gestured down at the mess of shattered earthenware. Each figure had been smashed with an exactness that did not look like an accident.

"You can see there's nothing worth salvaging."

She stared down at the broken shards then returned her icy gaze to him, the smile gone from her face.

"You seem disappointed, Ms. Asllani," he said evenly. "Not what you were expecting? Or perhaps there was something else you were hoping to find?"

A tension filled the air between them, and Mathias knew his suspicions had been correct. Then Marsela began to laugh, a soft tinkling sound. She leaned forward and pressed a palm against his chest, holding it there a moment too long.

"You really are a treat, Mr. Beauvais. It's a shame about the sculptures—things would have been so much easier." She reached into her purse and pulled out a card, which she slipped into the breast pocket of his suit jacket. "Call me when you change your mind about being difficult. You seem like a smart man. I'm sure you'll make the right decision."

She turned and strode out of the warehouse without another word.

Mathias tossed the plastic cover back over the crate and returned to the office. He pulled the card from the pocket of his jacket and flipped it over in his hand. It was blank except for a phone number and a stylized monogram printed on the back—an *O* intersected by a vertical cross.

Elise returned moments later with three cups of coffee and gave him a quizzical look. "Did you scare her away?"

"If she shows up again, you call me. Understand?"

Her forehead furrowed, but she nodded mutely, accustomed to his cryptic directions.

The woman was with the Albanians—Mathias was sure of it. The country played host to a handful of crime families who controlled a large part of the wholesale cocaine market in Europe and were primary distributors across the channel. With its proximity to the UK, an import business based in Calais was the perfect choice for an unsuspecting mule. He'd known someone would come for the drugs, but he hadn't expected someone like her.

Mathias tapped the corner of the card against his desk. It would take more than empty threats for him to cooperate with a bunch of puffed-up Eastern European gangsters. Marsela Asllani was forgetting one thing—he had what she wanted.

And this wasn't his first rodeo.

The Groupe d'action funding committee met once a month and allocated time for one proposal presentation per meeting. Karl must have pulled strings to get them onto the agenda for that afternoon. The organization's Calais headquarters was located downtown on the second floor of a drab commercial building. Rayan stood with Asmarina and Laurent in the corridor outside the conference room where the board was gathered. Karl had come to join them, looking almost unrecognizable in his navy suit and tie.

Rayan, too, wore a suit, the feel unfamiliar despite it having been his default uniform for years. He'd gone home to change before the meeting and had watched as his reflection in the mirror morphed before his eyes, a different person staring back.

"Remember, this is more a formality than anything," Karl said as they waited. "I've already had several discussions with management about the idea, but there's a process we need to follow."

Laurent paced the corridor with a nervous excitement. In his hands, he held a black portfolio book with the plans for the building and the prospectus they'd made to highlight their work at the center and the services they offered at the camp. He gave Rayan a jittery smile. "Stop me if I go on for too long. I don't want to mess this up."

"You'll do fine," Rayan said.

A young woman emerged from the conference room and held open the door. "Come on through. They're ready for you."

Once inside, they took seats across from a committee that mirrored their own—three men and a woman. The woman who'd summoned them sat at the end of the table behind a small laptop and appeared ready to take notes. The committee had copies of the plans from Laurent's portfolio, and as Laurent began to outline the scope of the project, they flicked through the pages, their expressions unchanging. In the chair beside Rayan, Asmarina began to tap her foot against the carpet.

Laurent had skipped ahead to the technical details of the construction process. Rayan knew that was what the man was most anxious about. It was a considerable undertaking, building from scratch, and while they'd taken pains to secure several different estimates, the cost remained significant. But in his rush to reassure the committee, Laurent had lost sight of the bigger picture—the reason why they were here.

Asmarina shot Rayan a glance, and he knew she was thinking the same thing. She inhaled audibly before clearing her throat. "If I may interrupt my husband, I'd like to take a moment to return to the root of the issue. We can discuss planning and consents and construction costs, but what we really need to be talking about is the people. You know as well as I do what they're up against. Both our organizations work on the front lines, and we see the reality—unaccompanied children, threats toward women, families who feel unsafe. The place is a hotbed for exploitation and frequently targeted by traffickers. We offer services and support, but we're tired of simply standing by. With a designated residence facility, we can prioritize the most vulnerable in the camp while they're in transition."

Several of the committee members were nodding. At the end of the table, the young woman tapped her nails briskly against the keys of her laptop.

"In the last six months, the police presence at the camp has doubled," Rayan added quietly. "But they're not stopping the violence or the smugglers. They're keeping people away from the A16 and making sure they don't stow away in freight trucks headed for Folkestone."

It was difficult to encapsulate the hope and suffering, the pain and resilience that he encountered each day in the camp—the weight of responsibility he felt bearing witness to it.

"The government is looking out for its own interests. Who is looking out for the interests of the people living there?" Rayan continued. "That's the gap we're trying to fill."

From his seat beside Laurent, Karl was bobbing his head in agreement. "The Calais Center for New Migrants has been an invaluable resource to the city's displaced population over the past few years, and they're well-placed to help manage a facility like this. Groupe d'action makes a point to prioritize efforts by local organizations, and I believe the funding would be well utilized here. It would also assist in reducing the movement of migrants across the Channel. You'll find my notes in the attached addendum."

The committee shuffled through their papers and began murmuring among themselves. One of the men removed his glasses and placed them down on the table. He fixed his eyes on Asmarina for a moment before speaking.

"We agree there is urgent need for a clean and safe residential facility to house the most vulnerable of those displaced people who've found themselves here. And I applaud your efforts to appeal on behalf of those unable to do so themselves. I'm not sure if Karl's informed you, but we've recently been awarded an aid grant by one of the EU's development programs. We, too, have been looking for ways to alleviate the delicate problem the Jungle presents, and with the government increasingly reluctant to get involved, I think this project represents a promising collaboration between our two organizations."

The man glanced over at his colleagues. "That being said, while generous, the aid grant isn't large enough to meet the full cost of even your most conservative estimate. We'll consult on the proposal, but if Groupe d'action decides to commit the funding, it will be contingent on you securing the remaining money for the project. Appealing to the city is the obvious choice. The council has the ability to apply for a discretionary grant from the French government for projects of humanitarian importance."

They spoke a while longer about logistics and timelines before the man got to his feet, and the rest of them followed. He rounded the table and reached out to shake each of their hands in turn.

"Karl has been following your efforts for some time, Monsieur and Madame Moreau. We're quite confident in your commitment to the cause. We'll have to go through the full consultation process, but I wanted to let you know that your proposal looks promising. This is exactly the kind of project that gives hope to those of us watching the development of this situation with great empathy. We'll be in touch when we have a decision. In the meantime, I suggest you make efforts to meet with the mayor and determine the city's involvement."

Karl thanked the committee, and the four of them filed back into the corridor. Laurent clapped Rayan on the shoulder, a grin splitting his face. "Promising. He said promising."

Rayan managed a smile but couldn't muster the same level of enthusiasm. Karl and Laurent began speaking quickly, already planning next steps.

"You don't look too pleased," Asmarina said at his elbow.

"That's not it," Rayan said.

He didn't want to voice his skepticism—not when the mood was so buoyant, when the wins were so few and far between. Yet the fact remained that they needed the city on board if they were to have any hope of breaking ground on the project. And knowing what he knew about Mayor Durand, that would prove a difficult prospect.

8

Mathias gritted his teeth against the growing panic. It lodged in his throat and rendered silent the caustic remarks, the protective objections. He had no one to blame but himself. He had actively, willingly chosen this—to peel it all back. To lay himself bare.

Rayan slid his hands to the backs of Mathias's thighs and pressed down, shifting his hips so Mathias could feel the pulsing heat of his cock pressed against him.

The blood thundered in Mathias's ears. He felt cornered, defenseless.

As if sensing his fear, Rayan brought Mathias's palm to his chest. Mathias could feel the man's heart hammering beneath his fingertips. So, it wasn't just him.

Rayan leaned in to kiss him, and his mouth opened around Mathias's own, sending a flood of warmth through Mathias's insides. He brushed his lips against Mathias's cheek, and when Rayan spoke, it was a whisper close to his ear. "I'll go slow."

The ease with which Rayan moved—his hands firm but gentle, the lines of concentration appearing on his forehead as he pushed against him—allowed Mathias to release his grip, to finally relinquish control...

Mathias jolted awake, breathing fast. Rayan lay in the dark beside him, his face serene in sleep. Mathias sat up to discover he was painfully hard.

The fuck was that?

He got out of bed and walked to the shower, more than a little unnerved. As he stood under the hot water, his erection refused to diminish. He reached down, practiced and efficient, the remnants of the dream lingering in his mind even after he came.

Mathias dressed and made his way downstairs to the kitchen. He flicked on the coffee machine then went to the front door to check for the newspaper. He spotted it poking out of a lavender bush by the roadside.

"The little shit," Mathias muttered as he went to retrieve it.

René was the infuriatingly unreliable paperboy who delivered to their street. Mathias had tried bribes and threats, but nothing seemed to encourage the dough-faced kid to do his job properly. Mathias was at the table, reading the salvaged paper, when Rayan appeared in the kitchen.

"You're up early," Rayan said, padding to the coffeepot and filling a mug.

Mathias kept his eyes trained on the international news section, in no hurry to reveal why. "I like to keep things interesting." He scanned an article about immigration reform in Greece.

Rayan came to join him at the table. "It's here before noon. René's outdone himself."

"I swear, that kid..." Mathias said.

"If you make an example of him, we'll have to move again."

Mathias gave him a warning look, and Rayan smirked into his coffee.

"Anything of interest?" Rayan asked.

"Parliament's proposed another round of tax hikes. What they get away with under the banner of public good... It's glorified protection money." Mathias had been forced to become more acquainted with that particular racket now that he ran his business aboveboard. Fortunately, he had a creative accountant.

"Still sore about that?" Rayan teased. "Thought you'd have embraced your new civic duties."

Mathias ignored him. "There was some story about the upcoming election in Canada."

Rayan stilled. "Piper's running again?"

"You should read what they're saying about him—like, he saved the country from itself, cleaned up its nasty image," he scoffed. "Canada, the poster child for peace and prosperity."

"It's not all peace and prosperity," Rayan replied carefully.

"No, not all of it."

Rayan lifted his cup to his mouth and took a measured sip. "Do you ever wonder what the Feds are up to these days?"

Mathias sometimes thought about where things had landed after they'd left—not with Inspector Allen's investigation but with the inquiries that would have undoubtedly followed. "Not really. And we're too far removed for them to take much interest. They have enough on their plate as it is."

"Right." Rayan's forehead furrowed, and he stared down at his cup.

"You miss Montreal."

Rayan gave a wistful shrug. "Yes and no. I feel like I gave it up long before I left."

Mathias studied the man. He briefly considered mentioning Charles and the postcard from De Luca but decided against it. He had no intention of involving Rayan in the lingering dregs of their past. It would only plant a seed of unease, and for what? He had no interest in resuming contact with the family.

Mathias folded the newspaper and finished the remainder of his coffee. "I'm heading to Belgium this afternoon to drop off a piece for a client." He would have sent Elise, but the client had called earlier in the week and specifically asked for him. "He's somewhat particular."

"Heylen?"

Mathias nodded and stood to deposit his empty cup in the sink.

Jacob Heylen was a Belgian shipping magnate obsessed with Napoleon Bonaparte. He'd spent years painstakingly decorating his three-story Gothic townhouse in Bruges's historic center with furniture sourced from the era of the French emperor's reign. Heylen owned JFH Logistics, one of the largest international container-shipping companies in Europe and, despite his questionable taste in antiques, was a shrewd businessman. Which put him in a different league from the majority of Mathias's clients, who solicited art as a means to ease their wealth-imposed boredom.

Mathias reached for his jacket draped over the back of the chair and shrugged it on. He felt Rayan's hand on his waist and turned to pull him close. As the man kissed him, Mathias was struck by a flash from the dream—the bold press of Rayan's hands on his thighs. When they parted, the headiness he'd tried to shake earlier had returned.

"Will I see you tonight?" Rayan asked, nestling his face against Mathias's neck.

"I'll be back before then."

"Good." Rayan released him with a smile.

It was less than an hour to the Belgium border and then another forty minutes to the bustling coastal city of Bruges. Heylen had arranged to meet him at the JFH Logistics headquarters building by the port. One of his assistants was waiting for Mathias in the underground carpark with a furniture trolley, which she used to transport the nineteenth-century wooden cabinet he'd brought up the elevator and into Heylen's office.

Heylen couldn't keep his hands off the thing when they arrived. He made a series of appreciative noises as he circled the piece Elise had unearthed at an estate sale in Bordeaux on their recent acquisition trip.

"It's remarkable," he gushed. "I don't know how you do it, Beauvais."

Heylen had certainly compensated him handsomely for his trouble. Mathias made a game of these sales, cranking up the figure Elise gave him by at least half. And still the man paid, not batting an eye. Mathias wanted to see how far he could push, but Heylen had yet to negotiate. He was the human equivalent of a blank check.

"Sit, please," Heylen said, ushering Mathias toward a plush seating area in the corner of the top-floor office, which boasted sweeping views of the port below. "Have a drink. You've come all this way."

Mathias sat down in one of the overstuffed chairs, and Heylen took a bottle of top-shelf whiskey from a nearby bar cart and poured two generous glasses.

"I'll be honest—I had somewhat of an ulterior motive in asking to see you today," Heylen said, handing Mathias his drink.

I wasn't born yesterday. Mathias had a sneaking suspicion Heylen's insistence on him making the trip out had nothing to do with neoclassical symbolism.

He accepted the glass and leaned back in his chair. "Is that so?"

Heylen took a swig and placed his drink down on the small table between them. "Tell me what you did before this. You're too savvy to be some humble antiques trader. I've worked with plenty of people over the years, and I know talent when I see it. I ask for something, and you get it faster than anyone else. And you charge an arm and a leg for it as well. I like that. You know your worth. You let the business come to you, not the other way around."

Mathias brought the whiskey to his lips. It was smooth and rich, the way he liked it. He gave a shrug. "Business is business, no matter the industry."

"And is this a hobby of yours? You made it big, retired early, and now you don't know what to do with your time?"

Mathias stared back at him. "Let me worry about the why."

Heylen gave him an amused smile then stepped over to his desk, where he retrieved a piece of paper and handed it to Mathias. "Out of curiosity, what would you make of this?"

Mathias narrowed his eyes. "So, in exchange for the drink, I perform like a circus monkey?"

"No, no. Think of it as an information exchange between one importer and another."

"I'm pretty sure what I import in a year, you write off on a single shipment."

Heylen chuckled, returning to his seat. "Humor me."

Mathias looked down at the sheet in his hand. It was a list of tariffs based on port locations. He glanced over the numbers, mildly interested.

"Well, you're getting gouged by the Dutch, for one. And the Finns are usually open to volume-based negotiations. They're not giving you nearly enough of a discount for what you're bringing in."

Heylen's grin widened, stretching across his face. "See? I knew it. I always trust my gut when it comes to these things." He waggled a finger in excitement. "We recently bought out a local competitor—nobody too impressive, but big enough to make a dent in our EEA revenue. Bruges is home to the second largest port in Europe. The sheer number of containers that pass through here, you wouldn't believe. I figure, with the new business under the right leadership, we could increase regional profit by at least forty percent. But there's the rub—finding the right person for the job." Heylen leaned forward in his chair. "I have a feeling you're the kind of man who could take a role like that and hit it out of the park."

He can't be serious. "I don't work for other people."

"I can understand that. I'm the same way." Heylen picked up his glass and took another sip. "What if I made you a partner in the new business? We're talking a fleet of three hundred, moving five and a half million containers per annum—oil, coal, timber, you name it. The commute's not too bad. You can come in when you want and run the rest from a satellite office. I don't need you down the hall. I need you managing—broad strokes, big decisions. The rest you can leave up to the team. And who knows? Perhaps at some point, we'll open a branch in Calais."

It was almost amusing how committed the man was to courting him.

"I haven't even mentioned the pay." Heylen pulled a pen from his breast pocket and jotted a number down on the back of the tariff sheet. "That's an indication of the kind of money you can expect."

Mathias glanced at the figure. *That many zeros, and it might as well be play money.* He gave a low laugh. "You don't know me. You'd hand over half your business to a man who sources your furniture?"

"I've had nine prospective CEOs come through my office in the past two weeks, and not one of them picked up on the fact that we're overpaying close to twelve million in tariffs—you being the notable exception." Heylen's expression turned contemplative. "You get to where I am, Mathias, and you realize you don't have to do everything by the book. I'm sick of dealing with people who look good on paper but can't deliver. Do you know what we used to do back before it was all about keeping the shareholders happy? Take a gamble and see how it panned out. Hell, it's my business. I can go out on a limb if I want to."

Mathias downed his glass and got to his feet. "I appreciate the drink, Heylen. You go on and bring that home to your wife. Give me a call when you're after another cabinet."

"Think about it, Mathias," Heylen called out as Mathias walked to the door. "It's there if you want it."

Despite his purported lack of interest, Mathias found himself mulling over the offer on the drive back to Calais. He didn't give a shit about the money, but Heylen's clout was impressive. JFH Logistics held a twenty percent share of the international container-shipping market, and Heylen would have connections that spanned the globe. The idea of partnering with the man played to Mathias's ambition, the part of him that had always wanted to see how far up in the world he could move.

His phone rang, and Elise's number appeared on the screen.

"Chief, there's been a small problem," she said when he picked up.

"What kind of problem?"

"They're holding the shipment from Dubai."

Mathias sucked his teeth. "Which shipment? A little more information so we don't have to sit around playing twenty questions."

"The pair of Bronze Age vases. The dealer in Dubai dispatched the order three weeks ago, and I received confirmation that it landed in Calais yesterday, but the freight company won't release it. When I called, the ship's master was gone, and I couldn't get a clear word from anyone. We'll have to go down in person to sort it. Otherwise, they'll probably send the whole shipment back."

Mathias knew that by "we," she meant him. Elise struggled to navigate the delicate workings of bureaucracy at the best of times.

"I'll stop by the port when I'm back in the city," he said and hung up without waiting for a reply.

9

Rayan was on his way home from his last class at the center when his phone rang. It was Mathias.

"I need you to come down to Bassin Carnot." He sounded annoyed, the way he did when he expected things to function as they should and then life went and threw a wrench in his plans. "Use the west entrance to the port, and look for berth six."

Rayan marveled at how little their phone conversations had changed since he'd worked as the man's second. *Is a simple greeting too much to ask for? Hello, how was your day?*

"I'm heading over."

The port wasn't far from the center, and it didn't take him long to find his way to the inner harbor and follow the signs to berth six. Mathias was standing with a man in a brown oilskin jacket, both smoking agitatedly. Behind them in the water, a small cargo ship was docked with its lights on. Rayan could hear the distant chatter of crewmen on board.

It was early evening, but the sky was already dark, transforming the ocean beyond into a vast inky blackness. He walked over to Mathias, taking in the surly looking man beside him with a full beard and skin the color of milky coffee. The bearded man scowled as Rayan approached.

"There's a shipment of mine they're refusing to unload," Mathias said tightly, tapping his ash. "The ship's master is AWOL and Kareem, here, is the only person available with any authority to speak on the matter. But he seems to have difficulty communicating. Perhaps you can translate."

Before Rayan could introduce himself, Kareem began speaking in rapid-fire Khaleeji, his meaty hands slicing through the air in a series of irate gestures. It wasn't a dialect Rayan was overly familiar with, common in the Gulf states and different from the Levantine Arabic that he'd grown up with, which more closely resembled that spoken by the Syrians at the camp. There were so many regional variations of the language, some more easily understood than others. Dialects aside, Kareem was certainly making his irritation clear.

"What's he saying?" Mathias demanded.

"Just insults at the moment. He says he doesn't like your face."

"Tell him I don't like his."

Rayan clicked his tongue. "I'm not going to do that."

He asked Kareem about the shipment, and the man launched into another tirade, this one containing a lot more salient information.

"He said your import license has been revoked."

"Fuck," Mathias muttered.

"He can't release the shipment until you're clean on the department's register."

"Tell him I'll sort it, but I expect him back here as soon as the paperwork clears."

When Rayan relayed this instruction, his tone remarkably different from the fervent crescendo of Kareem's, the man looked at him with a glitter of contempt. He sneered before giving his reply.

"He said, why should he listen to some arrogant Frenchman?"

"Tell him if his boss wants to get paid, he'll do what this arrogant Frenchman says."

This time Kareem didn't mince words. He launched a string of profanities at Rayan, flecks of spit gathering at the corners of his mouth. Apparently, Rayan was a half-breed, dog-faced, colonial bootlicker too pale to be a real Arab. But it was his final jab that made Rayan's stomach curdle. Without thinking, he advanced toward Kareem, his right fist clenched at his side, ready to make impact.

"Hey, hey!" Mathias barked, tossing his cigarette to the ground and stepping between them. He put a hand on Rayan's chest. "We're done here."

Mathias guided him away from Kareem, but not before Rayan let fly some choice insults of his own. They left Kareem leering by the dock and headed back in the direction of the port entrance.

"You'd think I trained you better," Mathias chided him.

"He called my mother a whore," Rayan said through clenched teeth.

"Nothing I haven't heard before."

Rayan shot him a look.

"What, you think it's less insulting when it's a fact?" Mathias's tone was easy, but there was a hard glint in his eye.

Rayan swallowed his careless reply.

"Come on. I'm parked around the corner," Mathias said.

The drive back to the house took them past the beach, dark and empty on a cold autumn evening. Rayan glanced over at Mathias and could tell from his pensive frown that he was preoccupied with this new information.

"Mathias," he asked carefully. "Is someone targeting the business?"

Mathias remained silent.

"Does this have anything to do with that crate of smashed figures at the warehouse?"

"Christ, Rayan," Mathias snapped. "Don't you have enough to do without meddling in my shit?"

Whatever was concerning him, it was clear he had no interest in discussing it. Rayan turned to look out the window and saw a flash of light out in the ocean. It appeared only briefly before disappearing into the darkness. It was too close to shore for a commercial ship and the wrong time of day for a pleasure cruiser.

"Stop the car," Rayan said.

"What?"

But Rayan was already pulling open the door. Mathias braked hard to bring the car to a stop on the side of the road.

"The fuck are you—Rayan!"

Rayan got out and heard a scream from the beach below. "A boat," he said. Squinting, he could just make out the shape of a capsized raft floating in the surf. Around it, a handful of people bobbed up and down in the water as the waves pushed them under. A jolt of fear gripped him. "They'll drown."

"Rayan!"

Ignoring Mathias, he vaulted over the barrier down onto the sand. As he sprinted toward the ocean, he threw off his coat before plunging into the freezing water. While his ability had improved—a benefit of living close to the coast—Rayan still wasn't a strong swimmer. But he knew who was on that raft—women and children without life jackets, weighed down by bags and heavy clothing. Whatever skill he possessed, it had to be better than what they were up against.

The waves battered him as he attempted to get closer to the boat. He could barely see in the dark, and the slap of salty water stung his eyes. He passed a man clearly struggling, his arms thrashing as his head dipped below water. Rayan reached for him and hooked a hand beneath one of his armpits, yanking him up. The man spluttered, calling out in a panicked voice what Rayan assumed were names.

He began tugging the man back toward where he thought the beach was, but it was impossible to tell. Everything was black and churning. The weight of the man kept pulling him under, and Rayan found himself swallowing mouthfuls of seawater, searing his throat. His limbs were impossibly heavy, already exhausted, and he had trouble keeping himself afloat. He felt the cold grip of panic and desperately tried to stay calm as he fought frantically against the unforgiving swirl of the sea.

After what felt like a lifetime, Rayan's feet brushed land, and he launched himself and the man onto the shore, coughing and heaving. Around them on the beach was a scatter of people, drenched and sobbing. The man staggered upright, wrenching at Rayan's shoulder, and repeated the names over and over, his face white with fear.

"Your daughters?" Rayan asked, still fighting to pull air into his lungs.

"Please help me find them."

Rayan's eyes snapped back to the ocean. The raft had disappeared, and the sea was an angry, frothing spray of waves. His heart dropped. If they were still out there, they didn't stand a chance.

"They might be here," Rayan offered weakly, gesturing at the people around them. "Do you see them?"

The man scanned the group gathering on the sand, shaking his head frantically.

Then farther down the beach, Rayan spotted a flash of yellow as someone emerged from the water, clutching a bundle of skinny limbs wrapped in a fluorescent life jacket.

"Amina! Zahra!" the man screamed and began running toward the figure.

Rayan followed closely at his heels. It was only when he got closer that he realized it was Mathias. The man's chest heaved beneath his sodden white shirt, and in his arms, two little girls clung to him for dear life.

Mathias had gotten out of the car and stared uncomprehendingly at Rayan sprinting down the beach toward the sea. His mind had clouded with a rapid succession of nightmare scenarios. Then he tore off his jacket, yanked his phone out of his pocket, and tossed both into the driver's seat. He left the keys in the ignition, pitying the poor soul brazen enough to steal it, then slammed the car door and headed down to the sand.

When Mathias made it to the black, turbulent water, Rayan had already disappeared. Cursing the man and his blind stupidity, Mathias surged into the ocean after him.

His clothes pulled him under as the waves crashed over his head. He refused to think about how Rayan, far less confident in the water, was faring. The sea was rough and choppy, which was likely why the raft had overturned. There was no shortage of stories about them in the newspaper—cheap and hastily constructed vessels that had little chance of staying afloat in a swimming pool, let alone crossing the English Channel. Smugglers often cut corners by refusing to provide life vests, leaving their passengers at the mercy of the elements.

It was just another sad fact among an avalanche of sad facts about the world that Mathias tuned out. He didn't see the point of languishing in other people's suffering. That was, until he unwittingly found himself in the thick of it, trying to save the reckless idiot of a man he happened to love.

As Mathias swam through the water, he passed several others heading back to the shore. He scanned their faces but didn't spot Rayan. He struggled to control his breathing, which quickened with exhaustion, his body no match for the unrelenting batter of the surf.

Mathias resurfaced to find a bundle of yellow bobbing beside him. His shoulder brushed against something solid, and then two small hands, the nails like claws, dug into his arm. Mathias grabbed the back of the life vest and pulled it up above the water.

It contained not one but two small children. The vest had been tied around them both in a crude attempt at protection. They clutched at him, gasping and spluttering, as Mathias attempted to keep their heads above the waves.

He scoured the ocean around him for any sign of Rayan, but it was almost impossible to see in the darkness. Hampered by the weight of the children clinging to his neck, he had no choice but to head back. Mathias fought a choking fear as he turned and began to make his way toward the shore.

He staggered onto the beach, panting. His lungs burned. Neither child had loosened their grip, and two pairs of brown eyes stared up at him, wide and glittering. Then he'd heard a series of yelps, and a frantic man with tears streaming down his face had hurtled toward them.

The children pushed against him, squirming for Mathias to let them go. He lowered them to the sand, and the man scooped them up, sobbing into their hair. The father wrestled the children from their shared life vest and Mathias saw they were both girls, long wet hair sticking to the backs of their dresses.

When he looked up, Rayan was hurrying toward him. He was soaked through, and his face was lined with concern. "Are you all right?" Rayan asked.

Mathias could barely hide the relief that surged through him. It was supplanted by an immediate rush of anger. "What the fuck were you thinking?" he growled, torn by the conflicting impulses to knock Rayan to the ground and crush him to his chest.

But before Rayan could answer, the father stood and began gesturing wildly at the sea and the other migrants gathered on the sand. Despite being reunited with his daughters, he didn't look any less panicked. He called out hoarsely in a language Mathias didn't understand.

"Mama!" One of the girls began to scream, ragged and piercing. "Mama!"

Mathias felt a dread in the pit of his stomach as he watched Rayan's face slacken and his eyes go dull.

"Mama!"

The sound seemed to rise above the rumble of the ocean, a single hollow point of pain. Rayan turned and took off toward the water. Mathias lunged forward and grabbed his arm, pulling him back.

In the distance, he could hear the approaching wail of emergency sirens drowning out the muffled cries of the people on the beach. Yet Rayan wouldn't relent. He struggled against Mathias's grip with an inhuman strength, like he would have torn off his own arm to break free.

"She's still out there—"

Mathias yanked him hard. "Listen, you hear that?" The sirens were louder now, and he could see the first police car pulling up along the shorefront. "That's the cops. We can't afford to be here right now. Do you understand? We need to go."

Rayan froze, his expression torn. He knew as well as Mathias that no good would come from them drawing the attention of the police. Mathias used the opportunity to drag him away from the family and back up to the road.

When they reached the car, Mathias looked down at the scene unfolding on the beach below. An ambulance and a second police car had joined the first, and several paramedics with thermal blankets were rushing over to the huddles of people. Out in the water, he could see the floodlights of an approaching coast guard ship. It would be searching for survivors. Or there to help recover bodies.

Mathias's throat was raw, and his drenched skin felt like ice in the cold night air. Beside him, Rayan bent over, one hand pressed against the car for support, and retched up a stomachful of seawater.

10

Rayan recalled nothing from the short drive back to the house. It was as though he'd blinked and found himself standing at his front door. He felt like an empty husk, his body a collection of dead limbs. Once inside, Mathias kicked off his wet shoes in the entranceway while Rayan stood, making a puddle by the door. As Mathias removed his watch, the hands frozen in place beneath the glass face, Rayan was devoured by a searing black fury.

"What the fuck did you do that for?"

"You're welcome," Mathias shot back. His drenched hair was plastered against his forehead, and his face was an angry mask. "Someone had to stop you from getting yourself killed."

"If it meant I could've saved their mother—"

"It would've been worth it?" Mathias hissed. "To whom?"

"You wouldn't understand."

"I understand perfectly," Mathias snarled. "You think I don't know what this is about—the center, working at the camp? This is all some fucked-up moral tally. You figure if you help enough people, you'll break even. Tell me, Rayan, how many more lives do you have to save to live with yourself?"

Rayan blinked, floored by his own transparency. "Fuck you," he spat. "This isn't about me."

His whole body hurt, and his mind swirled as if it, too, had been tossed about in the surf like a rag doll. He couldn't get the little girl's cries out of his head.

"I saw the look on your face," Mathias said, an edge to his voice.

Rayan had felt it—the familiar helplessness. Forced once again to stand back and watch someone slip away. It seemed Mathias was about to say more, but he pressed his lips together. Then he shook his head and began walking down the hall. Rayan was about to lose it. The anguish clawed out from inside him, refusing to be ignored.

"Didn't you ever wonder"—he hurled the words at Mathias's back, a shameful admission he'd kept buried all these years—"what I would've done if you hadn't picked me up that day?"

Mathias stopped. He turned to look at Rayan, his expression wary.

"I'd have thrown myself in after him," Rayan said.

Mathias strode forward and grabbed Rayan by the front of his shirt. He shoved him against the door. "Don't you ever do that to me." His voice was hard as steel, piercing through Rayan's fuddled brain with a violent clarity. "Do you hear me, Rayan?" A wave of conflicting emotions flickered across the man's face. "Don't you ever fucking leave me like that. Are we clear?"

Rayan nodded woodenly.

Mathias released him, his eyes shuttering. "I'm going to take a shower."

He disappeared into the house without another word, and Rayan stood dripping in the entranceway, his heart pounding in his chest. Then he wrenched open the front door and strode out onto the street. He didn't know where he was going, only that he needed to escape the thoughts. He could feel them circling, coming for him. It wasn't just his brother. He remembered the closed bathroom door, locked and silent. *Always too late.*

He made it to the end of the street and crossed over the road to the deserted promenade that followed the curve of the coast. Far off in the distance, he could see the flashing lights of the emergency vehicles that had gathered along the beach. Out at sea, the circle of light from the coast guard's boat lurched side to side as the cutter was jostled by the swells.

Rayan knew it was hopeless. She was gone. He sank down onto a nearby bench, and the memories found him, no longer able to be held at bay.

The past opened, swallowing him whole. He pressed his fists into his eyes, but the sobs rose, sharp and broken, squeezing through his clenched teeth. It was impossible to see where the pain began and where it ended, the tears coming for it all—two little girls who had lost their mother and the little boy who'd never gotten over losing his.

Mathias paced the floor of the study, his mind elsewhere. The sting, as his cigarette burned down to singe his fingers, snapped him out of his thoughts. He crushed the butt in the ashtray on his desk and ran a hand through his hair, which was still damp from the shower. In an attempt to distract himself, he'd come in here looking for the company's import-license paperwork, which was clearly in the filing cabinet at the warehouse.

After he'd left Rayan and climbed the stairs to the bedroom, Mathias had watched from the upstairs window as the man stalked from the house and down the darkened street. What had happened at the beach was a knife to a partially closed wound, and he'd thought it best to give Rayan a chance to regather. But standing in the silent, empty house, Mathias felt a twinge of unease. He'd still expected Rayan to come home.

The unease turned to dread lodged cold and hard in his chest. There was a part of Rayan so fragile it scared him. Mathias didn't trust himself to know what to do if it broke.

He strode down the hallway and threw on his coat then crouched to pull on his shoes. Not the ones from earlier—those he'd have to throw out. Italian leather didn't lend itself well to saltwater.

Mathias pulled open the front door and saw a dark shape on the steps outside. He reached behind him to flick on the porch light. It was Rayan, sitting hunched over on the top step. Rayan squinted as the light hit his face, and Mathias could see he was still in the same clothes, his eyes red rimmed.

"Must have locked it when I left," Rayan mumbled.

"Where are your keys?"

Rayan turned over his palm as if to show he was empty-handed. "In the water, I guess. Along with my phone."

How long has he been sitting here?

"Come inside."

Rayan looked away, staring out into the blackness. After a long time, he spoke. "I could have saved her."

The woman or your mother? Mathias stepped forward and held out his hand. "Get up."

Rayan took it, and Mathias pulled him to his feet. He led Rayan into the house and closed the door behind them.

"I don't want to think anymore," Rayan said hoarsely, digging his nails into the underside of Mathias's wrist. Sometimes he liked a roughness that bordered on pain, which Mathias was more than happy to administer. But the man was already hurting.

Mathias peeled Rayan's fingers from his wrist and linked them with his own. "Let's get you cleaned up."

Rayan yanked his hand away, his eyes darkening. "Don't coddle me."

Mathias had become better at it—knowing Rayan. He was less a puzzle than he'd once been. Mathias wrapped his arms around Rayan and pressed him tightly to his chest. Rayan wrenched against him, but Mathias held firm. Then Rayan's body began to sag as though he could no longer hold himself upright. He buried his face into the fabric of Mathias's shirt and went still, his arms hanging limply at his sides.

"I won't let go," Mathias said quietly as Rayan's breath hitched.

Later, Mathias ran a bath and helped Rayan wash the salt from his skin and rinse the sand from his hair.

"You think I'm pathetic," Rayan said, his eyes closed.

"I thought that already."

Mathias was granted the whisper of a smile. Then he'd toweled Rayan off and walked him to bed. They lay there, neither of them sleeping, waiting for the night to be over.

The office was empty when Mathias arrived at the warehouse early the following morning. After the night he'd had, it was a relief not to have to dodge any of Elise's small talk.

In truth, he'd been reluctant to venture from the house. He would have preferred not to leave Rayan, who'd eventually fallen into a fitful sleep, but he had this business with the import license to straighten out. The sooner he got his case in front of the stiffs at the trade office, the sooner he could get things resolved.

Mathias was flipping through the filing cabinet at the back of the room and had just located the folder with their current license certificate when the phone on his desk began to ring. He stared at it, wrestling with an unmistakable sense of foreboding. Then he tossed the folder onto the desk and lifted the receiver to his ear.

"*Oui?*"

"Evening, Beauvais. Or is it morning over there? I forget."

Mathias ground his teeth together. *The gall of the man.* "Think you can woo me like one of your side pieces? First love notes. What's next—flowers?"

De Luca chuckled. "When I heard your name come up, I couldn't help but be curious. You did just up and leave, after all."

"Why don't you ask Bianchi about that," Mathias said savagely. "See what he has to say."

De Luca's tone shifted. "The boss is proving less than accommodating these days," he said cryptically.

Has something happened? Perhaps life wasn't looking so rosy for the king in his kingdom. Then Mathias recalled the hot sting of betrayal that had accompanied his exit from the country and reminded himself that he didn't give a shit.

"Heard through the grapevine that you're working with the Albanians," De Luca said.

Mathias thought of Marsela sitting across from him with that self-assured smile, her tinkling laugh more ominous than amused. It was no coincidence that merely a week later, he'd found himself on the Ministère de l'Économie's blacklist. "Then you heard wrong."

"Careful with them. They're a shifty lot."

"What makes you think I have any interest in what you have to say?"

This seemed to dampen the man's peppiness. "Mathias, there's something we'd like to discuss—"

"Back off, De Luca," he warned in a low voice. "I'm done with the family." He dropped the phone back in its cradle and exhaled through his nose.

It wasn't as though Mathias was in hiding. He'd heeded Giovanni's warning and cut his ties. He didn't owe the family anything. But now—thanks to Charles's loose lips—they knew exactly where to find him.

De Luca's call hadn't been about retribution. In fact, he'd sounded almost deferential. They wanted something from him. And as far as Mathias was concerned, there was nothing the family wanted that he was willing to give.

He straightened, and his aching limbs grumbled in protest. It felt like he'd been flung through a spin cycle. He closed his eyes, and it took more effort than he expected to open them again. In addition to the restless night, he'd left the house without his morning shot of caffeine.

Mathias threw on his coat and headed to the café across the street. He ordered and stood to one side as he waited for his coffee. The smooth swell of jazz coming from the radio behind the counter faded abruptly and was replaced by the clanging intro music of the local hourly news bulletin.

"Last night, in yet another instance of its kind, a boat filled with illegal migrants setting out for Dover capsized not far from Calais beach. One woman is confirmed dead and another missing. Five people were transported to hospital with minor injuries, including three children…"

Around him, several people began to murmur.

"Another one?"

"What were they thinking, attempting a crossing like that with children?"

"They should just send them all back where they came from."

The woman behind the counter handed Mathias his coffee, and he stepped out onto the street. Instead of returning to the warehouse, he made his way to the promenade and took a seat on one of the benches facing the beach. Before him, the ocean stretched blue and tranquil along the coast. Gone were the giant swells they'd battled through the previous evening.

Mathias raised the cup of coffee to his lips. There had been a broken edge to the girl's voice as she'd screamed for her mother, a universal fear encapsulated in the sound. He wondered what the people in the café would have said if they'd heard it.

11

Rayan couldn't face the prospect of returning to the Jungle. He didn't want to think of the people living there and what awaited them. For several days, all he'd done was hang around the house, making excuses. The situation felt increasingly hopeless. The idea that he could possibly help was nothing more than a misguided delusion.

That morning, he was lying on the sofa in the living room, a book open on his chest, not even pretending to read, when Mathias appeared above him.

"Eat." Mathias shoved a bowl of oatmeal into his hands. "You're getting scrawny."

Rayan took the bowl and sat up. He'd been lost in his own thoughts and hadn't even heard Mathias in the kitchen. Rayan brought a spoonful to his mouth. It was hot and bland and oddly comforting.

Mathias sat down in a chair across from the sofa and lit a cigarette. He was shaved and dressed in his suit but apparently in no hurry to leave.

"Don't you need to get to the warehouse?"

"I don't need to do shit." Mathias stretched out his legs and took a long drag.

Rayan ate another spoon of what could have easily passed for prison gruel. Despite Rayan's pestering, Mathias was sparing when it came to the details of his childhood. Rayan did know that Mathias had spent much of it fending for himself, a fact that had revealed itself in his approach to cooking. Mathias prepared food with an austere efficiency, with flavor and variety coming second to practical considerations, like volume and nutrition. Food, for him, was a simple equation of empty and full—no different from the fuel gauge in a car—though he had a peculiar habit of ignoring the warning light, and then Rayan had to take it upon himself to feed the man before he self-destructed. Mathias hungry was a force to be reckoned with. Regardless, he'd been surprisingly receptive to Rayan's culinary dabbling. Not that he took obvious pleasure in the meals Rayan prepared, but he certainly ate them without complaint.

"What's happening in the world?" Rayan asked.

For three days, the newspaper had gone missing from the house. He knew it wasn't René's fault—despite the kid's less-than-stellar track record. Mathias had been deliberately shielding Rayan from the reporting on the latest incident. At this point, it was a common occurrence to find articles with confronting images and headlines detailing the number of people drowned. There existed a collective resignation at how normal these stories had become. The thought made his stomach turn.

Mathias shrugged. "New day, same stories."

"War, contested elections, environmental ruin?"

"That about covers it."

They sat in silence, the events of the past few days hanging over them. Rayan spooned more oatmeal into his mouth. He was ashamed by how much he'd leaned on Mathias. While he'd been humbled by Mathias's gracious handling of him, he was tired of his issues dominating their shared experience.

"Tell me about where you went to school in Montreal." Rayan could still conjure the photo of Mathias in his mother's entranceway, the powder-blue shirt and striped tie coupled with his cold expression.

"What's to tell?"

"It was a private school, right? You had to wear uniforms?"

Mathias smirked, exhaling twin streams of smoke from his nostrils. "Now, that's a troubling predilection."

Rayan snickered. "What were you like back then? When you were—"

"Young and innocent?" Mathias supplied. "I'll save you the suspense—I was never innocent."

"Did the teachers like you?"

"I think you can gauge the answer to that."

Rayan gave a soft laugh and took another spoonful of the porridge.

"They hated me. They would have expelled me if they could," Mathias said.

"What stopped them?"

"Proof. No one could ever pin anything on me." The man's mouth tweaked in what appeared to be quiet pride. "I once paid a kid a hundred bucks to fess up to breaking another boy's nose."

"What else did you do?"

"Ran a couple betting pools, sold pills. I dangled the class representative from the second-floor window for refusing to pay his tab. He never settled late after that."

Rayan shook his head with a grin.

"I told you it was baked in." Mathias blew smoke through his teeth.

Rayan looked down at the bowl in his hands, suddenly serious. "Why did your import license get revoked?"

"It's an empty threat. Nothing to take seriously."

Rayan frowned. "Who's sending you a warning, Mathias?"

Mathias seemed to consider his answer. "The Albanians. They've taken an interest in the business."

"As in, the Albanian mafia?"

"Like attracts like."

"Should I be concerned?"

"Do I look concerned?"

"No, but I've seen you smile staring down the barrel of a gun."

Mathias took another pull on his cigarette. "It's not working, by the way. There are simpler ways to distract me."

"What are you talking about?"

"What you said the other night."

Rayan felt a hot spike of discomfort. "I haven't had thoughts like that in a long time. Not since you." He swallowed, the bowl warm in his hands. "I don't do well without someone to live for," he said, the truth of it almost painful. "It was easy to make you that person. Even without you knowing it."

Mathias stared at him, the cigarette perched between his fingers. "You know..." he said after a moment. "It was a point of pride, how little people meant to me. Then you had to get under my skin." He leaned forward, elbows resting on his knees, not breaking his gaze. "Who exactly do you need to redeem yourself to?"

Rayan dropped his head. He thought of his mother's hopes for him, forever memorialized in her inscription. *Noble and kind. Someone to be proud of.* A reminder of everything he wasn't.

"She would have hated what I am."

"And what's that? Alive?" Mathias countered. "Believe me, that's an accomplishment in itself. And you're going to agonize over how you did it—that in the glut of options you were given, you didn't pick a cleaner way to survive? She'd take the end over the means—I guarantee it."

Rayan's eyes snapped back to Mathias, his mouth lurching. "You don't...?"

"I don't what?"

"Regret anything?"

When Mathias replied, his voice was hard. "I don't regret a fucking thing. This is how life works—you get dealt a hand, and then you make your move. You don't spend the rest of the game wondering if you should've made a different one." He crushed his cigarette in the ashtray on the coffee table, and a single column of smoke rose from his fingertips. "Stop playing hooky, Rayan. There's nothing wrong with your humanitarian crusade, but considering it a form of penance is a waste of head space."

"I needed a way make sense of things," Rayan said, unable to articulate the fear that had gripped him after leaving the family and looking out at the yawning expanse of life ahead. Even now, part of him still felt unworthy of his freedom.

"You don't have to make sense of it. Not every event needs to be assigned some greater meaning. You can either remain inactive or act. Forward momentum—live by that."

While he'd done so far less kindly when Rayan was a grunt, Mathias had always managed to bring the salient facts of a difficult situation into clear definition.

"So, what are you sitting around here for?" Mathias got to his feet. "Think of all the needy people you could be wasting your time helping."

He headed for the door but stopped as he rounded the back of the sofa. Mathias reached out and cupped Rayan's chin. He bent to kiss him, his lips warm and gentle.

Rayan closed his eyes, words deserting him, hoping only to communicate the depth of his gratitude in the sweetness of the kiss he returned.

Rayan arrived at the service office later that afternoon to find a relieved Asmarina sorting through files in the back room.

"There you are, Rayan." She wrapped him in a tight hug. "We were worried when you stopped returning our calls."

Rayan hadn't communicated much about his absence. He'd simply left a message at the center to say he wasn't coming in.

"Phone trouble," he offered feebly. It wasn't a complete lie. He'd had to pick up a new one and transfer his number.

"Right." Asmarina looked at Rayan as if waiting for him to say more. It wasn't uncommon in their line of work for people to disappear when the weight of the job got too much.

"I just needed a few days," he admitted.

She nodded and gave him a reassuring squeeze on the shoulder. "Well, we missed you."

Rayan smiled. "What do you have for me?"

"Some good news for one," Asmarina said, her eyes brightening. "We got confirmation of the funding from Groupe d'action."

"That was quick."

"Karl did say the meeting was more a formality. They were keen to get involved from the get-go."

"That is good news."

"And Laurent managed to pin down a meeting with the mayor for next week."

"Next week?" Rayan marveled. Contact with the mayor's office was usually painful and protracted. Maybe Durand had finally realized that ignoring the problem wouldn't help anyone.

"You'll come, of course."

"I'll think about it."

"Just so I'm not the only foreigner in the room," she teased.

Rayan laughed.

"I'm sure you've heard..." Asmarina lowered her voice, and the smile slipped from her face. "About the latest drownings."

Rayan could still recall the sting of seawater as it burned his throat. The panic as wave after wave broke over his head. He thought of the mother of the children on the beach—how frightened she must have been as the water filled her lungs.

He nodded wordlessly.

"There were several families hoping to reach relatives in Britain. But after the failed crossing, most of them ended up here at the camp. We've been trying to help them work through the process of applying for refugee status in France."

Rayan had assisted others with similar attempts, and he was well-versed in the requirements the French immigration system imposed on those applying for asylum. He would gather the information for the bid and then submit it with the assistance of an old school friend of Laurent's—a local lawyer who volunteered his services for a few hours each week. As cumbersome as the process was, it held more chance of success than setting out across the channel in search of better opportunities in the UK.

Asmarina led him out of the cabin and into the Jungle. They followed the dirt road that crossed through the middle of the camp toward a section of tents on the north side. "There's a family that needs some extra help with their application on account of their... situation." She paused by a blue canvas tent. "They're the family of one of the women who drowned."

Rayan knew, before she lifted the entrance flap, who he would find inside. Sitting on a frayed mat on the tent floor was the man from the beach, his younger daughter on his lap while the older one hung back.

"This is Farhan Taleb and his daughters, Amina and Zahra." Asmarina gave Farhan a warm smile and gestured toward Rayan. "Farhan, this is Rayan Ayari. He's here to help you and your family make a bid for asylum."

Farhan got to his feet with a look of shock, and the young girl slipped from his lap and hid behind the leg of his pants. He stepped forward to offer his hand, and Rayan shook it numbly.

Asmarina passed Rayan the folder with paperwork. "I'll leave you to it." She patted him on the back and stepped out of the tent.

"It was you, wasn't it?" Farhan moved to grip Rayan's shoulder. "On the beach. I didn't get a chance to thank you."

Rayan nodded and gently extracted himself. He didn't deserve the man's thanks. They stood in silence before Farhan indicated for Rayan to join them on the mat. Rayan sat down across from Farhan and his daughters, the folder deadweight in his hand.

"Your wife..." Rayan managed finally.

Farhan shook his head solemnly.

"I'm sorry."

"She'd have been grateful her daughters are safe."

The two girls stared at Rayan with large brown eyes. They were pretty, with angular faces and long dark hair tangled at the ends. He couldn't help but wonder if they took after their mother. Rayan felt his chest tighten.

"Let me help you keep them that way," he said, suddenly resolute. He opened the folder and pulled out the application, flipping to the first page. "We'll try and find a home for you here. Asmarina has talked to you about the process involved in filing?"

Farhan nodded. "Do you think it's a good idea?"

"It's the best chance you've got. That being said, it can take a long time, and the odds vary. I can't make any promises, but we will try."

Farhan gave him a tired smile. "Thank you, Rayan. It seems all we can do is try."

12

Mathias returned from picking up their newly reissued import license to find Elise and Vicente perched atop two crates in the warehouse, playing cards.

"You're very bad at this," Vicente was saying as Elise handed him a fold of bills.

"One more round. I think I'm getting the hang of it."

"Back to work!" Mathias barked as he walked past them on his way to the office. "I don't pay you two to sit around."

Vicente scrambled to his feet and pocketed the cards and his hard-won cash. Elise followed Mathias into the office and watched as he withdrew a folder from the filing cabinet and slipped the license inside.

"All sorted, then?" she asked.

It had proven more difficult than he'd anticipated—and far more expensive. He'd spent days cleaning up the mess with the trade office, which had demanded he provide six months' worth of customs-and-clearance records to remove the hold they'd placed on the company. Apparently, someone had reported them on suspicion of importing restricted goods. The irony wasn't lost on him.

"Don't encourage him," Mathias said, changing the subject. "He doesn't need any more excuses to slack off."

"Ah, but if he's good at his job, then who would you take your frustration out on?" Elise said smugly.

Mathias cocked his head. "You." The phone on his desk rang, and he picked it up.

"Mathias."

"Heylen."

"You're playing hard to get," the Belgian said.

Mathias eased into his chair. "The wife after a matching coffee table?"

Elise shot him a conspiratorial look and moved over to her desk, clearly listening.

Heylen chuckled into the receiver. "I just had a guy in here who was the former Minister of Energy and Mobility for the Austrian government."

"And...?"

"I asked him what he'd do if a high-ticket shipment couldn't get clearance to dock."

The man was so transparent. Mathias was almost enjoying toying with him. "Is this your idea of a riddle?"

"He thought we could leave it out at sea and wait for the slow churn of bureaucracy."

Hell, I'll bite. "So, in all his time in government, he didn't have a single contact capable of greasing a few wheels?"

Heylen let out a triumphant laugh. "I need you, Mathias. The new business—we'll split it down the middle. I front the cash, you run the show."

"I don't think you know what you're getting into."

"Prove me wrong, then."

"Take care, Heylen," he said and hung up.

From her desk, Elise gave him a sly smile and pulled a pack of cigarettes from her pocket. "I have questions. Come for a smoke?"

Mathias sighed. *Better to squash the curiosity before it gets the best of her.*

The clouds darkened in the sky overhead as he and Elise stood by the staff entrance, smoking. The muggy air clung to his skin, and Mathias felt a drop of rain graze his temple. He predicted it would be bucketing down within the hour.

"He called yesterday, too, while you were out." Elise brought her cigarette to her lips.

"What happened to passing on messages?"

"I don't remember *secretary* being part of the job description."

Mathias gave a dispassionate grunt.

"What's this about, then? Are you planning some sort of joint venture?" she asked.

He'd looked into the company Heylen had acquired. It was a family-owned operation run by a fellow Belgian businessman. While Heylen had only purchased it to limit competition with JFH Logistics, the business made a tidy profit and was a decent-sized player in its own right.

"Let's make this clear—I'm not working for Heylen."

"But if he's asking for you specifically, you must have done something to impress him."

Mathias tapped his ash. Partnering with Heylen would give him access to an entirely new tier of contacts. He'd be rubbing shoulders with the cream of Europe's corporate world. It was less a steppingstone than a springboard.

"That's not it," Mathias said. "He just can't stand for someone to tell him no."

Elise raised a skeptical eyebrow but wisely kept her thoughts to herself. She parted her lips to exhale a demure curl of smoke. "Did you hear about what happened at the beach? You know, before I moved here, I had no idea about any of it. I'm sure it was in the news. I was just so self-absorbed."

"Was?"

Elise shot him a look. "God, humans have made such a mess of things, haven't we?" She gave a woeful shake of her head. "I don't know how Rayan does it—seeing all the misery at the camp. It's so sad."

Mathias eyed her shrewdly. Rayan had a high tolerance for misery, built up like a muscle. "Well, the world's a sad fucking place."

There was a crunch of tires, and they both glanced over as an unmarked delivery van turned into the parking lot and pulled up alongside the warehouse.

Elise frowned. "I didn't know we were expecting a delivery today. Were you waiting on something?"

The driver got out, hoisted a small wooden crate from the back of the van, and placed it on the ground by the roller doors. Mathias and Elise dealt with enough shipments, many valued at six figures or more, that their delivery people knew to never leave one sitting outside. Mathias watched as the driver returned to the van and drove back out onto the road. He tossed his cigarette to the ground and walked over to crate, Elise at his heels. As he got closer, he could smell the fetid stink of decaying flesh.

"Don't touch it," he instructed Elise sharply. She recoiled and placed a hand over her nose.

His name was inscribed in large black letters on the top of the crate. He retrieved the folding knife from his pocket and extracted the blade, then used it to jimmy off the lid. A foulness filled the air, and Elise shrank back in horror.

"Holy shit," she whispered.

A severed pig's head stared up at them, mouth open and eyes a cloudy black. The crate was lined with a sheet of plastic to prevent the ooze leaking from the pig's neck from soaking through the bottom. A knife had been crudely shoved into the front of the animal's skull.

"Amateurs," Mathias muttered.

He would have drawn blood by now. Either Marsela was handling him with kid gloves, or she had another agenda. Regardless, he couldn't get a read on her intentions, which was unusual—and dangerous.

"This is about the drugs, isn't it?" Elise said, her eyes wide behind her glasses. "What are we going to do?"

"You're going to go inside and get Vicente to take care of this. Have him toss it in the dumpster out back," Mathias replied evenly.

His appraiser hovered beside him, unmoving.

"Go on, Dumont."

She started then turned and headed quickly back into the warehouse. Mathias flicked the knife closed and stowed it. Then he dropped the lid back on the crate, concealing its rank contents.

The next time Rayan went to visit Farhan, he brought a bag filled with food, clothing, and small gifts for the children. They'd found themselves irreversibly connected by the events of their meeting, and he felt a growing responsibility for the family's future.

When he arrived at their tent, Farhan had just made tea on a portable kerosene stove and invited Rayan to join him. Rayan unloaded his bag of treasures onto the mat in the middle of the tent, and the girls gathered around, their shyness forgotten as he distributed sweets and colored markers.

"Is this for me, *amo*?" Zahra asked, reaching for a package of rainbow hair clips.

Rayan nodded, and she gave him a wide smile.

While the girls used the markers to draw on a flattened cardboard box, Farhan poured tea into two dented metal mugs and handed one to Rayan. The tea was weak but hot, and Rayan appreciated the effort taken to prepare it. Tasks that only required the simple flick of a switch at home—washing clothes, heating water—involved an elaborate undertaking of time and resources at the camp. Rayan had worked with volunteers afraid to eat the food or drink the water here, turning down a resident's request to share bread or tea, unaware of the slight their refusal amounted to.

Farhan sat across from Rayan on the mat and gestured at the pile of items he'd brought. "This is very kind."

"If there's anything else you need, you can come and find me at the service office."

"Thank you, Rayan. We have plenty."

For a man whose life had been reduced to so little, it was jarring to hear him refer to what he had as plenty.

"Ayari—it's not a common last name," Farhan said after a moment, and he raised his chin curiously. "Back home in Aleppo, I have a friend from Beirut. He speaks in a similar way. Is that where you're from?"

"Canada, actually."

Farhan's face lit up. "Ah, I have a cousin in Canada. Which part?"

"Quebec."

"I don't know much about Quebec. But I hear Canada's a beautiful place. Very cold, though."

Rayan smiled. "It can get very cold. Do you also have family in the UK?"

"My wife has an uncle there. We weren't sure that would be enough to qualify for residency, but it was the only hope we had. Of course, now I don't know if I would've made the same choice."

He stared into his tea, and they fell silent. The girls chattered in the background, a harmony of voices amid the sounds filtering through the thin canvas walls that separated them from the Jungle.

"You're not Lebanese, then?" Farhan asked.

"My mother was."

Farhan nodded, and an unspoken understanding passed between them. "When did she die?"

"When I was a child."

Farhan looked down at his youngest daughter, who had climbed onto his lap and was using a tiny pink comb to brush the hair on a plastic doll. "So, they will be all right?" As he spoke, his voice cracked. He cleared his throat. "They will be all right even without their mother?"

Rayan couldn't make any promises. All he knew, from his own experience, was that children were resilient. "They're strong girls."

"They are," Farhan agreed.

"What was her name?" a voice piped up behind him.

Rayan glanced over to see that Zahra had stopped her playing and was looking at him as though she'd been listening the whole time.

"Samira."

"Our mama's Navine." She stabbed the toe of her sandal into the mat. "Do you still think about her?"

"Always."

"Was she nice?"

81

"Very. She loved to read me stories. What about your mother? What was she like?"

"Beautiful," Zahra said proudly. "She taught me how to draw."

"She would doodle in the girls' school workbooks," Farhan recalled quietly. "Write little notes in the margins, reminding them to study hard."

Rayan looked at the two children. Amina was the spitting image of her father, but Zahra's high nose and broad forehead must have come from her mother.

Farhan repositioned Amina on his lap. "The man who saved them from the water—is he a friend of yours?"

"Yes."

"Will you thank him for me?"

Rayan hesitated. "He might not be overly receptive to your thanks."

"That's the mark of a decent man—someone who does things without chasing acclaim."

A smile tugged at Rayan's lips. *So I'm not the only one who sees it.* "I'll be sure to pass the message on."

"Thank you. I'll feel better knowing you have."

"Of course." Rayan finished his tea.

Farhan lifted the pot off the stove to refill their cups. "What brought you here from Canada, Rayan?"

Rayan took the hot mug into his hands and turned it absently. "A change of circumstance."

"Good or bad?" Farhan asked, his eyes crinkling.

Rayan weighed the complexity of the question. "Both," he said finally. "How about you?"

Farhan's face grew serious. "Only bad. We would've stayed if we could. The girls loved their teachers and spending time with their *jadda*. But they closed the research center because of the fighting, and I lost my job. We were hungry more often than we weren't. That's no way for children to live."

"You're right. It isn't."

"There was too much violence, too much danger. We knew people who'd gotten out, and we decided we would too." He gave a sigh. "But who can say what we should have done? Leaving or staying, what would have happened either way? Maybe she would still be here, or maybe none of us would." He blinked quickly and looked away.

"The research center," Rayan said, careful to change the subject. "What line of work are you in?"

"I'm an agricultural scientist. We researched the development of sustainable crops in the world's dry areas."

"That's a rather specialized field."

"It is. I know more than any normal person should about soil and rocks."

They both laughed, and Amina squirmed on her father's lap. Farhan's expression once again turned pensive. "I just hope they will remember their mother, where they came from, who they are. I don't want them to lose everything."

"They won't forget her." Rayan shook his head, surprised by the conviction in his voice.

Amina lifted the doll in her hands to press it against her father's face.

Farhan moved the doll to one side and planted a kiss on the little girl's cheek. "I hope you're right."

13

Charles lived a half hour's drive from Calais, on a large block of land, where he tended animals and grew a selection of crops. It served as an idyllic cover for his less-savory activities. Casual drug runner, part-time farmer—who could want for more?

It was already dark when Mathias pulled up outside the main house that evening. He got out of the car and walked around to the covered porch, where Charles sat drinking, one hand dangling down to pet the black mutt lying at his feet. Charles spotted Mathias and reached for a bottle of beer from the cooler at his side. He raised it in offering.

"I'll pass." Mathias took a seat on the chair across from him. He'd never developed a taste for the stuff. As far as he was concerned, beer belonged in the same category as one's own piss.

Charles shrugged and returned the bottle to the cooler. "You a dog man, Mathias?"

"I barely have the stomach for people."

Charles let out a snort and ruffled his dog's ears. "There's no comparison. People are selfish sacks of shit. A dog will have your back to your dying breath."

They're also excellent conversationalists. "At least they don't talk back."

"That they don't." Charles drained the bottle in his hand and set it down on the porch. Then he lifted another from the cooler and reached into his pocket to pull out a bottle opener. He snapped off the lid, and it went clattering across the floor. "I've got everything set up, just like I told you. Want to take a look?"

"I didn't drive all the way out here for your company."

Charles chuckled and got to his feet with a grunt. Beer still in hand, he descended the porch steps with a series of short whistles that made the dog's ears prick to attention. "Here, Skip. Here, girl." The dog leapt up and bolted after him.

Less eager, Mathias stood and followed the man through the garden and out toward an old stone barn in the field beyond. The grass was tall and wet with dew, dampening the hems of his pant legs. Mud oozed up and around the sides of his shoes as he navigated the sodden earth.

"Should have said to leave your city clothes behind," Charles said, craning his neck to shoot him a grin. "I have an extra pair of work boots at the house."

Mathias scoffed. "I'll survive."

They reached the barn, and Charles slid back the barrel bolt on the door. It gave a loud creak of protest as he pushed it open. Inside, the space was empty except for a cluster of plastic feed drums. The dog surged past their legs and dropped its nose to the ground, sniffing around the perimeter. Charles moved to the far corner of the barn and tapped the toe of his boot against the floorboards in several places until Mathias heard a hollow thud. Then Charles crouched, placing his beer aside, and pressed down on a loose wooden board, which buckled beneath his hand. He slid it out and removed two other panels to reveal a large metal box that appeared to be bolted to the foundation. He fumbled beneath his shirt to pull out a key on a chain that hung from his neck. After unlocking the lid, he opened the box to reveal a neatly lined cavity that contained the stacked stash of powder-filled bags Mathias had asked him to pick up from the warehouse.

"It's all here. I've got commercial-grade lining to keep the moisture out so everything stays dry and cozy."

Mathias gave a satisfied nod.

Charles locked up the box and set the floorboards back in place. He straightened and wiped the dirt from his hands on his pants before bending to retrieve his beer. "I've had a chance to look into that business for you."

"How much are we talking?"

"I'd say you're getting close to twenty mil, street value," Charles said. "It's a premium product. Fetches quite a nice price on the open market."

Through the barn window, Mathias could see the darkened fields stretching out into the distance. Somewhere behind him, the dog let out a low whine.

"I have a few parties who're interested," Charles went on.

"And would one of those be our mutual friends up north?"

Charles eyed him carefully. "I've put feelers out on the mainland first, but I know for a fact they'd be in the running. They don't always get product of this quality out that way." He gave another whistle, and the dog appeared by his side. He reached out and rubbed its head. "Have you decided what you're going to do with it?"

Mathias hadn't. The last thing he wanted was to start a full-scale war with the Albanians. At the same time, he refused to be fucked over by Marsela and her group of opportunists. While he didn't have the manpower to match them, he sure as hell had the balls. The way he saw it, he was well within his rights to hold their product hostage and tack on his own penalty fee as punishment if only as a deterrent, so they knew not to mess with his business again. But Mathias wasn't going to make any sudden moves. Better to keep them waiting and see if he could get Marsela to show her hand first.

"Not yet. I'm keeping my options open."

Charles nodded and took a gulp of beer. "You can always find another buyer and pit them against each other."

Mathias's mouth curved into a smirk. "I underestimated you, Charles." He knocked the heel of his shoe against the barn floor, dislodging a clump of mud. "For a flannel-wearing redneck, you've got a real eye for this business."

Hôtel de Ville was an ornate building of redbrick and white limestone, which served as the seat of the Calais City Council. Commissioned by King Francis II, the building held official monument status and featured heavily in the tourist tat hawked to visiting holidaymakers. The mayor's office was located on the top floor. Rayan sat with Laurent and Asmarina in the reception area as they waited for their appointment with Durand.

"We've got this," Laurent said in an attempt at encouragement. His smile didn't quite reach his eyes.

Gone was the excitement of their meeting with Groupe d'action. Perhaps he'd begun to realize exactly what they were up against. After the recent fatal crossing and a string of violent incidents, the mood in the Jungle had become even more apprehensive. The lines outside the service office stretched farther than usual as people grew frightened about what was to come.

"Maybe we should have brought along one of the residents," Asmarina said, glancing over at the mayor's secretary, who sat behind her desk. "Listening to their stories, he's got to understand why this is so important."

"He'd probably see it as a gimmick, a way to make him look bad," Laurent said. "Durand's pretty touchy about the subject, especially with the election coming up."

Rayan tried not to let the cynicism show on his face. During his time with the family, he'd had a lot to do with the Montreal City Council. In his experience, those tasked with serving the city were often more interested in serving themselves. He didn't know whether to expect much else from Claude Durand.

"It's going to take all our efforts to get him to see the benefit of a permanent solution," Asmarina added. "Especially since the city seems determined to wash its hands of the problem."

Durand's secretary stood and approached them with a smile. "He's ready for you." She motioned for them to follow her, and together, they walked down the corridor toward a set of wood-paneled doors. "The mayor is quite busy today, so we're on a bit of a tight schedule. But I know he's an admirer of your work, Monsieur Moreau."

"My wife's the one who deserves the credit," Laurent replied. "She's the real force behind the organization."

The woman nodded vaguely before rapping on one of the doors and poking her head into the office. "Claude, I have your three o'clock."

Mayor Durand looked different from how he appeared on the campaign posters that had started cropping up around the city. He was tall and portly, with a prominent mustache and a rapidly diminishing hairline. The billboards gave him a glowing tan that matched the sun-kissed setting of the district he was trying to win, but in person, his skin had a pasty hue.

He greeted them with handshakes, and Rayan fought the urge to pull back when Durand clapped him on the shoulder like a schoolboy. They took seats as the mayor returned to his desk. Rayan's eyes fell on a framed photo of the man's family, perched on the corner of the desk. It was angled outward to reveal a short blond woman sandwiched between two teenage girls with matching toothy smiles.

Durand placed his clasped hands out in front of him. "I understand you've come to me today with a proposal."

Laurent paused briefly and tapped his fingers against his knee, which meant he was nervous, despite his earlier expression of confidence. "As you know, the situation at the Jungle isn't ideal for anyone—the residents of Calais or the people forced to live there. But with no real plan in place to address the situation, it's only going to get worse. The city's existing facilities are at capacity, and as more people arrive, they're going to find themselves forced into the hands of those looking to exploit them. We have a duty of care to those who come to our city. We can't ignore that responsibility."

Durand's face remained unmoving. "Then what would you suggest we do?"

Laurent reached into his bag and withdrew the portfolio he'd shown to the Groupe d'action committee. He placed it open on the mayor's desk. "We've had a bid for funding accepted by Groupe d'action, one of the national NGOs that's based out here. The situation in Northern France has drawn the attention of the

EU, and they've made available a development grant designated for a local project in Calais. Our proposal involves building a targeted housing facility that would accommodate the most vulnerable in the camp—the elderly, women, unaccompanied children. We'd use wait-lists and a priority vetting system."

The mayor flipped through the pages of the portfolio as Laurent went on.

"A significant part of the construction costs would be covered by the grant. However, we were hoping the city would provide the remainder. We believe you have mechanisms available to request assistance from the government on humanitarian grounds. It would cost far less than funding the project independently. All the figures are in there. We're also proposing a ground lease, which would be an additional source of revenue for the council. I hate to use the phrase, but it really is a win-win."

Durand stared absently at the plans. "And how much is the remainder you need the city to foot?"

"Around seven million."

The mayor let out a heavy sigh. "The council is struggling to finance a much-needed upgrade to our water-treatment plant, and you want us to pour even more money into handouts for these people?"

Asmarina leaned forward. "They've come here, having made a gamble on humanity, hoping we'll help shelter them in their time of need. And that camp is not shelter. For many, it represents danger, violence, and fear. The least we can do is give them a decent place to stay while they figure out their next steps. As if their journeys haven't been harrowing enough, now they're left to live like dogs? No—worse than that. There are animals in shelters around this city that are better taken care of than the people living in that camp."

Durand looked at Asmarina, somewhat taken aback.

She clenched her hands tightly in her lap. "Perhaps that was a rather strong analogy..."

"It doesn't make it any less true," Rayan cut in. "The forces bringing people here are large and complex, but what we do about them when they arrive says a lot about who we are and our priorities. It shouldn't be beyond our capacity as a city to provide people with a safe place to sleep."

The mayor's expression turned pained. "I understand the sentiment and truly appreciate the work you do, but the people of Calais have had enough. For years, they've had to put up with thousands of illegal squatters. And now you're wanting to give them a permanent reason to keep coming here? We build something like that, and we create a fixing point. They'll never leave. I'm not going to roll out the red carpet for these people."

"'These people,'" Rayan echoed sharply, "have children, parents, sisters, brothers. The woman who drowned at the beach last week has two little girls—just like you." He stood and stepped forward to turn the photo of the mayor's wife and daughters around to face him.

Durand reached out to steady the frame with his fingers. "I'm not denying that, but where do we draw the line?" His voice had gone quiet. "The refugees come from countries that should be looking after them. Why should responsibility fall to the residents of Calais?"

"Because they're here, in our city," Rayan said. "That's the reality of the situation. We have the opportunity to prove that not everyone has abandoned them."

The mayor gave him a pitying look, and Rayan fought against a bubbling anger. He knew how he would have dealt with a man like this before, but despite being back in his suit, Rayan had no power in this office. They had come with their hands out, hoping for his blessing.

"I think what Rayan's trying to say," Laurent interjected judiciously, "is that you get a chance to be the hero here, show the world Calais's generosity. It would be a testament to your legacy."

"I'm not concerned about my legacy. I only want to keep my constituents happy. Putting up with the camp is bad enough, but to use city money to build a migrant housing facility? There's no way residents will approve." He looked at Rayan pointedly. "That's the reality of the situation."

Rayan slammed his fist down on the desk, and both the mayor and Laurent jumped. "Can't you see that this is about more than votes? This is about people's lives."

Laurent stood and placed a hand on Rayan's shoulder. "It might be best if you waited outside."

Rayan's gaze traveled from Laurent's grimace to the shocked expression on the mayor's face, and he muttered something in the way of an apology.

"I think I'll join him," Asmarina said stiffly, and the two of them walked back out to the reception area.

Chastened, Rayan paced as Asmarina took a seat on one of the wooden benches. "I shouldn't have done that," he said.

"Better than sitting there smiling in that bastard's face." She tilted her head curiously. "You have a temper, Ayari. I wouldn't have guessed."

More than a temper. He had a violent streak refined to perfection. Rayan clenched his fists. He was still seething but embarrassed that he'd lost control like that. Especially with everything they had on the line.

Asmarina sighed. "It's always the same—the fate of the many placed in the hands of the few. And a clueless few at that."

When Laurent emerged from the mayor's office, he looked crestfallen. "He said he's required to bring the proposal to vote at the next council meeting, but he won't be endorsing the project. It's a no from him."

"Even with the majority of the funding secured?" Asmarina asked.

Laurent shook his head. "It was too ambitious. He's not interested in solutions." He began organizing the materials in his hands, slipping the letter of intent Karl had written for them inside the portfolio with the construction plans. "Durand holds the keys here. If he won't back it, I'm not sure there's any hope for the project."

They made their way outside, and Rayan declined Asmarina's offer of a ride home. He left on foot, hoping to dispel the bitter curl of defeat on his walk back to the house. He felt impotent, a fizzing ball of frustration. In his pocket, his phone began to ring. It was the number of the service office at the camp.

"Rayan," one of the volunteers said frantically when he picked up. "Can you come? We have a bit of a situation, and they refuse to talk to anyone but you."

They? He crossed the road and doubled back in the direction of the port. When he arrived at the Jungle, he hurried over to the cabin and found Farhan's daughters standing outside, holding hands, as Amina wailed hysterically. Around them, people went about their business, accustomed to living amid the full display of public emotion.

"Hey, hang on now," Rayan murmured as he approached, but the girls recoiled, frightened. In his suit, he must have looked like a stranger. "It's only me."

"*Amo?*" Zahra reached up to tug on the hem of his jacket.

"Where's your papa?" Rayan asked.

The girl shook her head. "Gone. They took him."

Rayan felt a cold realization dawn. "Who did?"

"The bad men."

14

Elise was at an estate sale in Dunkirk—some fashion heiress who'd spent her life collecting Baroque portraits. She'd left that morning, giddy at the prospect of picking through the woman's house for a bargain. Mathias had given her a generous upper limit and told her to use her best judgment.

It was amusing to see how flustered she got when he took his hand off the wheel. He had no doubt she'd come back with a decent set of purchases, but she didn't seem to share his faith. Her confidence had been knocked by the Indonesian-sculpture debacle, which wasn't necessarily a bad thing. If feelings of guilt helped secure her silence about the contents of the crate, then that worked in his favor.

Mathias was at the office, relishing the silence his appraiser had left in her wake, when the phone rang. He steeled himself for another pitch from Heylen.

"Changed your mind yet?" It was Marsela.

"Not something I'm in the habit of."

"I heard you ran into some administrative trouble. Such a shame when the government makes things difficult for hardworking businesses."

"Paperwork is easy to straighten out." Like he was going to give her the satisfaction of knowing he'd spent days jumping through hoops. "I wanted to thank you for the gift," Mathias went on. "You really shouldn't have." Even after Vicente had disposed of the gory delivery, the smell had lingered like a bad omen.

"Quit being coy, Beauvais. You have something that doesn't belong to you."

"I think you'll find it does. I have the bill of sale to prove it."

Marsela's teasing tone turned cold. "The product in the crate—we want it back."

"And by 'we,' you're referring to your small group of investors?"

"They're not as small as you think. And they're not afraid to throw their weight around."

"So who're we talking? The Bergs, Osmani?"

There was a long pause. "What do you know about the families?" she asked.

"Only what I've heard in passing."

"Then you've heard enough to know you're messing with the wrong people. If you don't return what's ours—"

"Then what?" he challenged, not about to be cowed by this woman and her crew of Balkan gangsters.

"You don't want to find out."

The line went dead.

Mathias thrummed his fingers against the desk. Despite her threats, Marsela's maneuvering felt toothless, almost tame. She was getting something out of their back-and-forth, and he couldn't put his finger on what.

Preoccupied, he was taken off guard when the office door swung open and Rayan strode in. He was wearing a suit, and his face was set in an angry frown. Mathias blinked, briefly transported to the past, as though Rayan had transformed back into his second.

"Didn't know it was dress-up day," he remarked, covering his surprise.

Rayan unfolded the piece of paper in his hand and splayed it out across Mathias's desk. It was a map of continental Europe that had been marked up in several places with black pen. "I went to see the mayor."

"And you two are planning a vacation?" Mathias asked as he peered at the scribbles Rayan had made across the map. Rayan scowled at him, and Mathias relented. "I take it things didn't go well with Durand."

"I'm here for a favor."

Mathias stilled. The man wasn't asking to borrow the car. What he wanted involved something from before. Rayan wasn't an idiot—he knew there were activities Mathias still dabbled in that stretched the definition of *legal*. Mathias was too pragmatic to let needless regulation get in the way of his success. They'd never directly discussed the topic, but Mathias had known to keep Rayan out of his affairs. And Rayan—for the most part—had chosen to look the other way. That was, until now. He'd been witness to enough of Mathias's negotiations during his time—IOUs carefully distributed and later meticulously collected. If he wanted something off the menu, Rayan would have to be willing to pay for it.

"You know how this works. I don't give them away for free. Even to you."

"I know. I intend to repay it."

"How, I wonder?" Mathias asked, leaning back in his chair.

"Let me worry about that."

"I'm not going to knock him off."

"Jesus," Rayan hissed, glancing at the door and lowering his voice. "I'm not asking you to whack the mayor."

"So, what is this favor?"

"There are smaller gangs—hustlers who prey on migrant encampments. They pick up men and take them to work illegally out east on construction sites, in mines and factories. The groups negotiate contracts with these businesses and profit from the forced labor." Rayan indicated to the points he'd marked on the map. "We're aware of several places in Poland and the Czech Republic, but there are many more. And without knowing which group is involved, it becomes almost impossible to find them."

Mathias could see where this was heading.

"I need to track down someone who's been picked up. I thought you might still have connections out east who'd have more information."

"You mean the Russians," Mathias said. The Bratva had a fair amount to do with smuggling people into Europe through the eastern borders and would no doubt be familiar with the groups that operated inside the continent.

Rayan nodded.

"Who is this someone?"

"Farhan Taleb." Rayan paused. "The man from the beach. He and his daughters ended up at the camp. He was taken from the Jungle earlier today."

"And you're going to go out there and bring him back?"

"Exactly."

"You're being stupid, Rayan."

"No, I'm taking action."

Mathias exhaled in frustration. *Trust him to twist my words.* "He's not your responsibility."

"He wanted me to thank you for saving the girls. Amina and Zahra are their names. And they need their father. They can't be alone in this world."

Mathias remembered the clench of those tiny arms around his neck. He clicked his tongue. "You're too soft."

Rayan fixed him with a steady gaze. "But you knew that already."

Mathias stared back. He'd been mistaken. Rayan might have looked like he had before, but this man was different. He'd come here not as a lackey, not as a lover, but as an equal.

Mathias stood and folded up the map then slipped it into his pocket. "I may still be in contact with the Bratva," he admitted finally. "I'll see what I can find out. But think carefully before you decide to get involved. There are more factors than you realize at play here. You don't get to dip your toe in only to pull it back out again."

"Don't worry," Rayan said tightly. "I have no intention of backing out."

Mathias kept his old phone in the safe in the study. He took it out later that evening and plugged it in to charge. It was like unearthing a little black book of Canada's seedy underbelly. Rayan's former number was the only one not saved. He'd had that memorized, dialed by heart each time.

He scrolled through the list of contacts, all coded so that at first glance, they appeared a strange mashup of unintelligible aliases. Police personnel identified by the last digits of their badge number, councilors by the name of their arrondissement, family members by physical features or famous fuckups. Belkov's number was simply saved under *Connard*.

When he got to it, Mathias stopped. He hadn't spoken to the Russian since he'd left Montreal. But he still remembered the man's promise: "The Bratva will answer." Perhaps it was time he tested that out.

The phone rang several times before Belkov picked up. "To what do I owe the honor?" He sounded amused and predictably inebriated.

"What do you know about the trafficking groups operating in central Europe?"

"Not even a 'hello, how are things'?" the Russian mocked.

"Not like you to waste time on pleasantries."

Belkov laughed. "Direct as always. Is this your new vocation, Beauvais? People smuggling? I figured you'd be running a resort in Cabo."

"I'm a man of many talents."

"That you are."

"I'm after information on who's shopping migrants around the industries for free labor."

"I'd say damn near all of them. You've got the Polish gangs, the Lithuanians... don't even get me started on the Bulgarian mafia. We don't have much to do with them once we get the people into Europe. We collect our fee and hand them over. But I know someone who oversees dealings along the Balkan corridor. He should be able to steer you in the right direction. Why the sudden interest?"

"I'm looking for someone who was picked up in Northern France within the last twenty-four hours."

"I pity the poor sucker if he's found himself in your sights."

"How easy will it be to track him down?"

Belkov sucked his teeth. "Not easy, but not impossible."

Mathias leaned back in his chair. "How about you tell me what you want in exchange."

There was a low chuckle in his ear. "You should have started with small talk. Buttered me up a bit. Then you'd have a better idea of what it is I want."

"Fine, I'll take the bait. What's going on in the city?"

"It's going to shit, Beauvais." The amusement was gone from his voice and replaced by a steeliness palpable through the receiver. "Russo kept the ship afloat for fifty years. Bianchi won't make it to five."

"What are you saying?" Mathias asked, his stomach tightening.

"He's started purging, from the bottom up. The numbers have gotten thin and morale even thinner. Rivals are circling the family like vultures with a dead carcass."

"You among them?"

Belkov paused. "If there's ground to be gained, it's in the Bratva's interest in staking our claim. My alliance with the family disappeared when you did."

Mathias's jaw clenched. Giovanni was a fool—muscling Mathias out, for one, and then letting paranoia inform his strategy. Even Russo had weathered pushback when he started trimming the fat. No one took it well when they thought they were next on the chopping block. Cutbacks had to be carefully executed, and by the sound of things, Giovanni had been far from judicious. With Mathias gone and the Quintino content to sit back and watch, no one had told the boss where to draw the line.

"So, what's the game plan?" Mathias asked.

"I shouldn't be talking to you about this."

"Why? You think I still report to them?"

"I don't know what the fuck you do. All I hear is that you're a ghost. Here one minute, gone the next. Some say you knew the ship was sinking, so you took your spoils and left. Others say you're a coward who couldn't stand up to Bianchi."

"A coward?" Mathias growled.

"Less are saying that now, what with how poorly the big boss has performed. The former seems more plausible."

"It was neither," Mathias snapped, somehow needing to put the record straight.

It stung even now. He'd known there would be talk after he left. Theories and rumors that spread like wildfire. But to be branded a coward? That was a special kind of humiliation.

"Bianchi tipped off the Feds to push me out. It was either leaving or prison."

"Or dead," Belkov added. "Don't pretend that wasn't waiting around the corner for you, Beauvais. I know how your kind works. Loyalty is everything until it isn't."

The Russian wasn't wrong. Giovanni had said as much that day in the cemetery before Mathias left Montreal.

"And what—you've joined the hordes trying to cut off a piece?" Mathias scoffed.

"All I'm saying is, if the opportunity arises, I know which side we'll be on."

Mathias stared out the window at the dusky night sky, struck by a sense of detachment. He would have solutions, ideas for how to turn the situation around, if he'd still been willing to put his life down for Giovanni, for the sake of the family. But none of that was true anymore.

"I have no sway with the family," Mathias said. "I can't help you there. What else?"

Belkov was quiet as though considering. "Then I'll leave my options open. Who knows how things will pan out? Can't hurt to have a favor from you in my back pocket."

"Suit yourself."

"I'll reach out to my man, and if I find anything, we'll be in touch," Belkov said. But instead of hanging up, he remained on the line. Static stretched between them. "What happens when the whole thing topples over? Will you come back and rise from the ashes?"

Mathias shook his head to dispel the possibility. "It will never fall. The family is too entrenched. The worst you can do is carve off the edges."

"It's not the edges we'll be carving."

Mathias ended the call, a heaviness weighing on him. He walked over to the window and yanked it open, letting the cool air brush his face. He could hear the faint crash of waves in the distance, a rhythmic whoosh that punctuated the evening silence.

He should feel nothing, yet it was as though he was staring down the face of looming disaster. He had lived through it once, and even now, cut off from his former life, he could conjure the feeling—the rising panic as the walls closed in. He knew what Giovanni was up against and could see the full extent of the mess he'd made. It shouldn't have bothered him, but it did. Mathias had invested too much in the family to feign indifference as he watched it teeter on the brink of collapse.

15

At breakfast, Mathias's phone buzzed from where it lay face down on the kitchen table. The man picked it up to glance at the screen, then pushed aside his coffee and stepped away to take the call. Rayan waited, his plate of eggs abandoned, willing it to be Belkov with news—any news. He needed something concrete to counter the crippling uncertainty.

When Mathias returned, his coffee was cold, and he was holding the map Rayan had given him. He spread it across the table, and Rayan could see he'd made a series of markings, outlining a route that went from Calais through Germany and into Poland.

"Belkov got word from his contact. The Łobuzi, a Polish gang from Lublin, have been active in France in recent weeks. Apparently, they're bringing a group back with them to Korczowa."

Rayan stared at the location Mathias had circled on the map. He felt the first tendril of relief since he'd arrived at the camp to find the girls alone. It meant there was still hope for Farhan. "He's headed to Poland?"

"The southeast, near the Ukraine border. There's no guarantee he's with them, but it's the only lead we've got. There are several factories in the area, where they put migrants to work. Belkov said his man has reached out to the local Łobuzi leader, Filip Zabawski, who'll meet us there. It's our best bet for finding your friend. But we need to move fast. They scatter quickly."

"We?" Rayan glanced up at Mathias. He'd been somewhat subdued since his conversation with Belkov the previous evening. It must have been difficult confronting the world he'd left behind. Rayan felt a twinge of guilt for his responsibility in that.

"I'm not going to pretend to understand what's going on with you right now with all of this," Mathias said. "But I'm not letting you go alone. If we're doing this, we're doing it my way. I need you to stay sharp, understand?"

Rayan nodded.

"Good." Mathias reached out and tapped Rayan's cheek with his palm. "Then listen up. Here's what we're going to do."

Because they had to move quickly, there was no time to get false papers issued. They would have to transport Farhan back the way the smugglers had taken him without documentation. Mathias hired a small box truck from a rental company on the outskirts of the city. He used a different name and paid in cash. Before getting on the road, they swung by the warehouse and loaded a large furniture crate into the truck.

Provided they managed to find Farhan, the plan was that he would only use the crate for the crossing from Poland to Germany. It had slits along the sides for ventilation and was just big enough to fit a man of Farhan's size. They tossed in a stack of padded moving blankets for him to use on the return journey. Being jostled about in the back of the truck would be far from comfortable, but it was better than the alternative.

"If anyone asks, we're traveling to pick up a Venetian credenza from my vendor in Krakow. The paperwork's in the glove compartment," Mathias instructed Rayan as they drove out of Calais and onto the highway heading east. "We'll pick up a few other pieces while we're there—fill up the truck to make it difficult for the border guards to poke around."

Mathias, familiar with flouting the rules of engagement, had thought of every detail. To him, hurdles were meant to be cleared, and when his mind was set on something, there wasn't much—legal or otherwise—that could stand in his way.

"We shouldn't have any trouble until Bademeusel. There's a checkpoint before leaving Germany." Mathias adjusted the rearview mirror, a grim line forming across his forehead. "Getting into Poland is easy. It's the way back we need to be concerned about."

The chance of customs searching the truck meant they were traveling unarmed, a prospect Rayan knew didn't sit well with Mathias. But between the two of them, they had enough experience taking people down—with or without a weapon. All he could do was hope they didn't encounter any obstacles on the road they couldn't handle.

"What's this?" Rayan asked. Sitting between them in the footwell of the cab was a sealed cardboard box.

"A gift."

Rayan raised an eyebrow. "Now we're rewarding these assholes?"

Mathias shot him a sidelong look. "Don't act so indignant. You know how this works."

Rayan knew all too well. He sighed and stared at the back of the caravan crawling along in front of them. "How is Belkov these days?"

Mathias frowned and tapped his thumbs against the steering wheel. "Same as always," he said, navigating the truck into the left lane to pass. "Looking for any God-given opportunity to take more than his share."

Rayan had a hunch Mathias was hiding something, or at least skirting the truth. It was frustrating, the way Mathias's first instinct was to withhold. But then, that instinct had been crucial to both his success and his survival. Rayan couldn't have one without the other, yet he wished Mathias would be a little more forthcoming so he didn't always have to guess what was going on in the man's head.

"I'm surprised he was willing to help."

"We developed somewhat of a mutual understanding in those last few years. When I left, he offered his assistance should I ever need it." Mathias made a sour face. "And before you say it, no, we're not friends."

Rayan laughed. It was strange to imagine the two men getting along, especially considering how much they'd hated each other during his time in Montreal. Rayan remembered several tense car rides back from Laval when Mathias had plotted aloud the details of the Bratva boss's takedown. Of course, city politics interfered with his plans. They made an odd pair but were also complementary, two underdogs determined to get their due.

Outside the window, France passed in a blur. Rayan hadn't been sure what would follow his request for a favor, but he should have known Mathias wouldn't attempt anything half-assed. He was well aware of the risks Mathias was taking by helping him.

"Thank you," Rayan said quietly. "For doing this."

"I shouldn't be."

"You are good at it, though."

"Smuggling people? You might be surprised to learn this is unfamiliar territory."

"No..." Rayan searched for the right words. "Finding creative workarounds."

"I believe the term is *breaking the law*. And yes, I've made quite a career of that." Mathias turned on the wipers as a splatter of rain speckled the windshield. "You think stroking my ego will make me forget about the idiotic wild-goose chase we're on?"

"It wouldn't be the first."

Mathias smirked. "No, it wouldn't."

"Tony always seemed to kick the real stinkers our way."

"No surprises there. That man was happiest when he had me knee-deep in muck."

Rayan grinned at the memory of standing outside Tony's office, raised voices traveling down the corridor, as Mathias and the Collections boss engaged in yet another clash of wills. "It feels like a lifetime ago. Hard to believe he's gone."

Mathias said nothing. Rayan knew a part of him was still sore about the circumstances surrounding Tony's death.

"He looked out for you, you know," Rayan said. "I overheard him a few times at Le Rouge, dressing down some of the old guard when they started talking shit."

Mathias's expression grew reflective. "I owed him more than I realized."

"I'm pretty sure he knew that."

"Of course he did." Mathias's mouth tweaked. "He'd have used anything to hold over me."

"It was his way of keeping you in line. Not much else seemed to work."

Mathias gave a snort and caught his eye, their shared past glancing between them. "Look at you, Rayan. So perceptive."

After eleven hours of driving, Mathias hit a wall. They'd just passed the German city of Cottbus when he exhaled heavily and flicked on his turn signal, guiding the truck toward a nearby exit. "We're done for the day."

Rayan shared the man's sentiment. His whole body felt stiff, and he was desperate to stretch his legs. Mathias pulled into an unassuming motel a short distance from the highway and parked in the deserted lot. They would spend the night here and make the crossing into Poland the following morning.

While Mathias went to pick up keys at the front desk, Rayan walked to the gas station across the road for coffee and cigarettes. It paid to be preemptive with Mathias. There was a glass case of hot food by the register, and Rayan took a carton and filled it with exotic convenience store delicacies.

Back at the room, Mathias eyed his selection warily.

"I think that's schnitzel," Rayan offered.

"It could be horse meat for all I care," Mathias muttered.

After they'd eaten, Rayan sat behind Mathias on the bed, working out the knots in the man's back. "I'll drive tomorrow."

"No," Mathias said. "I want to make the crossing."

"You don't think I can handle it?"

Mathias tilted his chin to look at him. "You're a useless liar. You'll be spilling your guts before the border guard even opens his mouth."

Rayan jabbed his thumbs into the muscle below Mathias's shoulder blades and was rewarded with a sharp grunt. "I'm an excellent liar."

Mathias chuckled. "See? Useless."

Rayan smiled despite himself and slid his fingers to the nape of Mathias's neck, gentle this time. His touch elicited the slightest of shivers. There was a line Mathias walked carefully—the division between resistance and submission. Sometimes, while Rayan had the man in his mouth, Mathias permitted him to move his hand lower. Then, just as quickly, Mathias would pull away, the flicker of something indeterminable in his eyes.

Rayan dropped his hands and pressed his lips to the warm skin behind Mathias's ear, leaving a trail of kisses. "Walk me through tomorrow."

Belkov's contact had arranged for the local Łobuzi head to meet Mathias outside a small town near Poland's eastern border. From there, they would determine whether the group had taken Farhan.

"We cross into Poland, make our way to Korczowa, and then find Zabawski. If he has your friend, we load him up and get the fuck out of there."

"And if he doesn't?"

Mathias moved to face him. "Then we turn around and go back. There is no second option. If he's not there, he's gone. We took it as far as we could."

Rayan shook his head, unable to accept that as a viable outcome. Yet at the same time, he knew Mathias was right. This was their only chance. If they couldn't find Farhan with the Bratva's help, what chance did they have on their own?

Mathias sighed. "What happens after this?"

"What do you mean?"

"I'm not running around Europe for every migrant you get attached to."

Rayan smarted. "Christ, Mathias."

"He's not the first person to find himself in this situation, and he won't be the last. You can't save everyone."

"I owe it to the girls." *Isn't it enough that they lost their mother? I can't stand by and watch them lose their father too.* "And we're working to try and stop this kind of thing from happening, or at least better protect people from it. We want to build a residence facility to safeguard vulnerable families like Farhan's. Someplace permanent."

That is, if we still have any hope of getting it off the ground.

Mathias raised a skeptical eyebrow. "How do you plan on doing that?"

101

Rayan recalled the mayor's pitying look and Laurent's glum admission that the project was too ambitious. Mathias would only say the same thing.

"What about you?" Rayan deflected.

"What about me?"

"What's next? Is this enough for you? The business, Calais..." *Me?*

"What are you talking about?" Mathias asked.

"You know what I'm talking about. This is a far cry from reporting to the head of the Fifth Family." Rayan paused, his voice lowering. "You're not exactly cut out for an ordinary life."

Mathias snickered. "Is that what you'd call this?"

"You would tell me," Rayan murmured, "if there was something else you wanted."

He waited for the man's denial, but instead Mathias seemed to be mulling over Rayan's question. "There might be other opportunities I'm considering."

Rayan frowned. "What kind of opportunities?"

Mathias was quiet for a moment, then he pulled away. "Enough, Rayan."

Rayan felt it again—the same prickle of fear as when Mathias had dismissed his concerns about the import license. *What else is he keeping from me?*

Mathias shed the remainder of his clothes and turned down the covers on the bed. "I'm tired."

Rayan decided now wasn't the time to push. If they wanted to have any chance of tackling what awaited them the next day, they would need their rest. But as he lay in the dark, a sleeping Mathias pressed against his back, the roar of the nearby highway rattling the cheap motel windows, Rayan couldn't help but think that, unlike him, Mathias was very good at lying.

As Rayan and Mathias drove up to the Bademeusel checkpoint the following morning, they were funneled into a steady stream of traffic headed for Poland. Germany had recently reintroduced checkpoints at several of their border crossings to combat the spike in illegal migration. The operation was efficiently run. Two guards flanked each barrier gate, and as a vehicle approached, one of them would step up to the driver's-side window to inspect documentation. If everything checked out, the vehicle was waved through. If it didn't, vehicles were directed to park in a separate lane and passengers ordered out for additional questioning.

Mathias took out his driver's license as he inched the truck forward in the queue. When they reached the barrier gate, a heavyset guard in a forest-green uniform stepped forward.

"*Deutsch?*"

"*Français,*" Mathias replied.

"License, please," he said, switching to English.

Mathias passed it to him through the open window. The guard asked where they were going and what was the purpose of their trip. Mathias provided a spare account, his expression bored yet his tone polite.

"You." The guard pointed a thick finger at Rayan in the passenger seat. "ID."

Rayan held out his driver's license, but the man shook his head.

"I want to see your national identity card."

Rayan returned the license to his wallet and removed his CNI.

The guard inspected the card as though he'd never seen anything like it before. "You live in France?"

"Yes."

"But that's not where you're from."

"Are you asking where I'm from?"

The guard made a face like Rayan had spat in his coffee. "I'm the one asking the questions."

Rayan kept his voice measured. "I'm from Quebec."

"Is that where you were born?"

"Yes."

Mathias let out a frustrated sigh. "Is the problem that he lives in France or that he comes from Canada?" He gave the guard a pointed look. "Perhaps the real issue is that you don't think he belongs in either."

The guard held Mathias's gaze. "It's my job to be thorough."

"Of course. Would you like to see my identity card?" Mathias asked. "I have it right here."

"That won't be necessary." The guard handed back Rayan's CNI with a scowl and indicated for them to drive on.

As Mathias drove through the border crossing, his eyes flicked to the guard in the rearview mirror. "Fucking idiot," he muttered. Then he turned to Rayan. "Your face was so distracting he didn't bother looking in the truck. Maybe we should try that on the way back."

Rayan could still hear his heart pounding in his ears. "No. Let's not."

It was another eight hours before they reached Korczowa. Rayan was beginning to feel the effects of almost two days on the road. He couldn't imagine what Farhan had been through, making this journey against his will and not knowing what would happen to his daughters back in Calais. Rayan remembered how adamant Farhan had been that Amina and Zahra be given a chance at a new life so that his wife's death wouldn't be in vain. They had to find him. Rayan couldn't go back empty-handed.

By the time Mathias drove the truck through the small Polish village, it was late afternoon. They continued out of town and along a single-lane road flanked by grassy fields. Above them, the sky began to darken.

At one point, Mathias pulled over to check his phone. He let out a string of curses as he realized they'd missed the turnoff. Mathias turned the truck around and headed back the way they'd come, slower now, peering out the window for any sign of the dirt road that would lead them Zabawski. Rayan spotted it first, and they veered off onto a crude gravel driveway.

At the end of the driveway was an old, weathered farmhouse, and behind it in the distance, two large grain silos came into view. Smoke curled from the chimney of the house, and Rayan could see light through the gaps in the curtains. Someone was home.

Mathias parked the truck out front, and they both got out, limbs aching, their shoes crunching on gravel. The door to the cottage opened, and a man moved into the doorframe. He was older than Rayan had expected, his dirty-brown hair streaked with gray. He had a curved nose that turned down at the end and dark eyes that squinted as Rayan and Mathias approached. Out of instinct, Rayan zeroed in on the pistol tucked into the man's belt and was immediately on edge.

"Beauvais?"

"Zabawski?"

The two men shook hands, and Mathias instructed Rayan to retrieve the box from the cab of the truck. Zabawski ushered them into the house, and Rayan set the box down on the dining table. Aside from two scuffed wooden chairs, the room was empty. Zabawski disappeared into the hallway and returned moments later with a dull steak knife. He used it to open the seal on the box and pulled out six pristine bottles of amber liquor.

He made an approving noise and spun one of the bottles in his hand. "Louis XIII? This would've set you back."

"A token of our appreciation," Mathias said.

The Polish gangster held the distinctive curved decanter up to the light. "Beautiful," he murmured. Then he placed the bottle on the table and gestured for them to follow him.

Zabawski led them back outside and around the house to a sprawling grassy field. At the far end of the field stood the grain silos, which was where the man appeared to be taking them.

"I was told you were looking for someone," Zabawski said as they walked.

"That's right," Mathias replied.

"We pick up people from all over—Germany, Spain, France. Some come willingly. Others need a little convincing." He glanced over his shoulder with a grin, revealing a set of golden canines.

Rayan had to work hard to keep the disgust from showing on his face. As they drew closer to the silos, he saw two men standing by the access door to the larger tower. One of them nodded at Zabawski and moved to unlock the door. He pulled it open with a metallic screech.

Instead of grain, the silo was filled with men. They sat on makeshift mats spread out across the concrete floor. Around them were backpacks, shopping bags, and all manner of hastily assembled possessions. They were of varying ages, most of them young, all of them gripped by a collective air of resignation. Rayan's stomach turned at the blatant lack of humanity.

"Well, here they are. There was a group from France that arrived in the latest cohort. See if your man's among them." Zabawski pulled a hand-rolled cigarette from his jacket pocket and lit it.

"Jesus," Rayan muttered as he stared out at the sea of faces.

He stepped inside, leaving Mathias by the door with the Łobuzi head, and began walking through the maze of people, searching for anyone who might resemble Farhan. He passed a cluster of men playing cards then stopped when he thought he heard his name called. He looked over, and there was Farhan, half rising from his seat on a flattened piece of cardboard.

"Rayan, is that you?" Farhan whispered in Arabic, his eyes wide with disbelief.

Rayan was overcome by a flood of relief. He couldn't believe their luck. After two days spent tearing through the haystack, they'd found their needle.

He reached for Farhan's hand and pulled him to his feet. "We're here to take you back."

There rose a chorus of murmurs from several of the men seated around them.

"There are others, from Calais, with families at the camp," Farhan said. "Can they come too?"

105

The other men began to stand, and Rayan was gripped with a sudden panic.

"Please," one man pleaded. "We want to go back."

"My wife is there, and my son," another said.

Rayan's pulse hammered in his throat. He glanced over at the door to see Zabawski deep in conversation with Mathias. *What the fuck are we supposed to do now?*

16

Belkov had told Mathias that Filip Zabawski was a connoisseur of expensive cognac. Mathias had a feeling that wasn't all the man had a taste for. In exchange for freeing one of his prized laborers, Zabawski would want more than a few bottles of top-shelf liquor. Sure enough, once Rayan had gone into the silo to look for Farhan, the Pole turned to Mathias with a shrewd smile.

"How about this: I'll give him to you for twelve thousand. I need to recoup the cost of getting him here and what we stand to make from him on-site. I would charge more, but out of respect for our mutual friend, I'm willing to give you a discount."

Mathias had done many things in his time, but negotiating the purchase of a person was not one of them. He nodded vaguely as though they were discussing interest terms on a loan. Despite having a reputation for never accepting an offer outright, his counteroffer tasted foul in his mouth. *Am I really going to stand here and haggle for Farhan's life?*

"Sounds fair," Mathias said, breaking his own rule. Fortunately, he'd taken precautions. He had at least twenty grand on him and another eighty hidden in the truck.

"A friend of the Bratva is a friend of mine." Zabawski raised his foul-smelling cigarette to his lips. His eyes caught on something, and Mathias followed his gaze to see Rayan helping someone to their feet. "Looks like you've found your man."

Thank Christ. It hadn't all been for nothing. Now if they could just get him out of here.

"Not sure what you want with that one, though. The Arabs don't bring in much. Is he from a good family? Some of them have relatives back home who will pay. Not often, but sometimes you get lucky."

Mathias felt a rising distaste for the Polish gangster. He wasn't a saint by any stretch of the imagination, but profiting off the backs of people like these—displaced and defenseless—required a certain kind of stomach.

"I have my reasons," he replied.

In the silo, several men had gathered around Rayan and Farhan and were engaged in an increasingly tense discussion. One of the men had a hand on Rayan's arm and appeared to be imploring him urgently.

"Thought you said it was just the one," Zabawski observed.

"I did," Mathias muttered. He strode toward Rayan, stepping around the people haphazardly strewn across the floor.

Rayan looked up when he appeared, his face lined with concern. "They're all from the camp. They were taken together. They want to come back with us."

"No," Mathias said in a sharp whisper, conscious of the attention they were drawing. "We got what we came for."

But Rayan remained fixed in place, his lips pressed together.

"What do you want me to do, cram them all in the back of the truck?" Mathias asked. The men were watching the interaction intently, their lives hanging in the balance. "I'm not here to fuck with Zabawski's business."

"It's not a business," Rayan hissed. "You know damn well what this is."

Mathias glanced over at Zabawski and his lackeys waiting by the door then at the sea of faces staring back at them. *I'm not seriously considering the logistics of smuggling a truck full of people across Europe...*

"How many are we talking?"

"Including Farhan, four."

The plan was to fill the cargo box with furniture from his vendor in Krakow. There were certain pieces that lent themselves to hiding a grown man—but four?

"He's going to want payment for each one." Mathias's voice was barely audible. "Twelve a head."

"I'll pay it."

Mathias looked at Rayan, and the man stared back, entirely serious.

"I could throttle you right now," Mathias said.

"Throttle me later."

The cash Mathias had on hand would be just enough to cover Zabawski's cost per head and a truckload of whatever his vendor had available to disguise their questionable cargo.

"Bring them out front. I'll take care of Zabawski," Mathias said.

It was a tough sell. The Łobuzi head wasn't too pleased about the prospect of losing four workers from his hard-won stock. In the end, Mathias threw in his Rolex, peeled still warm from his wrist, to sweeten the deal. They departed on their return journey to France with three more people than they'd bargained for crouched in the truck bed.

He and Rayan sat in tense silence as Mathias drove back along the bumpy gravel driveway and up to the main road. He made it several meters down the road before his fury got the better of him. Mathias pulled over onto the shoulder, got out of the cab, and stalked beside the truck, reaching into his jacket for his cigarettes. The passenger door slammed, and Rayan appeared, watching as Mathias unsuccessfully tried to coax a flame from his lighter.

"You realize this got infinitely more dangerous," Mathias snapped, rolling his thumb over the striker. "It's risky enough for the groups that do this for a living, let alone us out here winging it. One man, maybe you could plead ignorance—try to frame it as a stunt. Four? We'll be nailed for running a human trafficking ring."

"I know."

Fucking thing's jammed. He shook the lighter and tried again. "I'm not going to jail to appease your good conscience. Running into the ocean so you don't drown, coming out here—enough." He hit the striker once, twice. Still no spark. "Build your fucking residence center—hell, start a new camp in our backyard. You are far more useful to the cause when you're not putting yourself on the line. Because I won't have you throwing your life away. I need you more than they do." He closed his hand around the busted lighter and slammed it into the side of the truck. "Goddamn piece of shit!"

They stood, their breath pluming white in the night air. In the distance a bird called, breaking the silence. Rayan stepped forward and prized the lighter from his fist. Then slowly, methodically, he flicked his thumb against the striker, again and again, refusing to give up until the flame burst to life. He leaned in and held the lighter to the unlit cigarette dangling from the corner of Mathias's mouth. Mathias took a pull and exhaled a welcome lungful of smoke.

"You're right." Rayan slipped the lighter into Mathias's breast pocket. "I want you to fly back. I'll drop you off at the airport in Rzeszów—"

"What are you on about?"

"This was my idea. I don't want you shouldering any more risk."

"I already agreed. I don't go back on my word."

Rayan's expression grew conflicted. "I shouldn't have pulled you into this."

And Mathias couldn't help but think of all the situations he'd pulled Rayan into. Every time he had forced the man's hand, forced him to act against his better judgment. He reached out and placed his index finger on Rayan's forehead, right between the eyes. "Five years ago, this is where my skull would've blown open if it weren't for you."

Rayan blinked. Then he took Mathias's hand and brought it to his right shoulder, just below the clavicle. "And I would've bled out if not for you."

Mathias gave him a tight smile. "All right, then. Let's get this over with." He took one last drag on the cigarette before flicking it down at his feet and moving toward the truck.

"Mathias."

He stopped and turned.

Rayan was staring at him, his mouth a hard line. "This is it. No more crazy crusades."

Mathias shook his head with a snicker. "I told you, you're a useless liar."

They reached Krakow by dinnertime. Mathias parked the truck in the alley behind a row of brick storefronts, one of which belonged to his vendor, Jan Gorelik. Gorelik was an antique-furniture collector of some acclaim, and Mathias had commissioned several pieces from the man for a client in Geneva.

While it was well past closing time, Mathias had called ahead, and Gorelik had agreed to meet him at the store. Rayan would take their passengers out for food and supplies in the meantime. They had no idea how long it had been since the men had last eaten, and it was still a decent drive to the border. It would give them a chance to get comfortable before the journey ahead.

Mathias stood guard as Rayan helped the four men out of the truck. Back at the silo, they'd appeared gaunt and ghostly, but in the fresh evening air, their eyes were bright with relief.

"I'll let you know where we end up," Rayan said when Mathias finished locking up the truck. Then he set off with their charges on foot.

Mathias walked around to the service entrance behind the shop and knocked loudly on the door. Gorelik himself answered. He was a short man with sleek black hair and a matching mustache. He moved in a manner that was both curt and precise, and as soon as he'd ushered Mathias into the store, he swiftly turned and locked the door behind them.

The key thing he needed from Gorelik, besides a haul of furniture he'd have to enlist Elise to palm off, were customs and import papers for all the pieces he loaded into the truck. Arriving at the border without the correct paperwork was a good way to get the truck inspected—or worse, its contents seized.

"I must admit, Mr. Beauvais, I was a little surprised to receive your somewhat unconventional request. But as a valued customer, I'm more than happy to oblige. Now, what was it exactly that you were after?"

Mathias's tired eyes raked across the elaborately staged pieces that filled the showroom. "I'll take everything on this side," he said, indicating to a full bedroom suite and an enormous vintage cupboard that took up half the wall.

Gorelik pushed his glasses higher up his nose and made a humming sound between closed lips. "I see. There's a matching blanket chest in storage that goes with the bedroom set."

"I'll take that too."

"Of course." Gorelik cleared his throat. "Can Miriam get you some tea while I start putting the documents in order?"

A slight woman with a wheat-colored braid draped over one shoulder stood from behind the front counter.

"Do you have anything stronger?" Mathias asked, suddenly itching for a drink.

Gorelik gave him an indulgent smile. "For you, Mr. Beauvais, I have just the thing."

He spoke to the woman in Polish, and she disappeared up a narrow set of stairs tucked away at the back of the store. Gorelik indicated for Mathias to follow him into his private office. They each took a seat, and the man fired up the computer on his desk.

"Would you like the pieces on consignment?"

"No, paid in full. I'll settle in cash this evening," Mathias instructed.

Gorelik raised an eyebrow but said nothing more. He began tapping away on his keyboard. Soon the door opened, and the woman entered, carrying a tray with two narrow glasses and a crystal decanter. She poured the clear liquor into both glasses and held one out to Mathias. She left the other on the tray and took her leave.

"Please." Gorelik gestured and lifted his own glass.

The liquor burned on the way down, instantly settling Mathias's frayed nerves.

"And what about delivery?" Gorelik asked, his eyes trained on the computer screen. "Did you want us to arrange the shipment?"

"I'll take it all today."

This caught the man's attention, and his gaze flicked to Mathias. "I'm afraid our store hand has gone home for the day."

"That won't be a problem. I've brought my own muscle." He stood and reached for the decanter. "May I?"

"By all means," Gorelik said.

Mathias refilled both glasses then raised his to his lips and downed it gratefully. Several shots later, he settled the account with Gorelik and arranged to meet the man back at the store in an hour to load their purchases into the truck. Once outside, Mathias checked his phone to find a message from Rayan. He buttoned his jacket against the cold then headed down the alley and out onto the street.

He found Rayan, Farhan, and the three other men from the silo at a park several blocks away. They were sitting on two adjacent benches under the glow of a nearby streetlamp. Each had a polystyrene take-out container perched on his lap and was tucking into the boxes of sausages and chips like they hadn't eaten in days.

Mathias caught Rayan's eye as he approached, and Rayan held out a container of food. Mathias shook his head. He wanted to enjoy his buzz a little longer. He sat down across from Rayan and listened as the men attempted brief introductions, for Mathias's sake in a mixture of English and French.

Farhan, he knew. Then there was Ibrahim—a skinny kid from a small village near Nyala in Sudan—and Saif, who turned out to have lived not far from Farhan in Aleppo. The fourth man, Hayat, was Eritrean and said little. He looked to be several years older than the rest. They spoke of their wives and families, how they'd ended up in Calais, and how long it had been since they'd left home. When the conversation got too complicated, they slipped into Arabic. Rayan listened carefully as the men talked, interjecting occasionally in a quiet murmur and translating for Mathias when he deemed it necessary.

Mathias was less interested in their chatter and more in the way Rayan appeared to move between the two sides of himself, one he recognized, the other less familiar. They seemed more enmeshed these days. He heard Rayan mention his brother's name, and there was a harmony to the way he said it that hadn't been there before.

Mathias felt a rush of fondness. He became aware of the transience of the moment. How strange it was that they were here at all. He knew that whatever was going to happen would happen soon, but for the moment, he had this.

With four extra sets of hands, it didn't take long to load the pieces into the truck. Rayan and Mathias waited until the vendor had retreated into the store before making Farhan and the other men comfortable—or as much as possible, considering the circumstances. Using the moving blankets, they formed makeshift seats amid the cluster of furniture and strapped down the larger pieces to prevent them from falling over. They had a long night ahead of them. When everything was ready, Mathias secured the roller door at the back of the truck and stepped over to the cab. The man's face was stiff with fatigue.

He pulled open the driver's door, but Rayan took his hand and eased the keys from his grip. "Let me."

Instead of the expected brush-off, Mathias simply nodded, no longer possessing the energy to fight him. Rayan had barely maneuvered the truck onto the road before Mathias was asleep, his forehead pressed against the passenger window. Rayan made his way out of the city and onto the highway. It would be at least another five hours until they reached the German border. He would find a place nearby for them to stop and regroup. Then they'd wait for daylight before getting the men into position. Mathias had said they'd draw more attention as high-end antique dealers if they attempted the crossing in the dead of night.

Rayan drove along the darkened highway in eerie silence. They'd established a system before leaving Krakow. If the men in the back needed anything, Farhan would knock twice on the wall separating the cab from the cargo box. As of yet, Rayan hadn't heard so much as a whisper. He had a feeling their passengers were well aware of the stakes.

He stole a glance at Mathias's sleeping face, and his throat tightened. There was no way he could have done this without him. Mathias had taken each obstacle in his stride, operating with his usual unflappable efficiency. But even Mathias had his limits. "I need you more than they do," he had said. Rayan hadn't anticipated how hard those words would hit. They'd cut through all other concerns, leaving behind a renewed sense of clarity.

In the past, it had been Mathias who led and Rayan who followed, but they were tied together now. When he went one way, Mathias was tugged along with him. This trip had made that abundantly clear.

It was a responsibility Rayan had little experience navigating. He had to find a way to do what was needed—for Farhan and his family, for the people in the camp—without endangering what was most important to him. And while the desire to help hadn't lessened, the recklessness with which he'd approached that objective had. He'd meant what he'd said to Mathias. Rayan couldn't keep pulling him into situations that put his life on the line. He loved him too much for that.

Rayan gripped the steering wheel. His heart felt sore. While he would never know what his mother thought of him, in Mathias's eyes, there was nothing about who he was that needed redeeming. He'd spent so long hiding his love for the man. He'd never imagined there would be a time when Mathias would turn around and match it breath for breath.

17

Mathias woke to find the truck had stopped and the driver's seat was empty. He sat up in a haze of confusion. Through the foggy windshield he could see Rayan standing with Ibrahim in what appeared to be the parking lot of some kind of forest reserve. Fortunately, the place was secluded. There wasn't a car in sight, and they were surrounded by a wall of towering spruce trees. It must have been morning, because the sky was a muted gray.

Mathias rubbed his face with his hand. *Was I out the whole time?*

He pulled open the cab door and got out on achy legs. He'd never had the misfortune to fall asleep inside a moving vehicle, but there was a first for everything.

When Rayan spotted Mathias, he stepped over and passed him the bottle of water in his hand. "Sleep well?"

Mathias gave him a dirty look. "You're perky." He cracked open the bottle and took a long swig.

"I'll crash in about an hour," Rayan said with a tired smile.

Irked by the absence of his watch, Mathias pulled out his phone to check the time. It was almost seven. In a little while, they'd hit peak commuter traffic, which would serve as a convenient distraction.

"All right, gentlemen," he announced, and Saif, Hayat, and Farhan moved to join them, shivering in the early-morning cold. "We're clear on what happens next?"

The men gave a series of nods.

"We're going to wait another half hour then get back on the road. Use this opportunity to stretch your legs. It's going to be a tight squeeze."

Together, they'd scoped out several human-sized hiding places amid the tangle of furniture in the back of the truck. Mathias had no doubt the trip would be rough, but once they crossed into Germany, they'd be able to make their passengers more comfortable for the remaining journey back to Calais.

If we make it, that is.

The men dispersed, and Mathias's throat prickled with a growing apprehension. He took another gulp of water in an attempt to relieve it. He reached into his jacket to retrieve a roll of cash and turned to Rayan, pushing it into the man's hand. Back at Gorelik's office, he'd scribbled the number of a lawyer in Paris on a piece of paper and slipped it between the notes. Rayan would be able to call for assistance if they got separated.

"What's this?"

"Just a precaution."

Mathias knew he understood what remained unsaid: *Look out for yourself.* Rayan frowned, but he pocketed the cash and gave Mathias a reluctant nod.

Once they were ready to head out, he and Rayan helped their passengers get into position. Mathias couldn't help thinking, as he tightened the screws on the crate with Farhan inside, that it was not unlike sealing a coffin.

They drove the twenty minutes to the border checkpoint in silence. Rayan sat in the passenger seat, his eyes fixed on the road. As predicted, the crossing was clogged with utility vans and semitrailers heading to work in Germany and beyond. Their truck, packed with furniture for sale in France, would hopefully appear unremarkable to the border guards.

As they moved forward in the queue, Mathias reached into the glove compartment and retrieved the folder of paperwork Gorelik had prepared for him. When the barrier rose to let the vehicle in front of them pass, he and Rayan exchanged a brief look. Then the barrier lowered, and Mathias brought the truck to a stop, taking a slow, even breath through his nose.

Showtime.

He wound down the window, and a guard approached the vehicle. He was young, flaxen haired, and dressed in the same green uniform as the man they'd encountered on the way out of the country. Mathias handed over his license and waited.

"Where are you headed today, sir?"

"Calais."

"France?"

"That's right."

"For what purpose?"

"We're returning home."

"And what was the nature of your trip to Poland?"

"Business." Mathias passed him the folder. "I was collecting a series of pieces from a vendor."

The guard opened it and took a cursory glance inside. "Furniture?"

Mathias nodded. "Antique. Most of it Zakopane."

The guard handed the folder back. "Sir, if you could pull your vehicle into the marked area over there. I'd like to take a look in the truck."

"Of course." Mathias indicated right and eased out of the queue and into the inspection lane.

"Mathias." Rayan was staring straight ahead, his voice no louder than a whisper. "If something happens, I want you to know—"

"Don't you start with that shit," Mathias cut in, his jaw stiff.

The guard followed them and gestured for Mathias to get out of the truck. Mathias unclipped his seat belt and opened the cab door.

"Do you mind opening the back for me?" the guard asked.

"Not at all."

Together they walked around the truck, and Mathias unclasped the latches on the roller door. He pulled it all the way open, revealing the cargo box stacked with furniture.

The guard peered at the arrangement of pieces. He reached out to idly open and close the drawer on one of the nightstands and gave an appreciative grunt. "Some nice stuff in here."

"Let me know if there's anything that strikes your fancy."

The guard chuckled. "We'll see. You can close it."

Mathias refastened the latches and returned to the driver's seat. The guard handed him back his license through the window and slapped a palm down on the hood. "Off you go."

Mathias drove through a separate set of barriers at the end of the inspection lane and merged with the other traffic exiting the checkpoint. Only when they'd made it onto the highway, the signs now in German, did he allow himself to look over at Rayan. Their eyes met, and then they were both grinning, a shared relief bubbling to the surface. Mathias thumped his fist against the wall separating the cab from the cargo box.

"At ease, boys," he called out. "We're all clear."

They found a deserted rest stop just outside of Forst and removed the men from their hiding spaces. It was still a day's drive to Calais, but the mood was significantly more buoyant than it had been only an hour before. True to his word, Rayan—barely able to keep himself upright—passed out as soon as they were back on the road.

He woke several hours later to the rumbling of his own stomach. They stopped for food in Hanover and then pushed through to France. It was evening when they finally made it back to Calais. Mathias parked the truck outside the entrance to the Jungle, and he and Rayan walked the men into the camp.

"This is where you go every day?" Mathias muttered as they made their way down the dimly lit path that cut through the center of the encampment. A group of children ran past in mud-splattered clothes.

Rayan glanced at him curiously. "Were you expecting something different?"

Mathias wasn't sure what he'd been expecting. He'd seen photos in the paper and images on television, but he hadn't been prepared for what it was like in person. The noise, the smell. The sheer number of people crammed together like sardines in a sea of shoddily constructed shelters.

They reached a turnoff, and Saif and Ibrahim said their goodbyes and left for the other side of the camp. Hayat gripped Mathias's hand with a silent smile, then Rayan's, before disappearing into a nearby cluster of tents. Rayan led them to a portable steel cabin bearing the name of the migrant center on the front door. He pulled open the door, and there came a shriek from inside. Farhan's daughters flew down the steps and launched themselves into their father's arms. Farhan dropped to his knees and pressed the two girls to his chest, tears forming in his eyes. He pulled back to smooth their hair and spoke rapidly in a low murmur as they nodded along, smiles splitting their faces.

Mathias saw the way Rayan's expression softened, and in that moment, the past few grueling days were somehow worth it. Someone from the service office appeared in the door to the cabin, and Rayan turned to speak with them. Mathias felt a tug on his sleeve. He looked down to see the younger girl staring up at him. She stuck out her chin and said something he didn't understand.

"She says she remembers you," Farhan translated as he got to his feet.

Mathias recalled how she'd dug her nails into his skin, determined to live. She was scrappy, a fighter. He could appreciate that. The girl released his sleeve and skipped over to her sister.

"They had Amina and Zahra stay at the office to be safe," Rayan said when he rejoined them. "Someone kept an eye on your tent so you can return there tonight."

Farhan pulled Rayan into a tight embrace. When he broke away, they spoke briefly in muted voices before the girls swarmed Rayan, tugging at his wrists with questions.

Farhan held out his hand to Mathias, and he took it. "Thank you," he said, clasping Mathias's hand in both of his. "For saving me and my daughters. I'm forever in your debt."

"That's not a place you want to be," Mathias said, dismissing the sentiment with a shake of his head. "We're square."

After all, he hadn't done it for Farhan. He'd done it for the man standing before them, a little girl swinging from each hand.

They returned to the house, exhaustion settling in. Mathias brushed past Rayan in the doorway to the bedroom, and then their hands were on each other. It felt like weeks since they'd touched. They tumbled onto the bed, kissing, and then the urgency melted away, leaving behind a weary desire. They lay together, unfastening buckles and tugging out of clothes, unfazed by the dishevelment of three days on the road.

Neither of them was in the mood for games, both simply wanting the comfort of a familiar body. Face-to-face on their sides, they gripped one another and moved in tandem, relying on hands alone, only needing to take the edge off.

Tired, Mathias was impatient and efficient. Rayan matched the man's pace, yet even with his focus split, he was there too soon. He tried to catch his breath, tried to bring the swell of pleasure under control, but Mathias's fist around his cock laid waste to all remaining restraint.

His own hand stilled as he teetered on the brink, and Mathias slowed to draw it from him, gray eyes fixed on his as he pushed Rayan over the edge. The growl of release that erupted from Rayan's throat was enough to finish Mathias, and they both fell back onto the bed, panting.

Rayan leaned in to kiss him, their open-mouthed hunger fading to a soft brush of lips. Mathias rolled onto his back, and Rayan rested his head on the man's chest. He closed his eyes, sleep pulling at his heavy limbs.

"I saw you with the girls," Mathias said into the silence. His voice sounded far away. "I didn't know that was something you wanted."

Rayan opened his eyes, struck by Mathias's candor. It was a subject that had never come up, rendered fraught by their respective histories.

"No," he said quietly. "I've never wanted that." His childhood had left him with little faith in the institution of parenting. "What about you?"

"If I accomplish one thing in this lifetime, it will be to avoid that nightmare altogether."

Rayan stroked his fingers across the unfamiliar stubble that lined Mathias's jaw. "Your mother will be sad to hear it."

"Oh, she knows."

Rayan lay watching Mathias after he'd fallen asleep. At the camp, Mathias had exhibited an obvious discomfort at Amina's interest in him. Yet he'd pulled the children from the water like it was nothing. He possessed a kind of practical protectiveness that ran counter to his indifference. Rayan saw it in the way he handled his mother. As charged as their relationship was, Mathias continued to provide for her—reluctantly but consistently.

Gently, he pushed Mathias's hair back from his forehead. The fact that they were here together like this defied any logic. It was a clear departure from what his life had taught him to expect.

Rayan couldn't remember when he'd first started going to the clubs in the Village. But he knew what had brought him there—years of repressed desire and a loneliness that threatened to choke him. It would have been around the time his brother was working for Bastien. Tahir would disappear for days on end, releasing Rayan from his duties as his brother's keeper.

Initially, Rayan didn't go home with anyone. He preferred to retreat to the back rooms and fumble about in the dark. He fucked several men before he let someone fuck him, no longer able to ignore the pull he felt while watching them moan and writhe beneath him. The first time was with a man named Clément. He was in his late twenties, handsome, and friendly and had invited Rayan back to his apartment downtown. While Clément proved generous and accommodating in his instruction, Rayan found the experience tepid. He didn't want to be asked what he liked or how it felt or whether it was too much. He wanted someone to make those decisions for him. He wanted someone to own him. Only when he got close to that feeling did everything else begin to fade.

Afterward, when Rayan moved to leave, Clément asked him to stay. The following morning, he made him breakfast and gave Rayan his number. They saw each other regularly for several weeks, always at Clément's apartment. Sometimes the man cooked for him, or they would lounge around in bed while Rayan deflected questions about his life, sliding the truth out of view. Rayan had thought plenty about sex but not about the rest—the sharing of food and company, of feelings and expectations. He'd determined early on that he wasn't destined to enjoy the simplicities of life that came so easy to others. But those nights with Clément challenged his conviction.

Then one evening, he was downtown with his brother, who was high off his face, when Rayan saw Clément cross the street and head toward him.

"You're a fucking addict," Clément hissed, wrenching at Rayan's arm as if to confirm his suspicions. "Oh God—I let you into my house!"

He looked at Rayan like he was shit stuck to the bottom of his shoe. Rayan yanked his arm back, horror and humiliation churning in his gut.

"I know how this works," Clément went on. "You prey on unsuspecting men and get them to fund your habit."

Rayan had never asked the man for money. Never asked him for anything. All the assumptions about who he was hurt. It didn't matter if he refuted them—they were there now, lodged between them.

Rayan refused to allow the pain to register on his face. Instead, he let out a scornful laugh. "Don't flatter yourself. You were just an easy lay."

After Clément, there were others, but he knew not to stay. It was safer to keep the sex separate from the rest of his life. Still, the need ate at him. He wanted someone to throw himself against, confident they wouldn't sag under the weight. Rayan felt as though he was chasing a feeling, his fingers brushing the edge of it only to have it slip from his grip. It wasn't so much that he liked to be hurt but that he liked to be conquered, rendered obsolete. He'd grazed against it with some men, but never like with Mathias.

Mathias wielded power like it was his birthright, and Rayan had been drawn to his control, his purpose. With Mathias there was no hesitancy. Nothing about Rayan made Mathias so much as bat an eye. Mathias had owned him from the moment Rayan first reported as his second—long before the man ever laid a hand on him. For years, he'd been content to simply remain by Mathias's side. Rayan had never believed their relationship could be more than that.

As it turned out, that was only the beginning. Somewhere along the line, things began to change between them. The urge to be obliterated gave way to other desires, and they navigated these with a cautious back-and-forth. He discovered that Mathias's own needs were liable to bend and transform as he let Rayan in. It wasn't until they'd come to Calais that Rayan had started to believe that maybe life's simple pleasures weren't entirely out of reach.

Beside him, Mathias shifted, and Rayan felt his eyelids droop. He pressed himself against the man's warm body and let sleep come.

18

"What does it mean?" Rayan flicked through the menu, preoccupied. "*Bougnoule?*"

Mathias looked up. "Someone said it again?"

Rayan nodded, and Mathias exhaled loudly. He had no interest in validating the ramblings of some small-town zealot. "It's not worth wondering."

He didn't expect the flash of anger that crossed Rayan's face. Rayan put down the menu. "I told Farhan his daughters would be safe here. Safe from some things but clearly not others."

Mathias shrugged. "That's true of everywhere. France, Canada—take your pick. The world's got more than its share of bigots." He closed his menu and signaled to one of the waitresses.

The restaurant was several blocks from the house, and they came here sometimes when they got tired of cooking. Mathias suspected it was also because the place reminded Rayan of the restaurants in Montreal that offered classic country fare: *pate Chinois*, poutine, *fèves au lard*. While they didn't serve those dishes here, the hefty portions of meat, potatoes, and gravy had a similar affect.

It was still early, and the restaurant was not as crowded as it usually got during the dinner rush. Above the bar, a television played one of the mandatory weekend football matches on mute. It was hard to find a place in the city that didn't make a point of broadcasting the game.

Mathias glanced over at the older man seated at the bar across from them, shoveling a plate of fries into his mouth and washing each mouthful down with a swig of draft beer. *Calais certainly doesn't lack for fine-dining establishments.*

When the waitress arrived at their table, Rayan spoke carefully, consulting the menu as he ordered. Mathias noted how the woman, young with curly brown hair, shifted to look at Rayan, tucking her hair behind her ear. In an attempt to blend in, Rayan had begun eschewing certain Quebecois words in favor of the formal French equivalent—a futile pursuit, as it was clear as soon as he opened his mouth that he wasn't from around here. The locals seemed to find his dialect endearing, especially when the occasional Quebecois word slipped through. Then there were the words that meant something different. Rayan had been alarmed to discover that in France, *gosse* meant child and not—as in Quebec—a particular part of the male anatomy.

The food arrived quickly, and after the waitress had set down their plates, she lingered by the table, commenting on the weather and the local football team. Mathias found her blatant flirting amusing, particularly because Rayan appeared oblivious, as he often was about these things. She left the bill by Rayan's elbow, and Mathias saw she'd scrawled her number along the bottom.

"Seems not everyone's deterred," Mathias remarked, picking up his knife and cutting into his meat.

Rayan eyed the phone number like a message in an alien language. He picked up his utensils and began carving into his chicken then stopped abruptly. "Tony once told me you kept me on as a *fuck you* to the establishment. Was that why—because my otherness was a tool?"

"It is a tool. When someone doesn't know what to expect, it's easy to throw them off."

Rayan stared back at him, his expression guarded.

Mathias set down his knife. "Here's the thing about belonging, Rayan. It makes you complacent. You get used to believing you deserve things by the very fact that you showed up. The men in the family were like that. I worked with soldiers who heard their orders through a thick layer of entitlement. That wasn't the case with you. That's why I kept you on. You were more like me than they were."

"You never told me that."

Mathias returned to carving his beef. "That being said, I did enjoy ruffling a few feathers."

Rayan cocked an eyebrow. "A few?"

Mathias smirked. "You and Tony sat around gossiping about me like a pair of old women?"

"Mathias," Rayan said suddenly, his voice pitching. His eyes were fixed on the television behind the bar.

Mathias looked up to see the game had been interrupted by the hourly news bulletin. On the screen were scenes of a city he could re-create with his eyes closed. There was downtown Montreal, the camera panning to a group of armed police officers lined up along Saint Laurent Boulevard. The following series of shots were of buildings cordoned off by yellow police tape.

Mathias strode over to the bar. "Turn on the sound," he instructed sharply. The man behind the register picked up the remote and pointed it at the screen.

"Days of upheaval following the murder of Montreal mob boss Giovanni Bianchi. The city has descended into chaos, instances of infighting and retaliation occurring too frequently for police to intervene. It's unsure whether the killings are related or premeditated, but the crime family has pledged to counter any threats to its power..."

Mathias turned and wordlessly made his way out of the restaurant. He began walking down the street, unsure where he was heading.

"Hey."

He felt a pull at his elbow, and Rayan was beside him, breathing fast. "Do you know what happened? Was it an inside job?"

Mathias came to a stop. He remembered Belkov's ominous question: "What happens when the whole thing topples over?"

He was struck by an overwhelming urge to return to Montreal. He couldn't put his finger on why—the logic kept slipping. Mathias had thought he'd shaken the family's hold on him, but it remained, lurking silently in the background.

He continued toward the house, vaguely aware of Rayan following him. Perhaps a part of him still wanted it—the power, the respect. Knowing which rung on the food chain he occupied.

Mathias reached the front door and scaled the stairs to the bedroom. He heard the thump of Rayan's footsteps behind him. He took a small case from the wardrobe and began throwing things inside.

Mathias attempted to piece a plan together. There were glaring gaps—getting into the country, for one. Early on, he'd made some inquiries and discovered there were ways around Inspector Allen's bureaucratic blockade. Remarkable what you could do with money and a decent counterfeit passport. Still, that would take time.

What he would do when he got there was another matter altogether. Belkov had alluded to the rumors that had circulated in Mathias's absence, and Mathias wasn't sure what influence he had left in the city. And then there was this: the life he'd made in Calais.

"It's not your fight anymore," Rayan said from the doorway.

Mathias whirled around. "And a hell of a lot of choice I had there! Giovanni made sure of that."

Saying his name aloud sent Mathias's thoughts spiraling. He didn't know why news of the man's death brought him no satisfaction. Instead, it stirred a feeling akin to grief.

"Is that why we couldn't go back?" Rayan asked.

"It doesn't matter now."

Rayan stepped into the room. "Mathias, no good will come from you returning to Montreal."

"You don't fucking get it," Mathias snarled. "My whole life, I was a burden no one wanted. But I was someone there—more than my name, more than my history."

"The closest thing you had to a family."

Mathias froze, his hand on the zipper of the suitcase. He knew then why he'd been compelled into action. He felt it still—the need to act when his family was threatened.

"But they pushed you out, remember?" Rayan said. "That's not what a real family does."

"A real family?" Mathias sneered. "And what exactly does that look like?"

Rayan stood before him, searching his face. "This."

Mathias blinked. He recalled those paralyzing few weeks after they'd arrived in France. He had found himself unable to leave the house, the mere act of lighting a cigarette sapping the strength from his bones. He'd been felled by the past that had come to haunt him. Because, despite all he'd fought for and grown and accomplished, the family had cast him aside, just as his father had done—that first cardinal rejection. Mathias hadn't realized the hurt ran so deep until it stopped him in his tracks.

Yet it hadn't consumed him. Because for the first time in his life, he wasn't alone. And moving forward was as much an obligation to Rayan as it was to himself.

"I don't need you to prove that you're better or more deserving. You don't need to prove anything to me," Rayan said, his voice tight. "You think because your parents didn't want you that you're not worthy?"

Mathias felt a jolt as Rayan brushed against an open sore he had no business touching. "Don't—"

"Fuck them," Rayan whispered. "You are. Not by surpassing your father or your brothers and not because of some rank or title. You're worthy exactly as you are."

Mathias stood mutely, unable to conjure a response. Here was someone who had chosen him and, despite Mathias's best efforts to push him away, had stayed.

A look of resignation came over Rayan's face. "But if it's what you want, I won't stop you."

And Mathias knew he meant it. Rayan would watch him pack his bag and go back to Montreal if that was what he decided to do. That was what Mathias would be giving up if he left—the only person who truly gave a damn.

Mathias let his hands drop from the suitcase. His loyalty to the family, once a solid, irrefutable fact, withered in comparison. Having known something better, he could now see that what he'd held onto had been a hollow substitute.

Rayan woke in the middle of the night to find the bed beside him empty. Mathias had spent the evening holed up in the study, and Rayan thought it best to leave the man alone. He'd assumed Mathias was catching up on news of the developing situation, if only to better make sense of what had happened.

The images of Montreal on the television screen had been shocking. They'd made the right choice getting out when they did. He thought of having to watch those scenes from his apartment in Toronto, not knowing if Mathias was alive or dead and imagining the worst. Rayan had headed to bed on his own, figuring Mathias would eventually join him. But by the look of the undisturbed covers, that hadn't happened.

He got out of bed and threw on some clothes then made his way downstairs. There was a light on in the kitchen, and he found Mathias sitting at the counter staring into a half-full glass of scotch. Mathias wasn't one to be kept awake by errant thoughts, yet here he was, up in the small hours of the night, drinking. Since moving to France, Mathias had reached less frequently for his signature bottle of Macallan.

Rayan brought a hand to the base of Mathias's neck, and the man leaned into his touch. He combed his fingers through Mathias's hair, gently massaging his scalp. "What's on your mind?"

Mathias let out a sigh. "By the end of it, I hated the old man's guts. So I don't know why..." He stopped, his forehead furrowing. He lifted his glass and downed the rest of his drink then placed it on the counter with a purposeful thud. "It's the end of an era of greats—Russo, Tony, Giovanni—"

"You."

Mathias turned to look at him. "I wouldn't count myself among them."

Rayan dropped his hand to Mathias's shoulder. "I was there. You'd walk into a room, and the air would shift."

Mathias shook his head with a small smile. It was true. The old guard had hated how much clout he'd had for someone who wasn't full-blooded. Men on the ground, out in the streets, respected him. And it had always shown.

"You miss it," Rayan said quietly.

Mathias frowned and looked away. "The higher I got, the more I realized how precarious it all was. Walking the wire, trying to anticipate from which direction someone would come at you."

"Is that why Giovanni thought you were after his job?"

"The paranoia got to him."

"Was it ever something you wanted?" Rayan asked, almost afraid of the answer. "Maybe not then but someday?"

Mathias was silent for a moment. "It might have been."

Since their hurried exit from Montreal, Rayan had thought a lot about what might have happened if things had played out differently. Mathias had it in him to lead the family, but if he'd succeeded Giovanni, there was no version of that reality where he and Rayan could have occupied the same world.

"If you'd become boss, you never would have gotten out."

Mathias held his gaze as though he, too, understood the full implication of that decision. Rayan stepped over to the cabinet above the sink and took down another glass. He picked up the bottle of scotch and poured some into both glasses then held his glass aloft.

"To the greats."

Mathias raised his glass, and the two of them knocked back the liquor. It rushed hot and searing down Rayan's throat, and he resisted the urge to cough. Mathias chuckled, giving him a knowing look. Then he stood and pulled Rayan close. Rayan looped his arms around Mathias's neck and breathed him in. He was well aware of what Mathias had given up—was giving up—for him.

"Come to bed." Rayan tilted his chin to kiss Mathias, the taste of scotch lingering on his lips.

In bed, Rayan let himself be lulled by the even sound of Mathias's breathing as he drifted off to sleep. Still, a wisp of fear remained. He'd told Mathias he wouldn't stop him from going back, but that was a half-truth. Rayan would do everything in his power to hold him in place like an anchor—tether the man to him so he wouldn't be tempted to return to the darkness.

19

Asmarina beckoned Rayan over when he arrived at the service office the following afternoon. A donated shipment of medical supplies had arrived at the camp earlier in the week, and Rayan had been working with several residents to get access to medication.

"I've been meaning to tell you..." Her lips pursed, and tiny lines appeared around the corners of her mouth. "Laurent heard back from the council. They voted against the proposal."

"Right."

They looked at each other, the disappointment palpable yet not unexpected.

"I guess we'll head back to the drawing board and figure out where to go from here." Asmarina attempted a smile, but she sounded defeated. They'd put so much into this already. It was starting to feel like a pipe dream.

"In slightly better news, we had dinner with Jules on Sunday," she went on. Jules Lapointe was Laurent's lawyer friend from university. Rayan had recently met with the man to submit Farhan's bid for asylum. "He seemed pretty positive about the Taleb family's chances. Which is promising."

"Promising, maybe, but we've been let down before," Rayan said. "I don't want them to get their hopes up only for it to fall through."

Asmarina nodded. "Of course. I would hold off on saying anything this early in the game."

The door to the cabin opened, and there was a rush of noise from outside. Rayan glanced up to see Farhan with Amira and Zahra in tow.

"Something's happening," Farhan said, out of breath. There was a frantic look on his face.

The city had started sending surveyors out to the Jungle, and rumors were swirling about a potential forced closure. This only served to heighten the tension in the camp as residents confronted the possibility of losing their temporary home. The place felt increasingly unsafe, and Rayan had overheard Laurent telling Asmarina that he didn't want her coming anymore. Naturally, Asmarina had brushed off his concerns, so Laurent had asked Rayan privately to keep an eye out for her.

Rayan peered out the window and saw a stream of people moving through the camp with their belongings hoisted on their backs. Police in riot gear walked alongside, systematically pulling down tents and kicking over makeshift structures. Two officers in a motorized vehicle drove up. One of them held a bullhorn to his mouth and was instructing—in a combination of French and English—that everyone stay calm and vacate the southern side of the camp.

Asmarina's phone rang, and she answered it with a distracted mumble. "It's Laurent," she said to Rayan as she clutched the phone to her ear. "He said the government received approval from a court in Lille this morning to start demolishing part of the Jungle."

"They can't do that."

"This is public land. The government can do whatever they want," Asmarina said. "Laurent's at the center, but he's driving over now."

"He won't be much help."

Who could the people here call on to keep them safe? Not the police. They were the ones carrying out the government's orders.

Through the window, Rayan could see a group of men with sticks advancing from the other end of the camp. "There's going to be a riot," he said quietly to Asmarina, glancing at the other occupants gathered in the service office. "We need to get everyone out."

Asmarina turned and began instructing people to gather their possessions. There were several dull thuds and then a loud crash from outside the cabin, followed by a scream. Inside, unsettled murmurs rippled through the group. One of the girls let out a whimper. People began moving to the back of the office, shrinking against the far wall. Outside, the men with sticks had begun to throw rocks and other debris at the police, who'd raised their shields and arranged themselves into a defensive formation.

"It's not safe out there," Asmarina whispered. "How are we supposed to get through?"

They could only watch as more people joined in the violence. It had initially been directed at the police but was quickly becoming more indiscriminate. A group of teenagers were yanking at the poles of a nearby food-distribution tent, sending its occupants scattering. In the middle of the melee, a woman was struggling with the stuck wheel of a cart she was pulling. Her children pressed against her, crying and covering their faces against the onslaught.

"Lock the door when I leave," Rayan instructed Asmarina.

"Wait, Rayan—"

"I'll be fine."

Rayan strode out of the cabin. He heard the swift clank of the deadbolt closing behind him. He pushed through the crowd, and a man jostled him as he passed.

"Hey, *Croix-Rouge,*" the man mocked, taking in Rayan's aid-worker vest. "Haven't you heard? They're tearing this place down. We're nothing but roaches to be squashed."

"Animals in a zoo," another man chimed in.

"And how does acting like animals prove them wrong?" Rayan countered, shoving past.

He made it to the woman and her cart, only to find a cop had gotten there first. The officer was waving at her to move on while the woman pleaded with him not to leave her things behind.

"Hey!" Rayan called out, startling the cop. "Let her pass."

The man seemed momentarily taken aback, maybe because Rayan had come out of nowhere or perhaps because he was speaking to him in French. Rayan helped lift the woman's cart and pull it to one side so she could continue with her children.

"What are you doing?" the cop blustered. "Aid workers aren't supposed to be here."

"Must have missed the memo. I thought the whole point was to take us by surprise."

"Go on, get out of here."

"No," Rayan said, standing his ground. "I've got at least ten people in our service office who don't feel safe crossing your riot line."

A series of panicked shrieks came from behind them, and Rayan turned to see a plume of black smoke rising from deeper inside the camp. Someone screamed "Fire!" and then people began to run.

Rayan abandoned the officer and doubled back to the cabin. He thumped his fist hard against the door. "Everyone out—we need to leave."

Asmarina opened the door, and together they ushered the group out into the surge of evacuees. Rayan was helping an elderly woman down the steps when a rock hit the front window of the cabin, sending splinters branching across the glass. Rayan looked over to see a cluster of boys standing nearby, their hands filled with rocks and broken bricks which they were hurling at the police.

In the distance, Rayan heard the rising wail of approaching sirens. *When there's a chance the city might burn down, then they decide to interfere.*

The police were shoving people back, herding them into a single column. One cop had his baton out and was swinging it wildly through the air, telling people to move faster. He caught a young man on the back and sent him sprawling.

Rayan pulled the kid to his feet then snatched the baton from the cop's hand and tossed it to the ground. "Enough. They're already frightened."

The policeman's mouth twisted, and he knocked his riot shield hard into Rayan's shoulder, throwing him backward. "You—get out of here!"

Rayan flared with anger. He shoved against the shield with both hands, and it slammed into the visor of the man's helmet, snapping his head back. Within seconds, two cops had Rayan by the arms and were yanking them behind his back.

Asmarina elbowed her way through the crowd toward them. "Stop! He's an aid worker. You've got no right—let him go!"

Rayan heard someone yell, and then a brick whizzed past his ear and landed with a thud in the dirt by one of the officer's feet.

"Asmarina!" Rayan called out. "It's not safe. Keep walking. Go find Laurent."

"I'm not leaving you with these thugs."

Another projectile hurtled by, and she ducked. The two police officers pushed Rayan through the crowd. He could hear Asmarina following close behind. One of the cops began reading him his rights, and Rayan silently cursed his own rashness. Mathias was going to kill him.

"Unlawful force?" Asmarina echoed the charge the officer had cited. "I just saw you bludgeon a kid!"

"Would you like us to arrest you too?"

"Go ahead and try."

Rayan scanned the crowd ahead for Farhan and the girls. He'd just caught sight of Zahra's pink sweater when something slammed into the side of his head, causing his vision to go black. For a moment, it was as if he was falling, and then his sight returned, and he swayed on his feet, the chaos of the camp flooding back.

The officer dropped Rayan's wrists as he lifted his shield to protect himself. A river of warmth was running down the side of Rayan's face. He raised a hand to his temple, and it came away dark red. He felt a stickiness gathering in the dip between his shoulder blades, soaking through the neck of his shirt.

And then Rayan was back at the old house in Maskinongé, lying in the grass and staring up at the cloudless sky as the front of his T-shirt bloomed with blood. It had been a stifling summer's day. His mother had gone to lie down, and he and Tahir were slinking around the house, hot and bored. Their father was passed out in his easy chair with the TV on, head thrown back, snoring loudly.

Rayan's father had a utility knife that he always carried around in his pocket, the kind with little tools that folded out—corkscrew, knife, screwdriver. The knife was one of his prized possessions, and Rayan and his brother had long been fascinated by it. They would watch with rapt attention when their father took it out once a month and meticulously cleaned and sharpened each tool. That day, Tahir decided to steal it.

Rayan was reluctant at first, but his brother talked him around. They would only look at it and then put it back before their father noticed it was gone. In the years that followed, Rayan returned often to that ill-fated decision—the single flap of a butterfly's wings that set into motion a series of other, more horrific events. Because if he'd said no, Tahir wouldn't have taken the knife. Boyish rebellion was no fun without someone there to witness.

Rayan had kept a lookout, eyes trained on his sleeping father's face, while Tahir ducked behind the chair and carefully slid the knife from the man's pocket. They scurried off outside with their prize. Crouched in the long grass behind the house, they were so absorbed in the task of unfolding each tool and inspecting it that they didn't hear their father approaching. He was furious. Not the clumsy, drunken fury Rayan was used to but a dark, simmering anger.

"You're a pair of filthy thieves. And I didn't raise thieves, not under my roof. Whose idea was it?"

When neither of them answered, his father decided to forgo the belt he was partial to using and opted instead for his hands. As they cowered before him, crying and sniveling, he asked again.

This time Rayan answered. "It was mine."

His father looked at him for a long time, and Rayan's stomach squirmed. "You're a liar," he said finally. "A liar and a thief. I know it was him. You're always trailing around like his little accomplice." He reached into his pocket and removed the knife he'd retrieved from the grass. "And now you're going to learn your lesson, boy. Careful who you stick your neck out for. I'll make sure you don't forget."

Perhaps it was because he kept the knife in such good condition, as though needed for more than just popping the cap off a stubborn beer bottle. Or maybe his father had underestimated the easy give of a child's throat. He'd come at Rayan with the strength of a man, only to find his flesh soft and pliant.

The blood began to gush, and the front of Rayan's T-shirt turned sodden, sticking to his chest. He saw the fear in his father's eyes then. He remembered that look more than the pain. His mother came rushing outside screaming and pummeled the man with her fists. His father clumsily wrapped the gash across

Rayan's neck, and then they sped to the hospital in Montreal. Rayan had lain in the back seat of the car with his head on his mother's lap, staring up at the tears rolling down her cheeks.

"Rayan!"

He opened his eyes.

Asmarina's face filled his vision, her features flattened with fear. "Rayan!"

He returned to the present and blinked away the blood trickling into his eye.

"Are you all right?" she asked, gripping Rayan's arm to steady him.

"Farhan... where are the girls?"

"They've gone on ahead."

"Laurent told me to look out for you."

"You just worry about yourself, Ayari." Her hand was wrenched away as the police officer once again pulled Rayan's arms behind his back and led him out of the camp.

20

Mathias had visited the Calais Center for New Migrants only once. Rayan had just started teaching his acclimation course, and Mathias was curious. He found it difficult to imagine Rayan—a man who'd proven so good at following orders—in the role of instructor. The center shared a building with several other service organizations in a business park not far from downtown. There was little to distinguish it from the other office facades besides a sign by the door in French and English. Inside, he'd found the reception desk unmanned and continued down a hallway lined with posters for food parcels and legal support. Flyers pinned to the walls offered a selection of courses on cooking, budgeting, and finding temporary work.

He heard Rayan's voice before he saw the open door to the classroom. It was not the voice of authority. Instead, Rayan sounded like he did when he was telling Mathias about a book he'd just finished—impassioned but unsure if what he said made any sense. Mathias walked a little farther down the hall and could see the first row of students staring at Rayan at the front of the room. They comprised a range of ages, from younger kids to teenagers, and all were diligently taking notes. Mathias listened a while longer as Rayan explained about gendered nouns and then saw himself out. He'd never told Rayan that he'd come.

When they'd first arrived in France, Mathias had assumed Rayan would continue his studies, perhaps find work at a local university. But he'd been lured by another calling—one Mathias had viewed with cynicism until he began to realize how much the work resonated with the parts of Rayan that had never fit into their old world. Seeing him in front of that class, Mathias had caught a glimpse of who Rayan might have been had his life taken a different turn—had their paths never crossed.

"Did you hear?" Elise asked, poking her head into the office. She'd been out in the warehouse, supervising Vicente as he shelved a family of brass sculptures she'd found at a flea market in Versailles. If his appraiser was picky about the pieces she selected, she was even more fastidious about how they were handled.

Mathias was at his desk, moments away from abandoning the Turkish customs document he'd been attempting to decipher. His frustration didn't make him any more amenable to Elise's annoying habit of asking a question that required him to ask one back.

He gave an irritated sigh. "About what?"

"The police shut down part of the Jungle. Apparently, there was some kind of riot, and a bunch of people have been arrested."

Mathias took out his phone and dialed Rayan's number. When the man didn't pick up, he stood and pulled on his jacket. "Don't let Vicente out of sight. He gets distracted this close to clocking off."

He was about to head out when the phone at his desk began to ring. He picked up the receiver and heard a crackle of static before an automated voice announced, "This is an incoming call from the Calais Police Department. Please hold while you are connected."

There was a click, and when Rayan spoke, his voice sounded tinny. "Hey."

At least he'd had the sense to call Mathias at the office and not on his cell. "This had better not be what I think it is."

There was a long pause. "You're angry."

Mathias sucked his teeth, a harshly worded reproach ready to spew from his lips. Instead, he managed a clipped reply. "I'm hanging up."

If there was one place in the city Mathias had hoped to never set foot inside, it was the Commissariat de police de Calais. He strode into the station lobby to discover it packed with people. Several aid workers in blue vests marked with the names of charitable agencies were pressed against the front desk, engaging in a heated exchange with the harried-looking receptionist.

"He's been unfairly arrested," a larger man with a graying beard was saying to the woman seated behind the glass screen. "What happened today was an illegal raid."

Beside him, a dark-haired woman paced agitatedly. She wore a pale-green scarf around her shoulders that was mottled with smears of reddish brown. It took Mathias a moment to recognize Laurent and Asmarina Moreau, the couple who ran the new migrant center. He'd seen them briefly at a community fundraiser for local business leaders that he'd attended at Rayan's insistence. Mathias had left early but not before donating a chunk of cash that he'd later used as a tax write-off.

"If you don't release him, we'll go to the media. I'm sure the rest of the world won't hesitate to condemn this city and your actions—"

"Sir, Mr. Ayari's bail is set at five thousand euro. We can't release him until the bail is met."

"Five thousand euro?" Laurent echoed, incredulous. "We're a nonprofit organization. We don't have that kind of money lying around."

Mathias approached the desk and took out his wallet. He peeled a series of notes from the fold and slid them over to the receptionist. Laurent stared at him curiously.

"Can we move this along?" Mathias asked.

The woman behind the counter collected the money and shoved a clipboard toward him. "Fill this out, and we'll begin the procedure for release."

"Here." Mathias passed the clipboard to Laurent, in no hurry to commit his information to record.

"Do I know you?" Laurent asked as they stepped away from the front desk.

"No."

"You're a friend of Rayan's?" Asmarina asked.

"Something like that."

"Well, thank you. We'll reimburse you for the money. I'll be filing a complaint with the public prosecutor, and I intend to get back every cent." Her words were cutting, but she appeared upset. "You should have seen how they treated him. He did nothing wrong."

Mathias's eyes narrowed. *How they treated him?*

Laurent handed in the paperwork, and they stood around in the lobby, waiting. It was another half hour before the interior door to the station buzzed, and a burly cop with his gut hanging over his belt escorted Rayan out. Rayan looked pale and a little dazed, his shirt stained with dried blood. On the right side of his forehead, just below the hairline, was a large red gash. Mathias slid his hands into his pockets to hide the clench of his fists.

"Did you even bother to administer first aid?" Laurent berated the cop. "He could have a concussion!"

The man gave a shrug and turned away.

"Just wait. You're going to hear about this!" Laurent called out savagely to the cop's retreating back. He lowered his voice. "Bastards."

Asmarina moved to give Rayan a hug. "Let's get you to the hospital."

Rayan glanced over at Mathias. "You two should head home. I'm sure this is enough excitement for one day."

Asmarina seemed hesitant to leave, but Rayan assured her he was fine. Finally, she and Laurent said their goodbyes and stepped away.

"You've got something on your shirt," Mathias said when they'd gone.

Rayan gave him a weary smile. "It looks worse than it is."

Mathias leaned in to take a closer look. The cut was deep and jagged. He'd need stitches. "Come on."

They walked to the car parked on the street outside and got in. "You gave them your name?" Mathias asked as he eased out onto the road.

"I wasn't exactly thinking clearly."

"What else did they get?"

"Prints," Rayan admitted reluctantly. "But I used a different address."

"Fuck, Rayan," Mathias muttered. "One curious busybody runs those through the international system…"

"The charge will get thrown out. They know they were in the wrong. I was locked up with a priest, for Chrissakes. There will be pushback, and they'll want to cover up as much as they can."

At the lights, Mathias turned the car, heading away from the ocean.

Rayan shifted in his seat. "Where are you going?"

"Where do you think?"

Mathias saw a glimmer of panic cross Rayan's face. "No. Just take me home."

"You think you have a choice here?"

Mathias pulled into the hospital car park and found a spot. Throngs of people were gathered by the entrance. He and Rayan were in for a long wait.

They took a seat in the crowded waiting room, and Mathias fought the urge for a cigarette. Two of his least favorite places in one day. *What a fucking treat.*

He glanced again at the wound on Rayan's forehead. "The cops do that?" There'd be more than a letter of complaint coming their way if that was the case.

"No, it was… an accident."

"Your boss seemed rattled. What happened out there?"

"The police got orders to start tearing things down. They closed the south end of the camp."

"And you just happened to get caught in the fray?"

"I didn't feel like playing nice."

Mathias allowed himself a smile. "Attaboy."

Rayan leaned back and closed his eyes, and Mathias jostled him with his shoulder. "Not until someone's seen you."

"I won't fall asleep."

"Famous last words."

Rayan opened his eyes, and his mouth gave a slight tweak. "Keep me awake, then. Tell me a story."

"You must think I'm easy."

"Tell me about the time you lived in Paris or when you started out with the family. The first time you met Tony, anything."

"I don't do stories."

"Then read one from here." Rayan picked up a magazine from the pile on the table between them and handed it to Mathias.

Mathias flipped through. "You've got to be fucking kidding me... 'I left my husband for my blind brother-in-law'?"

"Sounds like a winner."

After what seemed like forever, a nurse holding a sheet of paper emerged from behind a set of swinging doors. "Mr. Ayari?"

Rayan stood, and Mathias followed him through the doors to a bustling room filled with curtained cubicles. The nurse gestured for Rayan to sit on an empty exam table and drew the curtain closed around them.

"Do you know what it was that hit you?" she asked, inspecting the gash with her gloved fingers.

"A rock, I think."

"Someone threw a rock at you?" Mathias seethed.

"Pretty sure it wasn't me he was throwing it at."

The nurse checked him for signs of concussion then cleaned the wound and inspected it closely. "It's quite deep. I will need to go ahead and close this up." She placed a tray down on the edge of the table and retrieved a small syringe. "It's just a local anesthetic. Do you have any allergies?"

Rayan shook his head.

The nurse pressed the needle of the syringe into the skin near the cut. "Give it a moment to kick in." She disposed of the syringe and returned to the tray, where she began threading a surgical needle. When she was ready, the nurse leaned forward and pinched the skin around the wound with one hand. "This shouldn't take too long. Bear with me, okay?"

Then, with the other hand, she gently inserted the needle. Rayan jolted, and his arm flew up, knocking her hands away. In her surprise, the nurse stepped backward and upended the tray, its contents clattering to the floor.

The color had drained from Rayan's face, and his chest rose and fell rapidly. "Sorry."

"Was there pain?"

"No."

The nurse bent to retrieve the tray that had fallen. "I should've asked. Things have been so chaotic today. Do you have a phobia of needles or any medical trauma? We can offer a sedative."

"No," Rayan replied carefully. "I'm fine."

It had been years, but Mathias could still conjure the look on Rayan's face when the doctor had dug the forceps into his shoulder. He could still recall the twisted cry that had torn from the man's throat.

"Take the sedative, Rayan."

Rayan's eyes met his, and he gave a resigned nod.

"All right," the nurse said and turned to Mathias. "You can come and see him when we're done."

Mathias went outside to smoke. His phone buzzed in his pocket, and he pulled it out to see a message from Elise asking if everything was all right. He ignored it and tossed the butt of his cigarette into a nearby receptacle. By the doors to the emergency department, a woman paced the pavement, wailing in a foreign language. When he was allowed back in to see Rayan, the man sported a white bandage on his forehead, and there was a soft plane to his features.

"He's a little out of it. Give him about twenty minutes for the sedative to wear off, and then you can go. No driving, though," the nurse instructed before drawing the curtain behind her and disappearing into the room beyond.

"Does it hurt?" Mathias asked.

Rayan shook his head groggily and reached up to touch his neck, where the scar stretched across his throat.

That was when Mathias understood. "Not a fan of hospitals, I take it?"

Rayan dropped his hand, and Mathias brought his fingertips to the scar. "Is this why she left him?"

It was a long time before Rayan spoke. "Child protection showed up at the ED afterward. They made it clear if she wanted to keep us, she couldn't stay." There came a shout from the cubicle next door, and then a baby's high-pitched squall filled the room. "If it hadn't happened, we wouldn't have left, and she wouldn't have ended up on her own." Rayan swallowed hard. "It was too much. She couldn't handle it. That's why—"

"You don't know why," Mathias interjected with a shake of his head. "You'll never know why."

"If we'd stayed, maybe things would've been different."

All this time, has he blamed himself?

Mathias moved his fingers to the hollow of Rayan's neck. "She did a brave thing, Rayan. She got you out." She'd done it to protect him, a feat not all mothers were capable of. *Just look at my own.* "And you can try to rearrange the past, but there's nothing you could've done to make it any different."

"I don't know if I believe that," Rayan said, his voice barely a whisper.

"It's true, whether you believe it or not."

Rayan looked up at him, his eyes still hazy. Around them, the room clamored with voices and beeps and the hum of machines. Mathias didn't move his hand from Rayan's neck, the man's steady pulse beating against his fingers.

Rayan stood under the hot water in the shower for a long time, watching the trickle of red at his feet run clear. He hadn't realized how much blood had caked onto his skin. It was a relief to be rid of it. As he dressed, he was careful not to make any sudden movements. His temple throbbed. The nurse had given him some pills for the pain, but he'd held off on taking them. He felt woozy enough from the sedative and needed a chance to get his bearings.

When Rayan came downstairs, he found Mathias on the sofa in the living room, nursing a glass of scotch while the news flashed on the television. He'd been quiet on the drive back to the house, and Rayan could imagine he didn't appreciate the way his day had derailed into chaos.

"Well, you got your international incident," Mathias remarked.

Rayan stared at the images on the screen—the cops in riot gear, the black smoke rising from the camp, the mess of destruction left behind. In the ticker tape along the bottom of the segment were a series of condemnations from international aid groups, politicians, and celebrities.

"What a mess," Rayan murmured. He sank down into a chair, and Mathias raised the remote to turn off the TV.

"They're saying it's only a matter of time before they're back for the rest," Mathias said, lifting his glass. "Surely, you knew that was coming."

The Jungle was done for. The writing had been on the wall for a while. They'd just been too stubborn to see it. Rayan thought of all the people he saw each day at the service office. *What will happen to them now?*

"When they tear down the camp, there'll be nowhere for the residents to go."

"I suspect the city doesn't care where they end up, as long as it's not here."

"Durand's just passing on the problem. It would mean putting children, families out on the streets."

And then Rayan's head was no longer fuzzy. In fact, he was struck by a strange clarity. His mind caught on an idea, crazy yet potentially feasible. "We don't need the city's money. I'll find a way to get it myself."

Mathias eyed him skeptically. "I think that rock hit you harder than you thought."

"We submitted a proposal to the council for the housing facility," Rayan explained. "It won't solve the whole impossible situation, but it will help at least. The majority of funding for the build has already been secured by an EU grant. We only needed the city to front seven million to get it off the ground."

"Let me guess—Durand wasn't too keen?"

Rayan nodded. "They voted it down."

"Seven million isn't exactly pocket change. Even I'd be hard-pressed to magic that kind of money out of thin air."

"We could fund it privately, reach out to donors here and abroad." Rayan gestured at the blackened TV. "You saw the backlash. There will be people who want to contribute. We wouldn't have anything to do with the city."

"That's where you're wrong." Mathias downed the rest of his drink. "You'll need planning approval from the council, permits for construction. You can try to skirt them, but as soon as the city figures out what you're using the building for, they'll shut you down."

Rayan frowned. There was the rub—Durand's opinions on the issue were too entrenched. Even if they removed all the obstacles and required nothing from the council, the mayor would still fight them on principle.

But Rayan was done waiting for permission. Durand's word wasn't the end of it. Rayan's time with the family had taught him that everyone could be persuaded one way or another. While intimidation was off the table, there were plenty of other routes they could take to get the mayor to reconsider.

"Then I'll make him change his mind."

"With your bleeding heart?" Mathias asked.

"Can't very well use my fists."

"Only two things speak to men like Durand—money and public sway."

"Laurent has contacts. We can get other organizations to petition the council, put pressure on him that way."

"And the money? You'll just go around with your hand out?"

Rayan bristled at his tone. Granted, it was different from how they'd gotten things done in the past. But that wasn't an option anymore. "That's how this works. Unless we call in another favor with the Bratva and see if they can extort Durand into submission."

Mathias scowled, and Rayan felt a splinter of remorse. The man had gone out on a limb by calling Belkov to help locate Farhan.

"No one gives a shit about a tiny town in France with a camp full of refugees," Mathias said. "It's a drop in the fathomless ocean of pain and suffering—"

"I give a shit," Rayan snapped.

"I'm well aware," Mathias growled. "I just spent the afternoon standing around while you got your head sewn up." He slammed his empty glass down on the coffee table. "What's next—someone shanks you for food rations? I'll be sure to show up in time to watch them shove your guts back in."

He stood and stalked into the kitchen. Mathias's irritation, his silence in the car—it was stupid of Rayan not to realize. He got to his feet and followed Mathias into the kitchen.

"I didn't mean to worry you," he said as Mathias opened the fridge and pulled out a bottle of water.

Mathias scoffed and placed the bottle down on the kitchen counter. His jaw tightened. "I wasn't worried."

"My mistake."

The sedative had well and truly worn off, and Rayan's forehead ached where the nurse had stitched up the skin. He recalled the sense of relief he'd felt at the hospital. He had given voice to his darkest fear, and Mathias had refused to accept his guilt, offering clemency instead.

"Thanks for coming to get me."

Mathias sighed, and the lines of anger on his face softened. "Next time, throw a fucking rock back."

21

"See the feathered strokes?"

Mathias peered at the small, framed painting of a hare poised on its hind legs. There was an eerie glint in the animal's eye.

"Dürer was famous for fashioning his own woodcuts," Elise murmured beside him, enraptured. It was almost endearing, how fascinated she was by this stuff.

They were at an auction house in Cologne, a morning's drive from Calais, and Mathias was about to bid on a private collection of paintings that had come to market following a patron's recent death. He had two clients on the lookout for an original Dürer, and if he was successful at the auction, he planned to find out which one wanted it more.

"Shall we?" Mathias gestured toward the bidding room, which was quickly filling with an even split of art enthusiasts and cutthroat procurers like him. He recognized several familiar faces among them.

He sat with Elise in the second row, and his appraiser began marking numbers on the bid sheet. She scribbled little notes about pricing and her suggested upper limits. They made a good team that way. While she relied on him for the actual bidding, she had an eagle eye for quality, and her estimates were never off by more than a couple grand.

When it came to securing what he wanted, Mathias employed an aggressive bidding strategy. He was confident he could foist whatever he bought onto one of his less discerning clients—those whose wealth eclipsed their general intelligence. Getting them to part with some of their money was practically a public service.

The auction started up, and Elise tapped his sleeve and pointed to the top figure on the sheet in her hand. Mathias inclined his head and raised his paddle, making the opening bid. He was soon engaged in a heated back-and-forth with a rival dealer, Jereon Klauss. He and Klauss had crossed paths at many such auctions, and Mathias found it almost impossible to back down. The Dutchman appeared to share this same fault.

The bidding stood at fifteen over Elise's upper limit, and she was making a cross with her index fingers to get him to pull back. She glared at Mathias as he once again moved to lift his paddle. He caught her look and reluctantly relented. The piece went to Klauss, as did the two other lots of Dürer paintings that were up for auction that morning.

Mathias was seething by the time the room broke for an intermission. He spotted Klauss in the crowd, and before Elise could speak, he strode toward the man and backed him against the wall. Klauss was a tall man who looked to be in his fifties. He wore his hair slicked to one side and had a confident little sneer that seemed permanently fixed on his face.

"What do you think you're doing?" Mathias snapped.

Klauss blinked in mock surprise. "What do you mean, Mr. Beauvais?"

"You're tailing my picks."

"I hadn't noticed."

"The fuck you hadn't," Mathias said.

"This is a fair auction, and I'm representing a client."

Mathias gave a snort and turned to leave.

"Just a moment, Mr. Beauvais." Klauss reached out to touch Mathias's arm and glanced around at the other auction attendees. "As it so happens, there's a piece you came into recently that I was hoping you might be willing to part with."

"So you thought you'd see if I'd cut a deal?"

"Well, not exactly—"

"Which piece?"

Klauss's eyes shone. "The pheasant still life you purchased at the auction in Luxembourg last month."

Mathias scanned his memory for the piece the man was talking about. There had been a painting in poor condition that Elise had convinced him to buy, with the reassurance that she'd arrange for its restoration. She'd said she had a hunch, and he vaguely remembered her prattling excitedly about it on the drive back to Calais. But he couldn't for the life of him remember why. He beckoned Elise over.

"Klauss," she said stiffly.

"Dumont," he returned, equally aloof.

"Klauss, here, says he's looking to trade the Dürers he just paid an arm and a leg for," Mathias said.

"Trade them?" Elise repeated, sounding confused. "For what?"

"Some still life we bought in Luxembourg."

"Is that right?" She inclined her head toward Mathias. "Can I speak with you?" They stepped away, and Elise lowered her voice to a fierce whisper. "That piece is a Cézanne. I just had it authenticated by a contact at the Musée d'Orsay. Klauss must have found out. It's worth more than a dozen Dürers."

Mathias shrugged. "So? We don't have anyone interested in buying it. I have two clients ready to pay me for these ones."

"Not yet, but wait until it's done being restored. You'll have people beating down the door—our friend Klauss included."

Mathias studied his appraiser. It was a bold move. Perhaps he was rubbing off on her. "It doesn't happen often, Dumont, but sometimes you surprise me."

"I'll take that as a compliment."

When they rejoined the anxiously waiting Klauss, Mathias gave him a complicit smile. "I'll think about it."

They returned to their seats, and the auction started up again. The painting in the next lot—some technicolor Cubist monstrosity—wasn't on their list. Mathias lifted his paddle. Almost immediately, Klauss followed.

"What are you doing?" Elise hissed beside him.

"Fucking with him," Mathias replied with a smirk.

It was late afternoon by the time they arrived back in Calais. Mathias knew as soon as he pulled the car up outside the warehouse that something was wrong. The roller door had been pulled all the way open, and a black BMW was parked out front.

Elise leaned forward in the passenger seat and squinted through the windshield. "Did we forget to lock up?"

"No." Mathias reached beneath his seat and pulled out his gun. *Here we go. Might as well get it over with.*

At least the timing had worked out. He'd finally decided what to do about his Albanian problem. But he would need all the leverage he could muster to pull it off.

Elise gasped and stared at him, wide-eyed, as he checked the chamber and tucked the pistol into the waistband of his slacks. "Where did you get that? Do you even know how to use it?"

"I think I can figure it out." He pulled out his phone and enabled the location-tracking function then slipped it back into his pocket.

"This is all my fault," Elise said, her voice rising in panic. "If I hadn't pushed so hard with the Indonesian dealer—"

"Shut up and listen."

Elise snapped her mouth closed. It was a tone he hadn't used with her before. Mathias had no more patience for theatrics.

"I need you to keep a clear head, understand?" he said.

She nodded.

"You're going to take the car to number nine, Rue Carnot. If Rayan's not there, go and find him. Got that?"

"He'll know what to do?"

Of that, Mathias had no doubt. He yanked open the car door. "Don't wait until I'm inside. Just drive."

"You're going inside?" Elise's face had gone white.

"I have what they want. They're not going to do anything to me until they get it back." *And they're not going to find it here.*

No sooner had Mathias made it halfway across the parking lot than he heard the squeal of tires. Elise banked a hard right and gunned the car toward the road. There came a loud crash from inside the warehouse, and he approached the open door cautiously, his hand resting on the handle of his gun.

Several shelves had been overturned, and a mess of merchandise was strewn across the floor. It was lucky he'd sent Elise away. She would have had a coronary. Mathias could see two men in sports jackets attempting to pry open the lid to a crate of packing material by the entrance to the office. The office itself looked undisturbed, which meant they hadn't made it that far yet.

"Afternoon, gentlemen."

The men looked up with matching sour expressions.

"You realize this isn't a junk shop. That's some pricey product you've tossed on the floor. Unfortunately, house rules apply: you break, you buy."

One of the men tossed his crowbar to the ground. Together they stalked over to Mathias. "Our boss wants to speak with you," the taller one said. He was lanky, with a prominent scar that cut through his left eyebrow. He had the same accent as Marsela but appeared far less innocent.

"I'll speak with her here."

The man shook his head. "You're coming with us. You and that little receptionist of yours." He sniggered and peered past Mathias as if expecting Elise to materialize.

Mathias contemplated the cost of the stock he currently had stored at the warehouse. The apes had already done enough damage, and if the situation got messy, the last thing he needed was for it to happen at his place of business. That would prove difficult to explain to the cops.

"Just me, I'm afraid. That's not a problem, is it?" He pulled back his jacket to reveal the pistol nestled by his hip.

The man scowled and glanced at his partner. He muttered something back, and they entered into a rapid-fire exchange in Albanian.

"I don't have all fucking day," Mathias prodded.

The shorter man nodded grudgingly, and together, they walked to the car parked outside. Mathias got into the back seat, and they headed out of town, driving south along the coast. Mathias kept an eye on the road signs, clocking them as far as Capécure before the driver turned inland and began a winding route through the countryside. They must have been near Saint-Léonard when the car made a sudden turnoff. The driver navigated a long, narrow road flanked on both sides by mature sycamores. At the end of the road was a large country villa crawling with ivy.

They slowed to a stop in the circular driveway and got out of the car. The shorter man thumped, heavy-footed, up the steps to unlock the ornate wooden door. He held it open and ushered Mathias inside. The house was tidy but unoccupied. Standing in the entranceway, Mathias could see into the adjoining sitting room, where the furniture was covered with white drop cloths and the chairs had been stacked neatly in one corner.

Scarface stepped forward. "All right, hand it over."

"I'm not giving you my gun."

"I wasn't asking."

The man advanced, and Mathias waited until he was within arm's reach before catching him flush on the nose with his fist and sending him sprawling on his ass. His partner rushed him, and Mathias blocked the man with his shoulder and hurled him into the wall. Mathias felt the sharp jolt of Scarface's knuckles as they made impact with his ribs. He staggered backward, and another blow landed, this time to Mathias's chin, splitting his lip.

Mathias recovered quickly enough to pull out his gun and smash the barrel into the side of Scarface's head. The man went down like a stone. His partner tackled Mathias, throwing him to the floor, and the gun lurched from his hand and slid out of reach. They wrestled across the marble tiles, the smaller man managing to land a fist just below Mathias's eye and a strike to the temple, breaking the skin and sending black spots dancing across his vision.

Mathias heaved him off and pinned the man beneath him. Fueled by bloodlust, Mathias felt his vision narrow, and he slammed his fist over and over again into the man's face. He felt two hands loop beneath his arms, and then Scarface was pulling him off with a frenzy of curses. Mathias snapped his head back and hit the man's jaw with a hard crack. Scarface gave a rasping howl and dropped to his knees.

Breathing hard, Mathias spat out a mouthful of blood and scanned the floor for his weapon. Behind him, he heard a distinctive click.

He turned to see Marsela standing in the doorway to the villa. She wore a red dress and heeled boots, a silk scarf tied chicly around her neck. She held his pistol in her hand, the muzzle pointed at his head, and let out an exasperated sigh.

"Now, boys. Must you always resort to violence?"

Laurent had forbidden Rayan from returning to work for the rest of the week. He wanted to be sure there were no lingering effects from the knock Rayan had taken to the head. In the lobby of the police station, and again when he'd called to check up on Rayan, Laurent had apologized for putting him in harm's way. He'd sounded so despondent over the phone that Rayan had held off on mentioning his idea about raising the remaining project funds independently. He would see what he could do on his own before putting the plan to Asmarina and Laurent, who had enough on their plate already.

"She's really cut up, Rayan," Laurent confessed. "She feels responsible for what happened."

Asmarina had insisted on accompanying him to the station in the back of the police van, pressing her scarf to his forehead until the bleeding stopped. She'd sassed the officers the entire ride, and when she ran out of words in French, she'd continued in Tigrinya.

"Tell her she shouldn't," Rayan said. Asmarina had nothing to feel guilty about. "And it's barely a scratch. I've had worse."

It was true. The bump had disappeared along with the throbbing pain, and he was pretty sure once the stitches were removed, he'd only be left with a faint scar. The injury was nothing compared to the lasting reminder on his shoulder.

Even if he was allowed to work, Rayan wasn't sure where he would go. Following the riot at the Jungle, they'd temporarily closed the service office, and Laurent had said that Asmarina refused to resume services at the camp until she was sure it was safe.

Which was why Rayan happened to find himself at home in the middle of the day. Mathias had left early that morning to attend an auction in Germany. He'd been reluctant to go, lingering in bed as their errant fondling turned increasingly impassioned.

"For fuck's sake," Mathias muttered when he caught sight of the time. He'd attempted to extract himself, but Rayan had proven less willing. "Cocktease."

He snickered and pushed Rayan away then got up from the bed to shower and dress. When Rayan went downstairs to see him off, he saw Mathias's gaze flick to his forehead. The bandage was gone, but the stitches were still clearly visible.

"At least they had the sense to keep you away."

"Not sure what I'm supposed to do," Rayan grumbled. He wasn't used to being idle.

Mathias shrugged. "Clean the house, bake a cake."

"Have dinner on the table when you get home?"

"Now you're getting it."

Rayan opted instead to return to bed. Later, he walked into town and wandered from store to store, buying things he didn't need. He'd just returned home and was finishing a late lunch in the kitchen when he heard the thud of someone banging on the front door. Peering through the peephole, he saw a flushed and frantic-looking Elise.

Rayan opened the door, and she spilled inside. "He told me to come here."

"Mathias?"

She nodded. "They came to the warehouse, looking for the drugs, and he's there right now with them. We have to do something—"

"What drugs?"

"The shipment from Indonesia. He didn't tell you?"

Rayan swallowed a barb of anger, recalling the crate of smashed clay figures. *No. Apparently, he doesn't tell me shit.*

"It was my fault. I sourced the pieces, and when they arrived, they were fake and filled with these plastic bags of white powder. Then this woman shows up, asking about Asian artifacts. Mathias must have known she was trouble because he told me to keep an eye out for her, but I didn't really make the connection until the pig's head showed up outside the warehouse—"

"That's enough," he said curtly, cutting through the panicked recap of information Mathias had blatantly kept from him.

Rayan strode through the house to the study, Elise trailing behind him. He spun the wheel on the concealed safe beneath the desk and opened it to retrieve a holster, a pistol, and a box of ammunition. He shrugged on the holster and began loading the gun, his fingers moving with surprising dexterity.

Guess it's a skill you don't forget in a hurry, he thought as he strapped the weapon to his chest.

"Christ, you too?"

Rayan glanced up. He'd forgotten Elise was in the room. She was staring at him in horror, like he was a complete stranger.

"What is going on here? Who are you?" she asked.

"That's a loaded question."

He pulled open Mathias's laptop on the desk and tapped in the man's password. Navigating to the location tracking app, Rayan synced it with Mathias's phone. He waited for the red dot to appear, but when it did, it was nowhere near the warehouse. And it was moving. Quickly.

"He's headed along the highway toward Capécure."

"How can that be? I have his car." Elise held up Mathias's car keys.

"Then he must be with them." Rayan took his phone from his pocket and connected it to the application, the little red dot now appearing on his screen. "Did he say anything about where he might be going?"

Elise shook her head wordlessly.

Not so chatty now.

He held out his hand for the keys, and she placed them in his palm. "Trust me—the less you know, the better." Rayan led her back to the entranceway and opened the front door. "Go home, sit tight. He'll be fine."

As he watched Elise walk down the path to the street, he stifled the fear that accompanied the lie. He had no idea if Mathias would be all right. He had no idea what the man had gotten himself into. He just knew he had to get him out of it.

For a second, he was gripped by a cold terror. *Did I kiss Mathias before he left this morning?* For the life of him, he couldn't remember. Rayan jerked his head to dislodge the thought. He refused to entertain the possibility that it might have been the last time.

He got in the car and reversed out of the driveway then sped down the street toward the highway. As Rayan drove, his mind trawled through the events of the past few weeks. There was the crate and the import license and the way Mathias had brushed off the interest from the Albanians when Rayan pressed him. And all that time, someone had been after him.

It was one of the man's exceptional skills. Rayan had seen it often enough in the time they'd worked together—the ability to find himself backed against a wall and still act like he held all the cards, his confidence alone wielded like a weapon.

Rayan cursed himself. He'd let Mathias do it again—placate him with his self-assurance as danger closed in. Rayan had been so preoccupied with his work at the camp and the housing project that he'd let Mathias shut him out and play him for a fool.

Rayan gunned through an orange light and headed toward the on-ramp. He glanced down at the screen of his phone. The little red dot was still moving.

This would not be like the dream. He would get to him on time. He had to.

22

Mathias sat in a wooden chair in the middle of the sitting room, his wrists zip-tied to the armrests. Once they'd picked themselves off the floor, the two Albanian half-wits had restrained him at Marsela's instruction. They weren't taking any more chances. Mathias tested the tautness of the restraints to find there was no give.

Marsela waited by the door to the room, his gun held loosely in her manicured hand. She'd kept it leveled at his head while her lackeys wrestled him into the chair, and it served as enough of an incentive for Mathias to play nice. With brute force off the table, he was going to have to get creative.

She said something in Albanian, and the two men slipped quietly into the entranceway, closing the door behind them. Marsela locked it with a flourish and walked over to place his gun down on the table by the wall. She stood before Mathias, studying him curiously.

"You must have really scared those boys. I gave them clear instructions to keep their hands to themselves." She let out a laugh. "But then, here I was thinking you'd come easy. I guess it can't be helped."

Marsela reached into the purse looped over her shoulder and pulled out a pack of clove cigarettes and a silver lighter.

"Do you like it?" she asked, gesturing at the cavernous room. "There are so many beautiful summer homes in the area. Used for only a few months, and then the rest of the year, they sit empty. The owner of this one was overjoyed to find someone willing to rent it out of season. And so quiet. No one for miles." She lit the cigarette and took a delicate draw through her pursed red lips. "As you've probably gathered, I have no interest in antiques. But I would very much like to know what you've done with our merchandise."

"I thought we'd already established what I knew."

"You're lying." She exhaled a thin stream of smoke. "The group I represent has a great deal of interest in where that product ends up."

"And what group would that be? It's hard to keep track of the Albanian mafia."

Marsela's expression flattened. "It would be unfortunate to involve an innocent man like yourself in something so unsavory."

"You already involved me by attempting to smuggle your narcotics through my business."

Marsela gave him a knowing look. "That's not really why you're here though, is it?" She moved toward him with an easy smile. "See, I know men like you, Mr. Beauvais. Men who go out looking for excitement. A beautiful woman takes an interest, and you think you can play on her level, dabble in things above your pay grade." Marsela reached out to brush the tips of her fingers across his bruised cheek and made a low tutting sound. "What a shame to mess up such a handsome face. They're a bunch of apes. There's a far cleaner way to do this."

She took one last drag before dropping the cigarette and crushing it with the toe of her boot. She withdrew a small syringe from her purse and uncapped the end. "I thought you'd like to sample the merchandise you've so brazenly stolen from us. It's very popular on both sides of the channel. It has a way of making people more cooperative. That's what I feel we've been missing from you, Mathias—a little cooperation."

He felt a sharp sting as she plunged the needle into his neck and released the contents of the syringe into his veins. Mathias gave a grunt when she pulled out the needle and tossed it to the floor. Despite his proximity to the stuff, Mathias had never been tempted to dabble. He knew a thing or two about the various highs and lows the family peddled, but he despised the humiliation that accompanied the drugs—how they rendered users sloppy, caricature-like. The loss of control alone was enough to put him off.

There was a slight tingle in his fingers. He clenched one fist and then the other, yet his head remained clear. Either the shit she'd injected him with was slow release, or he had a greater tolerance than she realized. But the woman didn't need to know that. Mathias relaxed his shoulders and sank lower into the chair.

Marsela's face lit up with amusement. "Look at you. Not a tiger anymore—just a tomcat. I bet if I scratched behind your ears, I could make you purr." She grazed his shoulder with the palm of her hand, her voice lowering. "Now that we're getting to know each other, I'll confess I enjoyed our first meeting. Your defiance was... unexpected. It made me want to see you again. That's what this is about, isn't it? Hiding what's mine in some elaborate attempt to capture my attention. Well, you have it."

Mathias almost snorted in disbelief. He remembered the way her hand had lingered on his chest at the warehouse and the look she'd flashed him. He'd assumed she was toying with him—a classic flex of soft intimidation. Yet it appeared she was completely serious.

Women like Marsela—bold, attractive, imperious—seemed to think they were entitled to whatever they wanted. He knew then the reason behind her puzzling pursuit—why she hadn't simply arrived with muscle and strong-armed him into returning what was hers. She'd drawn it out, a lioness playing with her food, because it wasn't just the drugs she was after.

There was a time when Mathias had made a game of picking up women. He discovered he could pull as easily as ordering a drink. While the encounters had left him cold, they'd aided him in his denial and bolstered the lies he told himself. For if this was true, surely the other thing wasn't.

Mathias cocked his head with a slow smile. "Was it that obvious?"

A pleased flush rose to Marsela's cheeks. She leaned in, her fingers at the nape of his neck. "You like to play with fire, don't you? You're not the first. I've fucked many men who want to see how close to the flame they can get."

His eyes locked on hers. "Close enough to touch."

Marsela let out a murmur of pleasure. "I thought so." She lifted her knee and pressed it between his legs. "I can't promise I'll be gentle."

"I didn't come here for gentle."

"But you're forgetting," she whispered, teasing, drawing her lips along his jaw. "Your hands are tied."

He angled his chin to press his mouth to her ear and felt her shiver beneath his touch. "I only need the one."

Then he felt it, a rush like he was falling forward headfirst. A liquid warmth spread through his limbs, expanding him. His body spilled outside the lines, feeling everything—the rub of the ties around his wrists, the chair pressing into his back, the brush of air against his skin.

Fuck.

Marsela straddled his lap and reached down to pull a small knife from her heeled boot. She used it to slice through the tie restraining his right wrist. "You'd better be right-handed," she said and crushed her mouth against his.

Despite the drug-induced euphoria, Mathias fought the immediate recoil. His head spun as the cloying scent of her perfume filled his nostrils. Through the haze, he became aware of the softness of her breasts pressed against his chest, her hand trailing down to the buckle of his belt. He pushed back against the demanding buck of her hips and returned the kiss with a leaden automation as he raised his hand to her neck and slid it beneath the silk scarf. She gave a mewling moan and thrust her tongue into his mouth, wet and probing. Mathias curled his fingers around the scarf and pulled taut.

Marsela's head snapped back, and her hands scrabbled at her neck, gagging as Mathias held firm. She slipped from his lap to her knees before him, the blood rising to her face as her eyes bulged. Mathias waited, an almost hypnotic calm coming over him. He knew how long to hold until her eyes rolled back into her head—knew how easy it would be to wait her out, listen for the last ragged breath before the silence that followed. He was outside himself, watching his movements like a character on a screen. It was unfortunate that she hadn't seen it—the darkness in him. She'd gravely underestimated his true nature.

Then, amid the addled mess inside his mind, an image arose from earlier that morning—Rayan splayed out in their bed, bathed in sunlight, the corners of his mouth turned up in a smile.

... exactly as you are.

Mathias was no longer observing himself but was back in his body, and the strength in his fingers slackened. He released his grip, and Marsela fell backward onto the floor, coughing. He reached for the fallen knife with his free hand and cut through the remaining tie, his actions sluggish and clumsy.

Marsela lay on the floor, sucking in jagged breaths. She held one hand protectively over her throat as the blood slowly retreated from her face. He crouched and unknotted the scarf from her neck, seeing where the fabric had cut into her skin, then used it to tie her hands behind her back. A strangled sound escaped her mouth, but whatever she was trying to communicate was unintelligible.

He thought about the two lackeys waiting outside the door. She must have had a history of these kinds of encounters if the thumps and gasps that had accompanied their little scuffle hadn't been concerning enough for the thugs to make an appearance. The noises had probably matched what they were expecting.

Mathias retrieved his gun from the table. It was clunky and unfamiliar in his hand. Another wave cascaded over his body, and it felt as though he'd been submerged in warm water.

"What the...?" His voice sounded different, not his own.

He'd come here with a plan, but the particulars had gotten lost in the swirl of sensation. His thoughts kept slipping as he tried to determine what to do next. He couldn't just stroll through the front door. He'd had enough trouble with Marsela's men while not doped out of his brain. He didn't trust himself with a gun, let alone behind the wheel, and commandeering the car he'd arrived in was the only way out of this godforsaken place. His eyes traveled to Marsela on the floor. Her oxygen-deprived stupor wouldn't last much longer.

As if to prove his point, she let out a hoarse laugh. "You're a big man, Mr. Beauvais. I may have been a little liberal with the dose."

Suddenly, there came a startled yelp from the entranceway followed by a flurry of thuds. Mathias heard a loud crack as something or someone struck the locked door. There was another crack, and the wood splintered, dislodging the handle. The door swung open, and Rayan appeared in the frame, his gun raised and his eyes dark with fury as he advanced into the room.

For a moment, Mathias wondered if he'd conjured him with his mind. He felt that powerful. He'd never doubted that Rayan would come for him. The idea that no one could be trusted—not even those whose job it was to care for him—had been instilled from a young age, but Rayan had proven, over and over, the exception to that rule.

For years the man had been chipping away at the barrier Mathias had built between himself and the world. Even when they were still only boss and subordinate, Rayan was the person he'd kept closest, granted access to the private workings of his life. After his resolve finally buckled, all Rayan had to do was press against the cracks he'd already made in Mathias's defenses to send the walls crashing down. And Mathias had let him walk right through the opening he'd created.

He stared at Rayan and felt a churn of something both light and heavy. He owed him so much at this point. His life for one—all those times Rayan had stood between him and a bullet. Then there were the more perplexing things—the simple peace he felt upon waking, the absence of that cold core of loneliness he'd carried for so long he thought it was part of him.

"Took you long enough."

"Consider your favor repaid," Rayan returned stonily. His eyes darted to Mathias's face, and his forehead furrowed in concern.

"Who is this?" Marsela asked, attempting to pick herself up from the floor. She began screeching at the men on the other side of the door, who were clearly incapacitated.

Rayan walked over to him. "Mathias?"

Mathias loved how he said his name and even more when he whispered it, his voice catching on the last syllable. What he wouldn't fucking do for this man, and here he was, right in front of him.

Rayan's frown deepened, and a grim recognition flickered across his face. Of course, for him, this was well-worn territory. "You're high."

This time when Mathias spoke, he wasn't sure if the words made it past his lips or if they were swallowed by the roll of thoughts in his head. "That appears to be the case."

23

The tracking signal from Mathias's phone had stopped dead at a large country house set back from the road several kilometers outside of Saint-Léonard. Rayan had decided against driving down the narrow lane that led to the house in case he was playing into an ambush. Instead, he pulled the car over to the side of the main road and continued on foot.

As Rayan walked, keeping to the grass on the edge of the lane, he removed his gun and flicked off the safety. This was where the little red dot had led him, but for all he knew, Mathias's phone could have been dumped, and the man could be halfway across the country.

Focus. It was too early for worst-case scenarios. And if Rayan knew anything about Mathias, it was that he wouldn't go down easy.

His breath sounded loud in his ears, and he worked to quieten it, channeling years of practice. He felt it again, the transformation into someone else, his senses heightened and his fear suppressed. One fact was certain—if something had happened to Mathias, Rayan would tear whoever he found to pieces.

Two cars were parked outside the villa, and as Rayan approached, he could hear voices coming from inside the open front door. They were speaking a language he didn't recognize. He saw a plume of cigarette smoke and gathered that the voices belonged to two men clearly off their guard.

Which meant that when he barreled around the corner and swung his fist into the side of the nearest man's head, Rayan caught him entirely unawares. The man staggered back several steps and then slumped to the floor, dazed. His partner seemed a little slow to catch up. His face was already bloodied and one eye swollen closed. It came as a welcome sight—proof Mathias had been here. Mathias must have scrambled the contents of the man's brain because he stood gaping while Rayan lifted his pistol and brought it down against the man's temple. He went down heavy.

Rayan turned to the man who was still conscious on the floor and leveled the gun at his head. "Where is he?"

The man didn't speak. He simply raised a finger to point to the closed door to left of the vestibule.

"Don't move," Rayan instructed the man.

He stepped over to the door and tried the handle. It was locked. Rayan stepped back and slammed his heel hard against the panel beside the keyhole. He heard a creak as the wood strained from the impact. He gave it another kick, and the door splintered open with a *crack*. Not stopping to consider what or whom he might find inside, Rayan launched himself into the room.

He wasn't prepared for the sight of Mathias standing impassively with his gun held slack in his hand. Mathias's expression was blank, and he appeared unhurried as though here of his own free will. Rayan caught a movement in the corner of his eye and saw a blond woman struggling to rise from the floor.

Is this the woman Elise was talking about?

His gaze returned to Mathias, and only then did he notice the bruises that mottled his face. Rayan felt a swell of anger and moved toward him then stopped short when he realized the reason for Mathias's apparent serenity. Rayan had spent enough time around his brother to know the signs—pupils large and unfocused, eyelids heavy, an easy roll to his limbs. When Mathias spoke, confirming Rayan's fears, his voice was slow and distant. They were in serious fucking trouble.

Rayan decided against grilling the man. Explanations would have to wait. Instead, he told Mathias in no uncertain terms that they were leaving.

"She's coming with us." Mathias reached down to yank the woman to her feet, and Rayan saw her hands were tied behind her back.

Rayan stood dumbly. "What?"

"Relax, I know what I'm doing."

Rayan gave a snort. "Sure, this all seems very well-thought-out."

Mathias turned to him, and in place of a terse remark, he gave Rayan a charming smile. There was an ease to the expression that was so foreign Rayan thought he'd imagined it. "Trust me."

Rayan was too taken aback to reply. He followed Mathias as he dragged the woman from the room and past the two men Rayan had immobilized by the entrance. Outside in the driveway, Rayan raised his gun and plugged the front tires of the Porsche and the black Beamer parked out front. That would buy them some time at least.

As they made their way back up the lane to the road, Rayan glanced over at Mathias. For someone pumped full of dopamine, the man appeared remarkably functional.

"Give me your gun," Rayan ordered when they got to the car.

"Why?" It dangled loosely from Mathias's fingers like a toy.

"Before you shoot your foot off."

Mathias smirked, but he relinquished his weapon and unceremoniously shoved their captive into the back seat. Rayan got in behind the wheel and turned to the woman.

"What did you give him?" he asked in English.

She pursed her lips. "Why should I tell you?"

He curved one arm behind him to press Mathias's gun against her forehead. "What did you give him?"

She seemed to be assessing Rayan. In his T-shirt and jeans, he didn't exactly appear threatening. "You wouldn't know what to do with it," she goaded him.

"Would you like to find out?"

Mathias was watching their little back-and-forth from the passenger seat and let out a laugh. "Don't push him."

The woman hesitated, a flicker of fear in her eyes. Then she exhaled through her nose. "It's a speedball. Our most popular export."

"So, coke and what?"

"Ketamine. They call this one Calvin Klein." She snickered as if the whole situation was amusing. "Lasts about an hour. Then see if you can pick him off the floor."

Rayan swore under his breath and tossed Mathias's gun into the glove compartment. He didn't know enough about the situation to trust venturing back to Calais. And then there was the minor issue of their unexpected companion.

They had to get moving. He needed to put some distance between them and the lackeys back at the villa. Rayan started the engine and pulled the car out onto the road. Beside him, Mathias wound down the window and leaned against the headrest, eyes half closed as the wind whipped his hair.

"Who is she?" Rayan asked quietly in French.

Mathias tilted his head to look at him. "It's a long story."

"I'm listening."

"Marsela Asllani. She's with the Albanians. They were behind the shipment."

"Of clay sculptures?"

"Right. I told you about that."

Rayan gritted his teeth. "I think you left out a couple details."

"Turn around," Marsela demanded from the back seat, no longer finding the situation amusing. "Take me back right now. You have no idea who you're dealing with—"

"Shut it," Rayan snapped.

"The smashed figures. They were filled with powder," Mathias continued, unfazed.

"And the Albanians came to get it back?"

"They tried."

"What did you do with the drugs?"

Mathias gave him a wide grin. "Wouldn't you like to know."

Rayan's jaw clenched, and he fixed his eyes on the road. *High, but still cagey.*

He drove in the opposite direction of Calais and found a run-down motel on the outskirts of Saint-Léonard. It was the best Rayan could come up with. Whatever Mathias had planned would be useless if he wasn't sober enough to execute it. All they could do in the meantime was hole up and wait.

He left Mathias in the car and went to the front desk. The only room available was a family suite. Not that it mattered. They weren't here on vacation.

Fortunately, Marsela didn't make too much of a fuss when he and Mathias escorted her from the car. Rayan found a tow rope in the trunk and restrained the woman's wrists to the headboard in one of the bedrooms. He used the abandoned scarf to gag her, finally silencing the tirade of multilingual curse words she'd spewed at them since being wrestled from the back seat. Once she was subdued, Rayan returned to the other room to figure out what to do with Mathias.

He found the man sitting on the edge of the bed, staring at the unlit cigarette in his hand as though contemplating its existence. Mathias had a split lip, and the right side of his face was speckled with blood, yet he was unnervingly serene, like someone had cleaved away the layers of his exterior. It was more than a little disconcerting. Rayan was used to what his brother had been like—antsy, hopped-up. Whatever Mathias was on seemed to have rendered him a placid and more obliging version of himself. Rayan wrung out a washcloth in the bathroom sink and sat down beside him on the bed, raising the cloth to the cut on Mathias's temple. He frowned as he inspected the bluish marks along his jawline.

"Don't worry—it'll heal," Mathias said. "I know you like me pretty."

"What I like has less to do with your face."

Mathias chuckled. "Cute."

"So, this was the plan? Show up and get the shit kicked out of you?"

"I had something a little different in mind. Wasn't counting on the zip ties."

"The what? Jesus..." Rayan tried to keep his voice even. "What are we going to do with her?"

Mathias opted against lighting the cigarette and tucked it into his breast pocket. "I've got it all worked out. Just give me a minute to clear my head."

Rayan pressed the cloth against Mathias's swollen cheek, tempering the rising guilt. He still couldn't see the man hurt without feeling like a failure. "Damn it, Mathias. Do you realize how reckless this is?"

The smoothness left Mathias's face. "Do you think I'm afraid of these people—of what they'll do to me? I've played worse odds in my time."

"Back then you had an entire organization at your disposal. Now we're on our own. You can't go around looking for trouble."

"I wasn't looking for shit," Mathias said, pushing Rayan's hand away. "I was holding my ground. I won't stand by and let someone fuck me over. Or have you forgotten that, *Nadeau?*"

Rayan stiffened at the callback.

"You may have succeeded in keeping me away from the family, but you can't take it out of me."

You think I don't know that?

"You blame me for leaving," Rayan said flatly.

"Fuck you, Rayan." Mathias's eyes narrowed. "You're using this as an opportunity. I know there's a million things you want to extract from me."

"No one's forcing you to answer."

"Except whatever's making this blanket feel like a hand job," Mathias said, splaying his fingers and running his palm across the comforter beneath them. "Christ, it's hot in here." He shrugged off his jacket and tossed it to the floor then started on the top button of his shirt.

Rayan launched himself to his feet, suddenly furious. "Stop keeping me out!"

He'd spent the last hour sick with worry, only to discover Mathias had deliberately kept him in the dark, concealing the true reason behind the Albanians' threats and his intention to venture out alone. "Tell me what's happening. I'm not your fucking subordinate anymore—I'm part of your life. If we're in this together, I need to know what you're thinking."

"So that's it?" Mathias scoffed. "You're entitled to my every thought because I love you?" His face lurched into a startled grimace.

Rayan blinked, momentarily speechless. It was as though Mathias had spoken in a different language. The words sounding both beautiful and improbable coming from his lips.

"Why don't you ever—" Rayan stopped, the rest stuck to his tongue. The question was so needy he couldn't get past the shame of asking for it.

Mathias scowled. "What does it matter? You know I do."

Rayan did know. A part of him had known as far back as Cyprus when Mathias had shown up, angry and addled, fighting against himself. He'd just been waiting to hear it out loud, as if that somehow made it more real. *But when have words ever been the way to understand Mathias?*

Rayan sat back down, silent.

Mathias brought a hand to his forehead and rubbed it roughly. "Even if sometimes I wish I didn't. Because I don't know who the fuck I am anymore. How does anyone accomplish anything when they can't keep their head on straight? I used to be efficient, god dammit."

Rayan fought a grin. "So you're a little less efficient."

"Among other things." Mathias sighed. "Still, it's better than before. I was convinced the only person I could rely on was myself. And then you had to go and change my mind."

"You know I would do anything..." Rayan swallowed the weight of sentiment that accompanied those words. "Anything you want, you have it from me."

"That's a dangerous proposition."

Rayan pulled Mathias close and kissed him, deep and tender. Mathias pressed against him, his hand curling around Rayan's neck. Then he broke away and flopped onto his back on the bed.

"Don't tempt me. I'm going to jump out of my skin on this shit. Feel like I could fuck you for hours and still not be done."

A slow smile spread across Rayan's face.

"You're taking advantage," Mathias warned.

"Because you wouldn't want that?"

"I would. But I'm pretty sure you won't once I'm done with you."

"Try me."

Mathias let out a short laugh, staring up at the ceiling. "You know, I had a dream about you."

"What happened in the dream?"

"I let you fuck me."

Rayan's breath surged from his lungs. "And did you like it?"

"You certainly seemed to know what you were doing."

"I do."

Mathias raised an eyebrow. "You gave me the impression you had a preference."

"With you, yes."

"But not with others?"

"Not always."

Mathias rolled over to look at him. "Exactly how many men have you fucked?"

"I'm not answering that."

There was an amused glint in Mathias's eye. "And women?"

"What are you getting at?"

"I'm asking how many women you've fucked."

There had been just one, when he was maybe fifteen—an ex-girlfriend of Tahir's who thought she could get back at his brother by going after him. Rayan hadn't been particularly interested, yet he also knew the chances of replicating such an opportunity on his own were slim. He felt a flatness around women that he thought would disappear when he was actually with one. It didn't. The experience had been clumsy and regrettable. Later, feeling like he'd broken some unspoken rule, he confessed to his brother. Tahir had found the whole situation hilarious, furthering Rayan's mortification.

"Enough to be sure I had no interest," Rayan shot back.

"You're adorable, you know that?"

"Do I want to know how many people you've fucked?"

Mathias reached up to graze his fingers across Rayan's lips. "No, you don't. But would it help to know that only one of them has ever meant anything?" He grabbed the front of Rayan's shirt and pulled him down. "Here's your chance, Rayan," Mathias murmured against his ear. "I'm all yours."

Rayan had never thought to consider the prospect because he loved what they had—nothing felt as good as submitting to Mathias—but also because he'd assumed that was a line of surrender Mathias was unable to cross.

He attempted to keep his voice steady while his heart pounded in his chest. "And have you not remember?"

"You'd remember."

Rayan kissed him hard. His hand found the curve of Mathias's jaw, tilting his head back as the man opened his mouth. He felt the warmth of Mathias's tongue against his own, urgent, wanting, and Rayan was struck by an unfamiliar surge of power. Their normal balance had flipped. He climbed on top of Mathias and pinned his arms to the bed. He felt, in that moment, like he could do anything he wanted. It was painfully arousing and, at the same time, scared him out of his mind.

Mathias was breathing heavily, and Rayan could feel the firm outline of the man's cock beneath the fabric of his pants. Then, slowly, Rayan sat up and moved his hands away. He rose from the bed and looked down at Mathias sprawled out before him. As intoxicating as this person was, he'd never longed for a cleaner version of Mathias. He'd always wanted all of him—the good and the bad, the rugged and the broken. The bruised heart beneath the layers of scar tissue. He would have all of him, or he wouldn't have him at all.

"Where do you think you're going?"

"Out." Rayan smiled. "You're going to want something for the comedown."

24

Mathias lay on his back on a cheap motel bed and stared at the pattern of water stains forming on the ceiling. His body felt unbearably hot beneath the fabric of his clothes, and his brain pulsed inside his skull. He blinked several times to dispel the fuzzy distortions from his vision, but nothing helped. Whatever Marsela had given him had done its work well.

He could only vaguely recall how he'd gotten here. His memory was a highlights reel in Technicolor with whole chunks missing. There were snatches of a conversation he'd had with Rayan, and the rest remained a hazy blur. In between the distorted snippets of memory were flashes of vivid sensation—the warmth of Rayan's lips, the impossible smoothness of the bedcovers. He felt the residual hum of desire in his bones. *Did we fuck?*

He staggered to his feet to discover a piercing headache, like nails hammered through his temples. He made it to the bathroom sink, where he splashed a handful of cold water against his face. Then he cupped his hands and drank from them, an unquenchable thirst rising in his throat.

Mathias studied his refection in the mirror, taking in the bruised skin and blotches of dried blood. He looked awful. He couldn't remember the last time he'd let someone work him over like that.

When he emerged from the bathroom, he found Rayan standing by the bed with a brown paper bag. Rayan handed him a bottle of water and a pack of painkillers, and Mathias popped out several and swallowed them then threw back the water as his thirst persisted.

"Where's Marsela?" he managed when he was done.

"She's in the next room."

Mathias picked up his phone from the nightstand and pocketed it. The movement sent splinters through his foggy brain, and he flinched.

"Maybe you should sit down," Rayan said.

"The sooner this is sorted, the sooner we'll be rid of her."

"The sooner what's sorted? What are you going to do, hold her for ransom?"

"Exactly."

Mathias moved through to the other room before Rayan could protest. Marsela sat on the bed with her knees tucked demurely beneath her. Her hands were tied to the headboard and the scarf fastened around her mouth. Like him, she appeared worse for wear. Her makeup was streaked, and strings of hair were plastered to her forehead. He sat on the edge of the bed and tugged down the scarf.

She gave a tinkling laugh, and her eyes flicked from him to Rayan in the doorframe. "I'm surprised you're standing."

"I'll be doing more than that."

She fluttered her eyelids suggestively. "Something to look forward to, if that kiss was any indication."

From across the room, Mathias felt Rayan's eyes on him. Mathias reached behind her and freed one of her hands. She winced and rolled her wrist. Then he pulled out his phone and handed it to her.

"Call your boss."

"My boss?" she sneered. "Is that what you think I am—hired help?"

Mathias leaned forward menacingly, and she drew back. "Call the person who decides whether you make it out of here alive."

Marsela paled and took the phone from him. She punched in a series of numbers with a trembling finger, and Mathias reached over and hit the speaker button. The whir of the phone ringing filled the room.

There was a click, and then a man's voice burst through the speaker. "Who's this?"

"*I dashur!*" Marsela cried out, her voice cracking.

"Marsela?"

Mathias prized the phone from her hand. "English," he instructed.

"Burim, please!" she pleaded.

"Now you have my drugs and my woman?" the voice growled in a thick accent. "Who the fuck do you think you are?"

"If you're smart, you'll get both back in due course. But I have no need for either, so I'd caution you to be careful. I tend to get rid of things that don't prove useful."

There was a long pause.

"What do you want?"

"Eight million for my trouble. The product you attempted to pass under my nose is worth twice that at least."

"You're out of your mind."

"I can see how she wouldn't be worth it."

"Fuck you!" Marsela snarled.

"You've wasted my time and disrespected me and my business. That doesn't come cheap."

"Who are you?"

"Someone it pays not to mess with," Mathias said in a low voice. "You don't want the product back? No skin off my nose. I'll sell it to the highest bidder. The girl will be a little harder to dispose of."

The man seemed to be mulling over that particular prospect. After a moment, he spoke. "All right. But she comes back untouched, you hear me?"

As if I'd be tempted to lay a finger on the harpy. "Eight o'clock at the abandoned maritime station in Boulogne. No funny shit."

"Let me talk to her—"

Mathias thumbed the disconnect button and leaned over to refasten Marsela's wrist to the headboard.

She glowered at him. "Just you wait. He's going to—"

Mathias raised the scarf to gag her before she could finish. *Nothing I haven't heard before.* He walked back into the adjacent room, and Rayan followed, closing the door behind them.

Mathias's head throbbed insistently, and he reached for the painkillers on the nightstand. When he saw the look on Rayan's face, he knew his sparing explanations would no longer cut it.

"That's what this is about?" Rayan strode over and shoved him hard in the chest. "Money?"

"Hey," Mathias protested half-heartedly. "Let's keep this civil. My head feels like a fallout zone."

"You almost get yourself killed to screw over a bunch of gangsters," Rayan snapped, his brown eyes flashing. "And now I'm part of a kidnapping plot?"

Mathias knocked another two pills back and swallowed them dry. "I thought we could diversify. It seemed a natural progression from smuggling people."

"Don't you fucking joke about this."

Mathias had to fight the urge to reach out and ruffle the man's hair.

"You told me you were considering other opportunities." Rayan was pacing, his hands clenched at his sides. "Is that what this is? A bid at your own group, a chance to get in on the game?"

"With these clowns? Give me some credit."

"I should have known it wouldn't be enough. That you would need something else. But this?"

Despite Rayan's tortured expression, Mathias couldn't help but laugh. "You're way off base here."

"Am I? Then why don't you tell me what you need with eight million euro—" Rayan's face went slack with understanding. "No..."

Mathias shrugged. "You were seven short, so I figured, why not round it up to an even eight?" That, and he'd have to cover the mess Marsela's goons had made at the warehouse. Charles would also expect a cut for his assistance.

Rayan's eyes were wide, and he was shaking his head. "No, Mathias..."

"Haven't you learned anything?" Mathias admonished him. "Life doesn't operate on some well-balanced scale of justice. It's a fucking wheel of fortune. You think the people in the camp don't know that?"

The crease in Rayan's forehead deepened.

"You spin the wheel, and sometimes you get nothing, and sometimes what you need falls right into your lap," Mathias went on. "You have no business questioning where it came from or whether you should take it."

"I swear, there's nothing you can't talk your way out of."

"You know as well as I do, Rayan," Mathias said, his tone hardening, "how unfair this world can be. You do what you have to do to look out for your own."

Rayan exhaled and ran a hand through his hair. "Do you have any idea the difference this will make?"

"If we can pull it off, that is." He tugged Rayan to him, but the man pulled away, his eyes darkening.

"You kissed her?"

The corner of Mathias's mouth tweaked. "Who knew entrapment was such a turn-on?" When Rayan scowled, Mathias chuckled. "It's a good look," he murmured, leaning in so their faces were almost touching. "I like you jealous."

Together, with one hand on each of Marsela's arms, Mathias and Rayan walked her out to the car. She went easily, as though resigned to her fate. Mathias suspected she'd grown tired of her own little game.

They left the motel shortly before eight and headed toward the coast. Rayan drove, as Mathias couldn't shake the pinpricks of black that remained at the edges of his vision. Mathias flipped down the visor and examined his bloodshot eyes in the small mirror. Worse than the lingering physical effects was the confusion that clouded his memory. Certain images had come back to him. He remembered Rayan appearing at the villa but not the drive to the motel. Then he'd get flashes of words exchanged and couldn't be sure if they'd been spoken or imagined. It was unsettling to know just how exposed he'd been.

He noticed Rayan watching him. "What?"

"What are we going to do when we get there?" Rayan had turned up the dial on his Quebecois, slipping into *joual*, the working-class dialect favored by garbage truck drivers and delivery men.

It was one of many things about Rayan that caught people off guard—how he could open his mouth and prove he was someone else entirely. Mathias knew he was doing it so Marsela wouldn't catch on. Even a French speaker would have trouble deciphering the thick, clipped variation of the language.

"Let me handle things," Mathias replied.

"You don't think they're just going to hand over the money?"

"If the man wants to know the location of his stash, then he'd better hand it over. And we have our collateral in the back seat."

"And if he proves uncooperative?" Rayan asked.

"Then we're both decent shots."

Rayan's hands tightened around the steering wheel. Mathias hadn't wanted to pull him into this, but here they were. There was no turning back now.

That thought jogged another. "Where's my gun?"

Rayan reached over and popped open the glove compartment. "I confiscated it."

"I was a trigger-happy dopehead?" Mathias mused, removing his pistol and tucking it into the waistband of his slacks.

Rayan smiled cryptically. "More like a careless one."

Within fifteen minutes, they were in Boulogne. Rayan navigated the car toward the city's old ferry port. Behind them, Marsela shifted restlessly, taking a series of short, panicked breaths. She'd been compliant enough that they'd done away with the scarf.

"You don't know what you're doing, Mathias," she hissed, her forehead shiny with perspiration. The sultry smugness had been replaced by an unfamiliar terror. "Burim is not a forgiving man."

"Neither am I."

But her obvious distress made his stomach tighten. *Who is this Burim, and why is she so nervous?*

He glanced over at Rayan, who was waiting for the light to change, and felt the sudden crushing weight of responsibility. "Hey."

The man turned to him, but Mathias seized up, the words catching in his throat.

If something happens, I want you to know...

Then Rayan gave him a knowing look. "Don't you start with that shit."

Mathias snickered. "Eyes on the road, kid."

Boulogne-sur-Mer had served as France's first commercial link with England and, up until the turn of the millennium, had remained an important transport hub between the two countries. The construction of the Channel Tunnel and the rise of the Port of Calais had put an end to that, and the rapid decline in traffic resulted in the closure of the city's maritime station.

In the dark, the station—which combined both a ferry terminal and a railway depot—was an eerie graveyard of mold-stained concrete. There were no barriers blocking the entrance, making it possible for them to drive up to the abandoned railway terminus and park behind the boarded-up building. Mathias ushered a reluctant Marsela from the car, and together, they waited for Burim to arrive.

Before long, two white Land Rovers appeared and continued through the deserted complex toward them. Mathias tempered a flash of irritation as the cars pulled up. Arriving with a convoy of cronies amounted to funny shit, in his book.

The Albanians emerged like clowns at a circus and formed a cluster around an imposing man with an artfully manicured goatee on his tanned face. He wore a collection of gold rings and chains, the currency of a low-tier gangster. All that was missing were the designer sneakers.

The man stepped forward to fix Mathias with a beady glare. "You the one called Beauvais?"

"That would be me," Mathias said evenly. "Where's my money?"

"It's here. But first, I have questions."

"Questions weren't part of the deal."

The man folded his arms. "I made a few inquiries about you, Mathias Beauvais. You're not some clueless antiques dealer. You're with the Sicilians in Canada."

Was.

"And not just a soldier either. Sounded pretty high up."

Where is he going with this? "If we're making introductions, mind telling me who the fuck you are?"

The man's face soured. "Burim Osmani. Maybe you've heard of my father? Most people this side of the channel have."

Mathias gave a shrug. "So your daddy's famous."

Burim scowled. "More than that. He's a fucking legend."

Mathias fought the urge to roll his eyes. Burim wasn't the first man he'd encountered who worshipped the legacy of his father.

"Do you know we work closely with the 'Ndrangheta? You'd be surprised how much the Italian families dictate the flow of activity in Europe."

"What's this, a history lesson?" Mathias scoffed. "When did questions turn into a sermon?"

"When you tried to fuck my wife."

Mathias froze. *God dammit.* His gaze flicked to Marsela who was pale as a ghost beside him. *She had to be his fucking wife.*

Marsela let out a stream of panicked pleas in Albanian, but Burim cut her off with a sharp rebuke.

"It seems my wife has grown bored of her pampered life," Burim went on. "First, she wanted more responsibility in the business. And I thought, why not? If it keeps her happy, where's the harm? Turns out that wasn't the only thing she was bored with."

The woman who'd had her tongue down Mathias's throat was married to the head of the Osmani family. That threw a wrench into their wager.

"It's been brought to my attention..." Burim said, looking at one of his men standing by the car. Mathias recognized Scarface, his face a broken, bloody mess. "That you're not the first man my wife has taken a liking to."

The mood took a sudden turn, and the other soldiers shot each other wary glances. Beside him, Rayan stiffened.

"Is that what this is?" Burim addressed Marsela. "A lover's arrangement? You take the cash, and the two of you disappear into the sunset?"

"No, *I dashur!*" Marsela cried.

Burim gave a scornful chuckle. "*I dashur?* You have some fucking nerve." He began speaking in a flurry of Albanian, his voice rising in fury. Marsela cowered, her tone keening when she replied.

Mathias ground his teeth. Here he was, caught in yet another lover's quarrel. This was getting old fast.

"I didn't try anything with your wife," Mathias said.

"You expect me to believe that?"

"That's exactly right."

Burim glared at him. "Do you know what happens when someone lays a hand on what's mine?"

"Please, Burim, it's the truth!" Marsela cried.

"Enough," Mathias barked, resting the heel of his hand on the handle of his gun. "I want my fucking money, or we're done here."

The ringing of a phone cut through the tense silence that followed. The melody, grating and insistent, filled the still night air. Burim reached into his pocket and pulled out his phone, his eyes widening when he looked down at the screen. He answered in a hushed murmur, suddenly reverent.

The call went on for some time, with Burim saying little and nodding as he was given what appeared to be a harshly worded dressing down.

"Mathias..." Rayan murmured beside him. His eyes were trained on the wall of Albanians as a hand rose to his holster.

Mathias knew what Rayan was thinking. If they were going to act, it would have to be now, unless they wanted to give this Osmani bastard a chance to follow through on his threat. But before they could make a move, Burim hung up and looked over at Mathias with unconcealed disbelief.

Then he gestured to one of his men. "Give him the money."

His subordinate walked over the trunk of the first car and pulled out a large black duffel bag.

"Seems you have friends in high places," Burim said as the Albanian soldier dropped the bag at Mathias's feet. "You should have told me you knew Leo Campini."

Mathias scanned his knowledge of Italian family politics. As far as he was aware, Leonardo Campini was one of the 'Ndrangheta's top brass. The Calabrian group wasn't on the best of terms with the Sicilians—which included their North American offshoots. How Campini had come to know about Mathias and his business, he had no idea. Mathias certainly wasn't acquainted with him personally. Even during his time with the family, he'd never had much to do with the 'Ndrangheta.

Mathias said none of this to Burim. He wasn't about to let an opportunity to one-up the Albanian slip through his fingers. Rayan retrieved the bag, and Mathias watched as he zipped it open to reveal layered stacks of bound five-hundred-euro notes.

Rayan flicked through the stacks then closed the bag and gave Mathias a quick nod. "It's all there."

It'd better be.

"Had I known..." Burim's tone had turned noticeably more cordial. "I wouldn't have let the woman near your business. And we wouldn't have shown you such disrespect. For that, I offer my apologies. We have a longstanding arrangement with the 'Ndrangheta, one I'm in no hurry to lose. We stay clear of the Sicilians to avoid stirring up trouble—something you both seem to do well enough on your own. That being said..." His eyes darkened, and he gestured down at the bag of cash. "I don't take kindly to people stealing from me. We had a deal. I want my drugs back."

Mathias withdrew a folded piece of paper from the inside pocket of his jacket. "Everything's here. A friend is holding it for safekeeping. I'll call ahead and let him know to expect you."

Burim's subordinate moved to take the slip of paper and handed it to his boss, who peered at the address contained within. "And if we show up and it's miraculously gone?"

"I'm a man of my word," Mathias said. "It'll be there."

Burim muttered something unintelligible.

"Or by all means, call Campini back," Mathias goaded him.

Burim pocketed the piece of paper and pointed to Marsela. "You, get in the car."

Rayan removed the restraints from Marsela's wrists, and she took a moment to compose herself, righting the hem of her dress and fluffing her hair. Then she strode over to the car Burim had emerged from. One of the Albanian soldiers opened the rear door and placed a hand on her arm to guide her inside, but she slapped it away.

Burim stood observing the interaction, his expression unreadable. When Marsela was safely stowed in the back seat, he turned to Mathias. "A man of your word, was it?"

"That's right. I wouldn't touch her with a ten-foot pole. You have my sympathy."

Burim's lip curled viciously. "Don't let me catch you near her again."

"Interfere with my business again, and this"—Mathias kicked the bag at his feet—"is just the beginning."

Mathias and Rayan watched the Albanians pile back into their cars. They stood in silence until the taillights of the two Land Rovers had disappeared into the distance.

"You had to try it on with his wife," Rayan muttered.

Mathias smirked. "Marsela couldn't leave well enough alone."

Rayan rubbed the bridge of his nose. "What the fuck just happened?"

"Looks like you got your funding."

They both stared down at the bag of cash, and Rayan gave a quiet laugh. "There's no way the mayor will approve."

"I'll take care of Durand."

"Thought you weren't going to kill him," Rayan teased.

"There's more than one way to skin a cat."

Rayan narrowed his eyes suspiciously. "Was this your plan all along? Call in a favor with the 'Ndrangheta?"

Mathias shook his head, still puzzled by the unexpected turn of events. "I have no idea what happened there."

Rayan's face grew serious. "Promise me, no more trouble. I'm sorely out of practice."

Mathias reached out to brush a lock of hair from Rayan's forehead. "No promises."

25

On the way back to the house, Mathias had Rayan drop him off at the warehouse. He had no doubt it would be as Marsela's lackeys had left it— wide open to the world, a treasure trove of high-value art sitting around for some light-fingered opportunist to help themselves.

He'd called Charles from the car on the drive to Calais and told him to expect a visit from the Osmani group. He'd given Charles clear instructions to hand over the stash without incident. At least Burim would succeed in setting right one of the evening's wrongs. Mathias had to give it to her—Marsela had pluck. That or a death wish. He wasn't entirely sure.

As expected, when they pulled up outside the warehouse, the roller door was still raised.

"I can wait outside while you lock up," Rayan offered as Mathias got out of the car.

Mathias shook his head. He wanted to have a look around and inspect the damage. Not to mention there was eight million in cash currently sitting in the trunk. The sooner that made its way into the safe in the study, the better. "Go on ahead and secure your little windfall. I'll meet you back at the house."

He watched Rayan drive away then walked into the warehouse and pulled the roller door closed behind him. Mathias surveyed the floor strewn with fallen frames and shattered ceramics and decided to leave the wreckage until the next day. For the time being, he'd see if the office remained intact. They didn't keep much in the way of cash on-site, but that was where someone would go to look.

Mathias stopped dead in his tracks. From where he stood, he could see a light on inside the office. They'd left the warehouse in the afternoon, and there was no way the lights had been on then. Someone else had been here. Or perhaps they still were.

He reached for the pistol tucked against his hip and held it in front of him as he approached the door to the office. Through the window, he could make out a squat figure in a gray suit sitting behind his desk.

Mathias froze mid-step. Then he dropped the hand with the gun and pushed open the door. "Enzo fucking Carbone."

Enzo was reclined in Mathias's chair, a cigarette dangling from his lips. He looked the same as he always had, right down to the boxy cut of his suit. The man gave him a knowing smile and straightened up to stub out his waning cigarette in the ashtray on Mathias's desk.

"De Luca was kind enough to let me know where I might find you." He gestured at the office around them. "Nice little operation you've got here, Beauvais. What are you pulling in each month?"

Mathias returned the gun to his waistband, making no attempt to hide it. He knew better than to assume this was a social call. "I know you didn't come here to talk shop."

He walked over to the desk and reached for the half-empty bottle of Macallan standing on the corner. He and Elise were partial to the occasional glass on nights they found themselves working late. "So they sent you."

"Could you imagine if Gabriele had come? You'd have plugged him between the eyes before he could open his mouth. You and I always seemed to have somewhat of an understanding."

It was true. Of the three old men on the council, Enzo had been on the same page as Mathias more often than not. Mathias poured a generous serving of scotch into two tumblers. After the day he'd had, he would have preferred to drink straight from the bottle.

Enzo accepted his glass with a nod, and Mathias pulled up a chair, surprised at how much his body hurt as he sat down. Tomorrow would be painful. *If I make it that far.* There was no telling why the councilman was here or what that meant for him.

"You look a little worse for wear," Enzo commented.

"I had to take care of a small problem."

"An Albanian problem, by any chance? Trouble seems to follow you everywhere."

There they were—the missing pieces falling neatly into place. "I have you to thank for that?"

Enzo shrugged. "The Albanians worship the 'Ndrangheta, and I still have a few friends in Calabria. They won't be bothering you again."

"You have my gratitude. I can only imagine what I owe you in return." Mathias fixed him with a hardened glare. "Why don't you tell me why the fuck you're here?"

"I see your self-imposed exile has left you rough around the edges."

"I was always rough around the edges," Mathias snapped. "And it wasn't self-imposed. Bianchi pushed me out."

"I figured as much. I don't think he quite realized the pressure that came with the position. Russo made it look easy. But that's because he was a ruthless bastard. He had us all under his thumb. Things got to Giovanni, and he started making some bad calls."

"Yeah, well, looks like he got what was coming to him."

Enzo's face darkened, and he placed his drink down on the desk with a dull thud. "The city is in chaos, Mathias."

Mathias took a long swig from his glass and let the liquor burn his throat. "That's not my problem anymore."

Enzo studied him carefully. "That's a rather shortsighted view. I think you're missing the bigger picture here. Can't you see it's ripe for the taking? Not just Montreal—I'm talking the whole fucking country."

Mathias was beginning to understand why the man was here.

"We need to right things, for stability's sake. There are a lot of interests at play, some from far afield. This upheaval does no one any good, and the quicker it's squashed, the better. None of the Quintino are strong enough to make a bid at leadership. We don't have the skills or the sway. We'd only end up easy targets. But you, on the other hand…"

Mathias would be lying if he said he wasn't tempted. A part of him itched at the prospect of that much power, the whole organization laid down at his feet. *If my old man could see me now.*

But the sentiment passed quickly. His father no longer had any hold over him. Instead, he thought of Rayan. *Would I hide him away, put him up in a nice apartment like some glorified* goomah? Just like his mother—who'd spent his whole childhood sequestered so she could be ready and waiting any time his father wanted her.

Mathias would be expected to marry someone the council approved of, to keep up appearances as he drowned in a farce of domesticity. And children. That would be expected too. Perpetuating the torment that was supposed to end with him.

No. Even if he was the most powerful man in the country, nothing was worth that.

Mathias let out a low laugh. "You were just telling me how taxing the job was."

"For some. I have a feeling you would prove the exception. You have what it takes, Mathias, you're—"

"A ruthless bastard?" he said coldly.

"Well, yes, if you excuse the word choice."

"Interesting, considering how quick the family was to overlook me for that very fact."

Enzo sighed. "I know you're still sore about how you were treated—"

"The family didn't want me until I showed you what you were missing. And then you needed me because I worked harder than anyone else. I broke my back giving you exactly what you wanted."

Because I needed it too. I needed to prove that I could.

"But that's nothing new, is it? Using me, knowing there was nothing I wouldn't do. Knowing how desperate I was to be more than some illegitimate afterthought. And I did it all. After Piero sent Junior to whack me, I didn't retaliate, as was my due. Piero fucked me over, and I spent six months sitting on my hands for the good of the family. Waiting just long enough for Tony to get himself killed. Left for dead, face down on the concrete." Mathias's jaw clenched, and he swallowed the hard lump of guilt. "Giovanni wanted me six feet in the ground or rotting in prison, and now you expect me to come back for more? For the good of the family?" Mathias shook his head ruefully. "The faces change, but you're all the same. I needed it once. I don't need it anymore."

Enzo scowled. "Have you fooled yourself into thinking that this menial life is worthwhile? That it makes up for everything the family has to offer?"

"Maybe I have."

Enzo began to laugh. He lifted his glass to his lips and downed the contents. Setting the glass back on the desk, he stared at Mathias with a vague sort of curiosity. "Then perhaps I'm the fool."

He rose from his chair, and Mathias did the same, steeling himself for the repercussions that would follow. It wasn't as though they could force him into the position, but they could make his life difficult for turning them down. Mathias had been lucky to disappear this quietly in the first place—he figured Giovanni had something to do with that. Enzo might decide that courtesy had lapsed.

Instead, Enzo offered Mathias his hand. Mathias hesitated, gauging the man's intent, before reluctantly extending his own. They exchanged a firm shake.

"So long, Beauvais," Enzo said with a smirk. "Hope it's worth it."

Mathias stood in the doorway to the office and watched Enzo make his way across the warehouse to the staff entrance. He listened for the click as the door closed behind him. Then Mathias returned to his desk and knocked back the remainder of his drink. He gripped the glass in his hand and waited for the regret to surface, but all he felt was a calm clarity.

He didn't have to hope. He knew.

Rayan parked in the driveway beside the house but couldn't muster the energy to get out of the car. The clock on the dashboard said it was almost ten. Had it only been six hours since a frantic Elise had come to their door? He felt like he'd been up for days.

He let out a long breath. There was nothing for it. He was sitting on a veritable fortune that wasn't going to hide itself.

He flicked the lever to open the trunk and got out to walk around the back of the car. It took both hands to lift the duffel bag and haul it into the house. He'd been surprised to discover, in Boulogne, that the thing weighed a ton.

Once inside, he headed for the study and unlocked the safe beneath the desk. First, he removed his holster and stowed the gun, then he began emptying the bag, lifting each stack of notes one by one. Rayan kept a mental tally as he went. He got two-thirds through the bag before the safe was full. He locked it and headed upstairs.

There was another safe, in the closet in their bedroom, that contained Mathias's cash reserves and a series of questionably legal documents—passports and citizenship papers that secured them freedoms in a handful of countries. Mathias liked to plan for contingencies.

Rayan hadn't given much thought to what would happen with the money, but Mathias was a magician when it came to that sort of thing. He'd probably launder the money through a Swiss-owned company then funnel it back to his various accounts here and abroad. At least, that was the extent of Rayan's knowledge on the subject. He would leave it in Mathias's capable hands.

He finished stashing the remainder of the cash and had just returned downstairs when the front door opened, and Mathias appeared in the entranceway. Mathias kicked off his shoes and walked past Rayan into the living room, where he sank onto the sofa. Rayan moved to join him, not sure, once he'd sat down, whether he could pull himself up again.

Mathias leaned his head back and closed his eyes. "Christ, what a day."

"That's one way to put it."

Suddenly, Mathias stiffened, and his eyes snapped open as though something had just occurred to him. He turned to Rayan with a veiled stare. "I asked you to fuck me, didn't I?"

Rayan faltered, a flush rising along his neck. "Not in so many words," he replied carefully. "But if it's something you want—"

"That's another conversation." Mathias sighed and raked a hand across his face. "Anything else I'll have the misfortune of remembering later?"

Rayan shot him a look.

"Right. That." Mathias's expression shifted. "I've never said it to anyone."

Rayan reached out and tilted Mathias's chin toward him. "I don't need words. I only want you."

"You have me, Rayan."

Rayan felt a pang in his chest, hot and tight. He pulled himself onto Mathias's lap and took the man's face in his hands. Mathias winced as Rayan made contact with his bruised skin.

"Sorry."

"Do your worst." Mathias looked up at him, eyes unflinching, and Rayan lowered his mouth to kiss him.

The jolt of sensation cut through his exhaustion and sent his body humming. He was no longer tired. Mathias wrapped his arms around Rayan's waist and parted his lips with a sudden urgency. Rayan rocked against the growing bulge between Mathias's legs, and the man broke away, letting out a sharp breath.

"That shit messed with my brain. I've never been this pent-up."

"Let me help with that."

Rayan rubbed a palm across the front of Mathias's pants, baring his teeth to graze the man's neck. When he began on his zipper, Mathias stopped him. "Shower first."

In the shower, Mathias could no longer hide his untamed arousal. His cock stood tightly between them, pressing against Rayan's stomach as Rayan rubbed soap across Mathias's chest. He gently cleaned the last remnants of dried blood from Mathias's face then knelt under the thunder of water and took him into his mouth. *Pent-up* was an understatement. Mathias lurched past his lips, and Rayan could already taste the salt from his slit. He was rough and needy, drawing his cock in and out of Rayan's mouth at speed.

Rayan pulled back to catch his breath, and Mathias shot unexpectedly, glancing across his cheek. It was sluiced away in seconds, and Rayan got to his feet with a wry grin. "Don't get used to that."

Instead of a snide retort, Mathias crushed him against the shower wall in a passionate kiss. The man had lost his edge, his body no longer tense but warm and pliant, and Rayan melted into him, opening his mouth around the press of

Mathias's lips. Then Mathias lifted him, wet and dripping, from the bathroom and tossed him onto the bed. With his hunger momentarily satiated, Mathias turned his attention to Rayan.

In the time he spent edging Rayan with his mouth and fingers, leaving him slick, open, and desperately wanting, Mathias's cock had returned to its earlier glory—thick and hard, kept at the ready as Mathias lowered a hand every so often to give it an absent stroke.

No longer patient, Rayan rolled Mathias onto his back and straddled him. He took a palmful of lube and slowly lowered himself onto Mathias's cock, taking a moment to ease into the feeling. Mathias steadied him at the waist and waited, staring up at him, his gray eyes smoldering, letting Rayan call the shots.

Rayan rolled his hips, biding his time before he started to move. Mathias captured the head of Rayan's cock in his fist, and he thrust forward into the man's hand as he clenched and released. Rayan moved faster as the pleasure grew, spreading through his chest and causing the heat to rise to his face. He leaned down, and Mathias slid a hand around the back of his neck, bringing Rayan's mouth to his.

Then Mathias released him altogether and gripped Rayan's hips. He raised his knees so that his feet were planted flat on the bed and began to slam Rayan down on his cock. Rayan groaned, the intensity of the angle sending him hurtling toward the limits of his restraint.

"Fuck—" He dug his fingers into Mathias's shoulders, leaving marks in the skin, and was rewarded with the man's quickened pace. His mind began to fracture as the illusion of control slipped out of reach. He thought of Mathias pressed beneath him at the motel, his lips brushing Rayan's ear.

I'm all yours.

It wasn't just Mathias who'd been pent-up. Rayan came in forceful arcs across Mathias's chest, reaching as far as the man's chin. Despite being entirely spent, his cock gave a jerk at the sheer audacity of the sight of his former capo marked with his pleasure.

Mathias drew a thumb through the slickness and brought it to his mouth. Rayan felt a shiver run through him, and he bent to kiss Mathias, tasting himself on the man's lips. Then strong arms looped around his waist, and Rayan was swung down onto the mattress—Mathias now above him but still inside him.

Rayan moaned as Mathias began to thrust, powering toward his release. Mathias had him doubled over on his back, and Rayan's hands clenched the sheets beneath them. Rayan's vision blurred. He was aware of little but the merger of their bodies and how desperately he needed this man, how much he loved him.

"Yes... please—" Rayan choked out.

Mathias gritted his teeth, his lips twisting into a snarl as he came. His body gave a shudder, and he buried his face into Rayan's shoulder. Rayan reached up to stroke the man's hair, the wet strands sliding through his fingers. Mathias raised his head to kiss him deeply, and they lay like that, still joined, mouths pressed hard together. In the soft warmth of their embrace, Rayan found it difficult to imagine needing anything but this—Mathias beneath his fingers, in his bed.

Mathias eased himself onto his back, and they lay in a silence punctuated only by the sound of their breathing as it slowed. Mathias was the first to speak.

"Enzo was at the warehouse."

A cold panic pierced Rayan's insides. "Enzo Carbone?"

"The man himself."

"For fuck's sake, Mathias," Rayan snapped, sitting up. "I told you not to keep this shit from me."

"I'm telling you, aren't I?"

"Tell me first. That's what you should have led with."

"I wanted to fuck you first. There's a natural order to these things."

Rayan let out a snort. *How am I to supposed to argue with that?*

He lay back and tried to curb his racing thoughts. "I presume he's not here to clip you, because you're very much alive."

"They want me to head the family."

Rayan felt as though a crate of lead had been dropped onto his chest. He realized he'd stopped breathing. When he finally spoke, he couldn't hide the fear in his voice. He'd been too long out of practice.

"And what did you say?"

Mathias's eyes scanned Rayan's face. The man had him figured out. Rayan had said he wouldn't stop Mathias from doing what he wanted, but this was the one thing Rayan couldn't bear for him to want.

"What do you think I said?" Mathias asked.

"I know why they want you, and I know you could do it. You'd do a better job than Giovanni—hell, better than Russo even. You'd bring the whole city to its knees—I don't doubt that for a second. This is your chance to become everything you've ever wanted to be, prove once and for all that you're in an entirely different league from your father." Rayan's throat tightened, and he swallowed hard. "But please... don't fucking do it."

He turned away. He didn't want to see Mathias's face when he told him he was leaving.

"I said no."

Rayan exhaled shakily and closed his eyes. "Why?"

"You know why."

"Tell me."

"Thought you didn't need words."

"Tell me," Rayan whispered. He felt Mathias move so he was above him. Rayan opened his eyes, meeting the man's steady gaze.

Mathias cupped Rayan's face, his thumb running softly across his cheek. "Because you're my family now."

26

"Furthermost limits."

"How many?" Mathias asked.

"Four across."

Not parameters, then, or boundaries.

"Ends," Mathias said, taking a sip from his mug of coffee. Rayan sat beside him on the sofa, filling out the boxes of the crossword in his careful hand. Mathias noticed the date at the top of the newspaper. "That's yesterday's paper."

"René hasn't been yet."

"One job. That kid has one fucking job," Mathias muttered.

The next time he saw René, he figured, a touch of friendly intimidation might do the trick. If they ever saw him again. There was no logic to René's so-called service.

"How do you feel?" Rayan asked.

Mathias's head was still fuzzy, and his whole body ached. He'd inspected his face in the mirror that morning and concluded that nothing was broken. But he did look like he'd run headfirst into a pole.

"Fine, considering." Mathias raised his fingers to the small purplish bruise on the side of his neck and recalled the sting of the needle going in. "Not a trip I'm in any hurry to repeat."

Rayan observed him quietly. They hadn't touched on his familiarity with the subject. "You were surprisingly mellow. I used to tail my brother around the city to make sure he didn't do anything stupid. Not that I was any good at stopping him."

"You were pretty good at stopping me."

More had come back to Mathias about the events of the previous day. The scenes felt like dreams, crudely sketched, but Mathias knew—with a spike of humiliation—that he'd given Rayan permission to do as he pleased. He'd placed his pride in the man's hands, and Rayan had gently handed it back.

Rayan gave him a guarded smile. "I figured you might feel differently once you'd sobered up."

"How chivalrous."

Despite the flippancy of their exchange, an unspoken shift hung between them. He saw it in Rayan's eyes. Mathias had opened a door that hadn't been open before. And he wasn't sure he wanted to close it.

"Heylen asked me to run his new business," Mathias said, deftly changing the subject. "As a partner."

Rayan lowered the newspaper. "When?"

"A couple weeks back."

"You're doing it again."

"Look, you don't get to know everything."

"Even if it's something that might get you killed?" Rayan asked.

"Please, Heylen's as tame as they come. And if you're referring to that business with Marsela, I was never in any real danger."

"Bullshit. If that was true, you wouldn't have sent Elise to get me."

"It was merely a precaution," Mathias lied.

Rayan's voice softened. "You don't need to deal with everything on your own anymore, Mathias."

It landed right where he intended, and Mathias prickled defensively. "I can handle myself."

"I know you can. But talk to me."

Mathias grunted. "Christ, you're a broken record."

"Have you spoken with Elise?"

"Briefly." Mathias had contacted his appraiser the night before. She'd been beside herself. When her panic subsided, he would have to address what had happened.

"She'll have questions."

Mathias shrugged. "Then she can ask them."

"Did she know about Heylen?"

"You've met her. She inhales all information in her direct vicinity."

"So I should pry more?" Rayan asked.

"You pry plenty."

"You don't sound too thrilled about the idea of partnering with him."

"When have I ever sounded thrilled?"

Rayan tossed the paper onto the coffee table and cocked his head. "I know how important it is for you to push yourself. Just look at what happened with the Albanians. You get bored enough, and you start making your own fun."

"I wasn't bored. I was proving a point."

"You took it as a direct challenge."

Mathias leaned back against the sofa cushions. He had to admit there was some truth to Rayan's observation.

"It might be an interesting venture," Rayan offered. "Worthy of your talents."

Mathias recalled the figure Heylen had scrawled on the back of the sheet of paper and the man's promises of market domination. Something about it scratched an itch—the same itch he'd felt when Enzo had offered him Montreal on a silver platter. Power, respect. A part of him that small-town living hadn't managed to satisfy. Perhaps his hesitation stemmed from not wanting to upend the life they'd so carefully constructed together. Especially for Rayan, who'd known enough turmoil. Yet here the man was, giving Mathias his blessing.

The night before, Mathias had heard the tremor in Rayan's voice as he made his plea. Rayan had always been judicious when it came to his feelings about Mathias and the family. He'd never before attempted to force Mathias's hand. What Rayan didn't know was that the decision had already been made. Rayan had made it for him.

Mathias's gaze fell on the book he'd given Rayan, perched on the edge of the coffee table. It wasn't the only one either. There were more stacked on the floor by the sofa and another two on the end table.

Rayan was watching him. "It bothers you."

"The books?"

Rayan nodded.

"You don't think I'm used to it by now?"

"Used to it doesn't mean you like it."

"I like it, then." Mathias leaned over to pluck the red hardback from the table. "How many times have you read this one?"

"I've lost count."

Mathias flipped the novel open, and it landed on a page with a slip of paper lodged against the spine. He knew Rayan kept markers in his books of his favorite passages and often returned to reread them. "What's it about?"

Rayan seemed to consider the question. "A man who doesn't belong. Camus likes to play with the idea of societal rejection as a form of rebellion."

There was a thud at the front door, and Mathias snapped the book closed. He pulled himself up with a grumble.

"Go easy on him," Rayan cautioned.

Mathias yanked open the front door to find the rolled-up newspaper lying on the top step and René nowhere to be found. *That fucking kid.*

186

He bent to retrieve it, and as he straightened, a taxi pulled up outside the house. The back door opened, and a woman stepped out. She wore sunglasses and a camel coat over her billowing paisley dress. Mathias's stomach seized. Unthinking, he strode down the steps toward her, unsure whether the quickening of his pulse was from anger or fear.

"What are you doing here?"

His mother removed her sunglasses and blinked at him uncomprehendingly. "Mathias? What happened to your face?" She glanced around at the open front door and the car parked outside. "I came to see the old family house. What are... Do you live here?"

He hadn't mentioned Calais on any of his visits, and she'd never asked where he was living. She probably assumed he had an apartment somewhere in Paris. By the vitriolic way she'd talked about her father, Mathias hadn't pegged her for the type to make a nostalgic pilgrimage to her former childhood home.

His mother's face furrowed in confusion. "How...? They told me it was sold after he died."

"It was. I bought it."

"That's not possible."

"Why? Because both you and my father seemed intent on severing any claim to my heritage?"

At that moment, Rayan appeared on the front step, and Mathias watched the slow-motion collision of two separate worlds, two entirely different parts of himself. His mother's eyes widened even further, and the three of them remained unmoving, part of some absurd tableau.

"This is Rayan," Mathias said flatly. "I believe the two of you are acquainted."

His mother nodded. Rayan raised his hand in greeting and threw Mathias a tense glance before mumbling something about coffee and disappearing into the house.

Mathias stared her down, trying to read her expression. Was it disappointment? No, that would assume she'd ever actually given a shit.

But none of that mattered now. He'd found what he needed. Or more accurately, it had found him—the thing he'd tried, despite his best efforts, to convince himself he'd never wanted. And she was left with their hopeless double act—she, the unwilling mother, and he, the accidental son.

Mathias let out a resigned sigh. "Well, you're here. Might as well come in." He turned back to the house, but his mother's hand on his arm stopped him.

"Mathias..." she whispered.

187

He met her blue eyes, clouded and shiny, and Mathias felt a sharp stab in his chest. It wasn't disappointment he saw. Instead, she looked at him like it was the first time she'd seen him. As though, after a life spent lurking in her periphery, he'd finally come into view. The stab turned into an ache, tight and pulsing, yet Mathias couldn't bring himself to pull away. He hadn't realized how painful it would feel to know just how much he'd missed.

27

athias was barely awake when Rayan left the house that morning. The man had kissed the crook of Mathias's neck and murmured something in his ear about Laurent and the center, the words just touching the fog of half sleep. After he was gone, Mathias lay in bed and found his thoughts returning to his mother's surprise appearance, not for the first time in the days that had followed it.

To Marguerite's credit, after the initial shock had worn off, she'd become unusually animated. They'd sat at the kitchen table while Mathias smoked and Rayan made coffee, and she'd regaled them with tales of her father and their family growing up—spending summers at the sea as a little girl, breaking her wrist falling out of the tree in the backyard. Then she walked through the house room by room, making astonished exclamations and murmuring to herself. She showed them a hidden doorway to the attic that Mathias hadn't known about and her name carved in a child's scrawl on the inside of the wooden frame.

It was his mother as he'd never seen her, and Mathias didn't know how to reconcile this one with the version of the woman he'd spent his life reviling. When she finished her impromptu tour, she made her way back downstairs and announced that she was leaving. True to form, she'd discussed nothing salient, but she did ask him if she could visit again.

Mathias shrugged. "We'll see."

And she beamed as if he'd issued her an open invitation. He remained by the door after she'd left, his fingers lingering on the handle. Rayan stood watching from the hallway.

"That was unexpected," he said finally.

"Hmm."

"If she comes again...?"

"Lock the door."

Rayan frowned, and Mathias gave a short laugh.

"I think I can handle my own mother, Rayan."

"Do you think—"

"She knows."

Rayan let out a slow breath. "And are you...?"

"Fine."

They exchanged a look, Rayan clearly as caught off-balance as he was. "At least this time, she didn't ask where I was from."

"That woman, I swear..." Mathias said.

"You know, I'm probably not..." Rayan stopped, his eyebrows pulling together. "Someone she'd approve of."

"What a relief," Mathias said, stepping away from the door and reaching out to give Rayan's shirt collar a tug. "I've always considered it fortunate we don't see eye to eye."

Yet that wasn't what Mathias had gathered from his mother's visit. In fact, he'd had the distinct impression that she understood that neither Rayan nor their life together would ever be up for discussion.

Mathias rolled out of bed and stretched his stiff limbs. Standing in front of the bathroom mirror, he saw that the bruises on his face had already begun to fade. He showered and dressed then pulled out his phone and headed downstairs to the study. He took a seat at his desk before dialing.

Heylen picked up almost immediately. "Mathias, it's been a while."

"Here are my terms," he said, wasting no time on small talk. "I'll agree to the partnership, but ownership is split clean down the middle—none of this sixty-forty shit. I want full day-to-day control and compensation proportional to profits."

Heylen chuckled. "You're not saying anything I wasn't expecting."

"And I want to relocate the business to Calais."

There was a pause. "Now, that might be harder for the board to get behind."

The corners of Mathias's mouth curved upward. No need to make it too easy for Heylen. He wanted to see how far he could push. His terms, or he'd walk— simple as that.

"It's a decent port. Not Bruges, but big enough to meet the margins you're after. And this way, you'd be diversifying. Something shuts down operations in Belgium, and you've got a nice little alternative ticking away over here."

Heylen appeared to be thinking it over. "It's a fair point."

"You'll get your results. There'll be a longer lead-up, but I'll deliver."

"I don't doubt it," Heylen said. "Look, with me, you're golden. I just need to run it by the board. But, Mathias, this could be big."

Mathias allowed himself a smile. He felt it again—the rush of ambition, the thrill of the hunt. "It will be."

The fire that started during the riot swept through a large section of the Jungle, destroying tents and shelters and leaving hundreds of people homeless. They began to spread out into the city, squatting in parks and other public spaces. The camp hadn't even been closed yet, and Calais was already feeling the effects of what would happen if no thought were given to the future.

Rayan took no pleasure in the fact that the predictions they'd given the mayor were becoming a reality. And that reality didn't truly hit home until Rayan ran into Amer on his way back from the center one evening. The elderly schoolteacher had moved with his daughter and her children to a park near the beach after their shelter had gone up in flames. Rayan offered to help them find alternative arrangements, but Amer politely refused, too proud to accept his charity. Amer bid him good night, and Rayan walked the rest of the way home with a rock in his stomach.

"Patience," Mathias counseled him when he'd returned to the house, frustrated and disheartened. "I'm meeting with Durand on Friday. Things will get underway soon enough."

Mathias's certainty rankled him. Rayan remembered how powerless he'd felt standing in the mayor's office, listening to Durand refuse to commit city resources to a problem that wasn't his. "I don't think you realize how adamantly against this he is."

"I'm about to bring a nice chunk of Belgian profit to our fair city. The mayor won't want to see that go up in smoke."

"You've accepted Heylen's offer?"

"That's the plan, provided the board agrees to my terms."

Rayan was unable to hide his amusement. "Why am I not surprised you're making him come to you on his knees?"

"It wouldn't be a deal if he didn't."

Mathias had already taken care of the money. The stacks of cash had quietly disappeared from the house and were replaced by a folder that appeared on the kitchen table one morning. Inside the folder was a certificate of registration for a Canadian charitable trust and, beneath the certificate, a series of backdated statements detailing over a dozen meticulously recorded donations of varying amounts into the trust's account. Rayan didn't need to do the math to know that together they would equate to a tidy sum of seven million euros.

Later, when Mathias came downstairs, dressed for work, Rayan pushed the folder across the table toward him. "What's this?"

Mathias lifted the coffeepot and took his time filling his mug. "You didn't think I'd just drop it in your bank account, did you?"

"No."

"The lawyer's details are in there. If you want to move things around, give him a call, and he'll arrange it. You're not connected to the trust publicly, but you have executive control as the grantor."

Rayan felt a swell in his chest. He looked at Mathias. "You don't know what this means."

The man held his gaze, and Rayan could see that Mathias knew exactly what it meant. "Now she has no choice but to be proud."

While Farhan's tent had remained intact following the riot, the violence he'd seen that day had strengthened his resolve to find another place to live, for the sake of his daughters. At the center, Rayan had been working with Asmarina to put together a list of charitable organizations and private volunteers willing to open their doors to migrants waiting on immigration appeals. Among them was Madame Laborde, an eccentric widow who owned a large estate just outside of Calais and had been a longtime supporter of Asmarina and her work. She'd offered several of the rooms in her stately home to young families, providing them with a temporary place of refuge until other arrangements could be made.

With Asmarina's help, Rayan had managed to secure a room for Farhan and the children at Madame Laborde's estate. They'd moved out there several days earlier. When Asmarina called Rayan with an update about the progress of the family's application, he decided to deliver the news to Farhan in person. He took a taxi from the city and met Farhan at the door to a towering country house.

"The girls think they're living in a fairy tale," Farhan said with a laugh as he led Rayan through the sprawling villa.

Farhan's family had been assigned a room on the second floor. He and Rayan passed a handful of other residents on their way up the stairs. Amina and Zahra squealed when Rayan stopped in the doorway to the room. He had brought along another bag of goodies and was aware he'd practically purchased their affection by this point.

While the girls pulled each item from the bag and arranged them in a careful display on the floor, Rayan sat with Farhan on the window bench and retrieved his folder of paperwork.

"The good news is that you've been granted provisional residence status while your asylum application is being adjudicated," Rayan said, taking out the letter the lawyer had received from the immigration department on Farhan's behalf. He passed it to the man, who scanned the clunky legal terminology with a frown of confusion. "It means you can start accessing some basic social services and enroll the girls in school."

"School?" Zahra exclaimed from the floor, a box of colored pencils in her hand.

"That's right. We can get you both enrolled in one of the schools nearby."

This was exciting news for Zahra and less so for her younger sister, who was busy sorting the selection of fruit Rayan had brought in order of size.

"But how will we afford it?" Farhan asked, lowering his voice so his daughters didn't hear.

"The public schools are free."

"Even if the asylum claim isn't approved?"

"These things take time—sometimes years—and there are multiple steps involved. But with temporary residence, you can start applying for housing, even a job. You're not waiting around in limbo."

Farhan allowed for the slightest of smiles as he better understood what this meant. "So, I can work?"

Rayan nodded. "At the center, we have listings for jobs in several local industries—construction, hospitality, seasonal agriculture. Not exactly what you're used to back home—I don't think there's much going in the way of scientific research."

Farhan gave a laugh. "Work is work. I'd be happy to do something again. Madame Laborde has said we can stay here for a little while, but I'd like to find somewhere more permanent. Build something for the girls."

Rayan thought of the plans for the residential complex and the trust account with the eye-watering balance. Laurent and Asmarina had been wary of his suggestion to fund the remaining cost of the build privately, mainly because they didn't believe the center was big enough to draw the kind of mainstream appeal that larger aid agencies commanded. But Rayan had no intention of making a flashy bid for support. As far as he was concerned, the less buzz, the better. There was no need to draw attention to where the money came from. All he had to tell Asmarina and Laurent was that he'd been approached by some old contacts in Canada who'd seen coverage of the Jungle and wanted to help. Rayan would have no choice but to honor their request to remain anonymous. After all, it wasn't unusual for wealthy philanthropists to avoid the public eye. Many people preferred to do their good work on the quiet.

"Working toward something's important," Rayan agreed. "And there is hope—you're not alone. We're looking to make things better one step at a time."

Amina appeared at her father's side, a half-eaten apple in hand, and Farhan tucked a loose strand of hair behind her ear. He turned to Rayan and shook his head, perplexed. "Rayan, you've done so much already."

Now it was Rayan's turn to shake his head. "There's more to do yet."

28

Elise had been skittish around Mathias ever since Marsela's lackeys had shown up at the warehouse. He hadn't bothered with much in the way of an explanation, but she was smart enough to draw her own conclusions. The last few days, she'd been handling him with a nervous caution, sometimes forgetting long enough to make the occasional witty quip, only to catch herself and throw him a panicked look. He'd grown tired of her awkwardness, so when she arrived at the office that morning, he beckoned her over to his desk.

"Sit." Mathias gestured toward the chair across from him. He reached for the bottle of scotch and poured two small glasses.

Elise's eyes widened as she took a seat. "You're here before ten, and we're already drinking. I'm getting fired, aren't I?"

"The thought of firing you is tempting. I've certainly considered it enough."

"That's comforting."

Mathias handed her one of the glasses. "So, ask me."

Elise gripped the glass, and her mouth gave an anxious quiver. "About what?"

"Don't play dumb, Dumont. You've been tiptoeing around me all week. What do you want to know?"

Elise lifted the liquor to her lips and took a generous sip of courage. "Are you one of those Israeli secret agents?"

"You got me."

Elise scowled at his mocking tone. "You told me once your father was Italian. Do you have connections to... you know? Do you know anyone...?" She raised her eyebrows in silent implication.

Mathias shrugged. "Everyone knows someone."

"What about the gun?"

"It's for protection. We have valuable merchandise stored here."

"Rayan had one too. And he looked like he knew how to use it."

Mathias snapped his fingers. "That's right—he's with the Mossad."

Elise narrowed her eyes. "I see what you're doing. You're not going to give me anything, are you?"

"If that bothers you, go ahead and walk."

She appeared startled. "Why would I do that? I mean, it's not like you're a bad person."

"A bad person," Mathias echoed. "Now that, I can guarantee."

Elise looked at him for a moment then shook her head. "I don't believe you. Anyway, that depends, doesn't it?"

"On what?"

"Your definition."

Mathias gave a low laugh. "Well, if you're not going to walk away, I'll make you a proposal."

"A proposal?"

"I want you to take over the business."

"What?" Elise blinked. "I can't do that."

"Why not? We'd start you off with a couple shares, and over time, you can buy me out. I'm not precious. You'll get it for a bargain. And whatever profit you make, it's yours."

Elise turned the glass in her hands, chewing on her lower lip. "I don't know the first thing…"

"You know the market, the product, how to price. While you do lack a basic level of business sense, that can be taught."

"But negotiating with clients, navigating import laws—I have no idea where to start."

"So do what I did—hire someone who knows more about it than you do. Then make them do all the legwork." Mathias leaned back in his chair. "You told me yourself you liked the freedom of the job, choosing what to buy and who to sell it to. You can specialize or diversify, depending on your interests. The nature of the work was always more appealing to you than it was to me."

"This is crazy," Elise whispered. "I can't believe I'm even considering this. What are you going to do?" Then she flashed him a knowing look. "You're going to take Heylen up on his offer."

He'd received a call from Heylen the previous evening. Everything was set. The board had agreed to Mathias's terms, and the company's legal team was drafting up the partnership documents. Heylen had sounded giddy over the phone, confessing that he'd grown tired of playing it safe and had been looking for the right opportunity to make a bold move. If only he knew how bold a move he was making.

"Maybe I am."

"I'm not surprised. He's right up your league. A pair of cutthroat capitalists."

"I take that as a compliment."

Elise laughed. "You would." She shifted in her seat, and her foot hammered nervously against the floor. Mathias could almost hear the whir of her mind spinning. "Fuck it, I'll do it," she announced. "On one condition."

Mathias cocked an eyebrow. "And what's that?"

"You said business sense can be taught. I want you to be the one to teach me. I want you to be my mentor."

Mathias snorted. "I'm not going to hang around here and hold your hand, Dumont."

"That's the condition," she said, raising her glass. "I get to call you when I need help."

What's the alternative—stand back and watch her burn everything to the ground? Better to stick around long enough to make sure she has a decent run at it.

"Fine," he relented. "But I get to decide whether to answer."

"Deal." She clinked her glass against his. They threw back the scotch, and Elise broke into a grin. "We have to celebrate. This stuff's way too strong. I'm going to grab us some bubbles." She glanced at the clock on the office wall. "And maybe some orange juice."

She stepped out of the office and disappeared into the warehouse, only to return moments later, the grin gone, and her face stricken. Mathias stood, immediately on guard. He recalled the black BMW parked outside the warehouse when they'd returned from Cologne. Surely, the Albanians weren't stupid enough to come back here. He'd confirmed with Charles that they'd picked up the shipment, but that hadn't stopped him from stashing a gun in his desk just in case.

He walked past Elise into the warehouse. Through the small window on the staff door, he could see a dented blue hatchback pulled up out front. Beside it, a man was pacing agitatedly.

The ballsy little fuck. Well, Mathias was nothing if not a man of his word. He returned to the office and found Elise pressed against the far wall, her nails digging into the flesh of her forearm.

"I don't know how he found me here," she mumbled frantically. "I've been so careful."

Mathias unlocked the top drawer of his desk and pulled out his gun.

"No, Mathias!" Elise cried in horror.

"I told you if you didn't sort this, I would."

Back in the warehouse, Mathias pushed open the staff door and strode out into the parking lot.

Theo stopped pacing and glowered at him. "Where's Elise?" he called out. "Is she inside?"

Mathias continued toward him.

"You don't scare me," Theo taunted, clearly not having clocked the pistol at Mathias's side. "I know you're not fucking her. You're just a—"

Mathias slammed him against the side of the car and shoved the muzzle of the gun hard against his throat. "Go on," he said, leaning in. "Say it."

A high-pitched whimper erupted from Theo's mouth. His eyes opened so wide Mathias could see the whites all around.

"Let's hear it, you sniveling piece of shit. What were you going to call me?"

Theo shook his head rapidly. "N-Nothing."

"That's what I thought." Mathias increased the pressure so that the metal dug into the man's skin. Theo began to splutter, spittle forming at the corners of his mouth. "If you come anywhere near her again, I will string you up by your ankles and gut you like a pig. Are we clear?"

Theo nodded.

Mathias released him and raised his gun to fire one shot through the windshield of the man's car. Theo screamed, his arms flying up to protect his face as the window shattered, splinters of glass tinkling to the ground.

"Now, fuck off. The next shot won't miss."

Theo practically tripped over his own feet, trying to get back into the car. He slammed it into reverse and took off, squealing, across the parking lot toward the street. Mathias waited until the car had disappeared from view before making his way back to the warehouse. Elise stood by the staff entrance, watching him.

"Okay, first lesson," she said when he closed the door behind them. The wobble of fear was gone from her voice, and her eyes were fixed on his, cold as steel. "Teach me how to use that."

Mathias smirked. She was proving a fast learner. "There's hope for you yet."

As Mathias drove through the city toward Hôtel de Ville, it was impossible to ignore the collection of tents dotting downtown. Since the Jungle's partial closure, small camps had begun to pop up across Calais. Through the window, his gaze was caught by a woman with a baby strapped to her chest and a child in hand. Watching her, he felt a glimmer of Rayan's rage.

While Mathias tended to dismiss the man's social conscience, he also admired Rayan's refusal to simply sit back and let the situation play out. If there were a few strings Mathias could pull to nudge things along, then he was more than willing to do so. He'd been ambivalent about the opportunity to profit from Marsela's misguided venture. A deterrent was necessary to ensure that the Albanians didn't try anything like that again, but neither the drugs nor the money he stood to make from them held much appeal. Then, somewhere between returning Farhan to his daughters and Rayan announcing his plan to fund the remainder of the residence build on his own, Mathias had seen it all click into place—a way to help Rayan get what he wanted while allowing Mathias to get rid of his Albanian problem in the process. And if it meant that the likes of this woman and her two young children ended up with a better deal, well, what did that matter to him?

Mathias parked the car on the street and glanced at his watch. Right on time. When he'd contacted the mayor's office to request an appointment, he'd done so as a valued member of the Calais business community. While Durand's concern for the thousands of displaced people crowding his city was questionable, he made sure the corporate suits he hoped would bankroll his upcoming election campaign received his full attention. And as of yesterday, Mathias sat squarely in that demographic. Heylen had sent through the completed paperwork, and Mathias was now joint owner of a two-billion-euro container-shipping business headed for the Port of Calais.

Mathias walked past groups of photo-snapping tourists milling about outside the town hall. He scaled the steps to the building and strode into the lobby, where he cleared security and made his way upstairs to Durand's office.

The mayor's assistant greeted him with a bright smile. "Good morning, Mr. Beauvais. Go on through. He's expecting you."

Mathias pushed open the set of wooden doors at the end of the corridor and stepped into the office. Durand stood from behind his desk and moved to shake his hand.

"Mathias. Always happy to make time for a hardworking party supporter."

Early on, Mathias had established himself as a generous donor to Durand's affiliated party, Alliance Nationale. He'd found that front-loading favors worked best to engender credibility. It paid to be the person owed and not the other way around.

Mathias took a seat across from the mayor's desk as Durand lowered himself into his plush leather chair. "What can I help you with today?" Durand asked.

"I believe the council has been approached about the construction of a migrant residential complex."

The mayor made a face. "Don't worry—you're not the only concerned member of the public who's come forward. I made sure to shut down that idea pretty quick."

"Did you?"

"What would the rest of the country think if we were seen to roll out the welcome mat for these people?"

If the man's worried about the city's image, perhaps he should look outside his window.

"That's a shame," Mathias said. "I'm here to make you change your mind."

Durand began to laugh, glancing at Mathias as if to see if he would do the same, but Mathias remained impassive. He took a nervous sip from his steaming mug of coffee and placed it back down on the desk.

"You can't be serious, Mathias."

"Do I look like I'm joking?"

"The council vetoed the proposal. It's a nonstarter."

"Have you walked through the city recently? The camp isn't even closed yet, and there are people on every corner. What do you think Calais will look like when you bulldoze the rest?"

"There's no way we'd get public approval to fund something like that. Residents are tired of their hard-earned tax dollars being wasted on this problem."

"This problem isn't going to go away just because the people of the city are sick of it." Mathias leaned back in his chair. "I've been informed that the remaining funding has already been secured. As it turns out, the activities of our little city have caught the attention of several Good Samaritans abroad."

Durand gave a disapproving grunt. "Oh?"

"It's an embarrassment, really, having to rely on foreigners to solve our problems," Mathias went on. "What would make the situation even more embarrassing is if the local council was seen to be blocking much-needed humanitarian efforts."

The mayor's mouth flattened into a thin line.

"So, now that funding is no longer an issue, we can expect the project to be treated like any other build. The council doesn't have to pledge its support. You can remain as indifferent as you want, but when planning applications begin to trickle in, I'm sure they'll make it through without delay." Mathias reached into his jacket pocket and pulled out his cigarettes. He placed one between his lips.

"I'm afraid you can't smoke in here," Durand said.

Mathias brought the flame from his lighter to the tip of the cigarette and waited for it to catch.

The mayor shifted uncomfortably. "I don't quite understand what you're getting at, Mr. Beauvais. Perhaps it's better if—"

"I've already told you. Regardless of your views on its intended use, you will make sure the building is approved for construction. That's all. As for the hardliners, you can handle a few complaints. You're no stranger to them, after all."

The mayor shook his head. "I'm not sure I can do that."

"You're not sure?" Mathias took a pull on his cigarette and exhaled a stream of smoke into the air between them. "But you're aware of Joseph Fillon, owner of the Mermaid? I heard he got planning approval for his expansion into the building next door. Now, Fillon has twenty-odd girls on his payroll, and you and I both know they're doing more than dancing. I don't see the council getting worked up about the nature of that particular establishment."

"I'm sorry, Mr. Beauvais. But as mayor, it's my job to have the city's best interests at heart. And giving these people a reason to stay in Calais is not in its best interests."

Mathias studied the man's pensive expression. Durand sat forward in his chair, a sheen of perspiration visible along his hairline.

"Remind me, who is it you're running against this year—Gérald Dupuis? He's quite the popular candidate. A Socialist Party supporter, very progressive. It would be difficult, wouldn't it, if his campaign received sizable financial backing?"

Durand paled.

"It was only by a thin margin that you won the last runoff. Money makes all the difference in a close race like that. And it so happens I'm looking to bring a substantial amount to Calais."

"What do you mean?"

"You're familiar with Jacob Heylen."

"The Belgian billionaire? Isn't he big in the container-shipping market?"

"That's right. I can give you the numbers—the kind of revenue a company like his brings to the local economy—but I'm sure you have a fair idea. He's recently acquired a new business that he'd like me to run from here."

The mayor's eyes lit up. "Heylen is looking to open a branch in Calais?"

"Unless I convince him otherwise." Mathias held up his cigarette in demonstration. "I don't like being told no, Durand. And if I feel the city isn't overly accommodating to the needs of its business community, I may find myself backing another candidate."

Durand's forehead creased with confusion. "Why do you care about what happens to these people?"

Mathias shrugged. "Like you, Mayor, I simply want what's best for the city. But I'm less concerned with politics than I am with solutions. And what I see on the streets of Calais is not a good look for prospective investors."

Durand's expression turned contemplative. "If someone like Jacob Heylen is considering setting up shop here, that would be an enormous opportunity for a place like Calais."

"The least we can do is make a decent impression."

The mayor fell silent, his fingers idly tapping against the edge of the desk. Then he licked his lips. "Like you said, a fully funded proposal is an entirely different story. I'm sure the council would be open to reassessing the merits of a residential housing complex that doesn't require any capital investment on our part. After all, it would be in the city's interest to have a means to deal with this particular issue." He shot Mathias a complicit look and lowered his voice. "That is, assuming I can rely on your continued support."

Mathias gave a slow smile. "That wasn't so difficult, was it?"

He took one last drag on his cigarette then leaned forward and dropped it— still smoking—into the mayor's coffee.

29

Mathias gave a disapproving click of his tongue as he surveyed the tailor's handiwork. "You need to take it in here, and the cuffs are too long. He looks like a kid wearing his father's suit."

The stooped, white-haired man beside Rayan nodded rapidly.

"And here..." Mathias made a slicing motion with his hand along the hem of the tuxedo jacket. "Bring it up."

As the tailor went back to work with his tray of pins, Rayan tugged at the bow tie cutting into his neck.

"Stop fiddling with it," Mathias scolded.

"I feel ridiculous."

"You'll look ridiculous if we don't get the fit right." Mathias tilted his head, eyes narrowing. "Not this one."

He deftly unknotted the bow tie and yanked it off then selected another—slimmer, the fabric less glossy—from the row of boxes on the table and looped it around Rayan's neck. Mathias took an end in each hand and tied it expertly, pulling the knot tight against the collar of Rayan's pristine white shirt. He stepped back and gave Rayan a once-over.

"Now we just have to figure out what to do with that mop on your head."

"I'm growing it out."

"The fuck you are. Keep this up, and I'll take Elise instead."

Mathias was representing Heylen and the company at a European business summit in Copenhagen. The congregation would be joined by the Danish crown prince for the opening gala dinner and had been given strict instructions on dress code.

When Mathias had asked Rayan to come with him, Rayan had assumed he would hang around the hotel, maybe explore on his own for a bit. Rayan hadn't anticipated his attendance at the black-tie function. Secretly, he'd been overjoyed, partly because of the sheer extravagance of the event but mostly because Mathias wanted to share it with him.

"Go ahead," Rayan said. "I'm sure she'll make a wonderful impression." Elise was many things, but poised and muted in company, she was not.

Mathias scowled. "You're as bad as each other. At least you double as security."

Elise had taken over Importations Fleurdelisé, and from the little Rayan heard about it from Mathias, she hadn't yet set the warehouse on fire. Mathias still got calls from her occasionally. Some of them, he picked up, using the opportunity to remind her of her staggering ignorance. Other times, he would glance at her number on the screen and hang up without answering. Rayan knew Mathias got a kick out of leaving Elise to deal with her own problems. He didn't want her getting too comfortable.

When Mathias was satisfied with the fitting, Rayan went behind the curtain to change. He emerged to find Mathias standing outside the boutique, his phone pressed to his ear and a sour look on his face. "I need to stop by the office to sign some papers," he said after he hung up. "It won't take long. I'll drop you home first."

"I can wait."

Mathias shrugged. "Suit yourself."

They got into the car, and Mathias pulled into traffic, heading in the direction of the port. The office Heylen had commissioned for the company in Calais encompassed the top floor of a large operations building that overlooked the outer harbor. Mathias oversaw a staff of sixty—customs brokers, marine technicians, dock workers. He'd thrown himself into the partnership with his signature proficiency and blown all of Heylen's earnings predictions out of the water. Something had settled in him, the restlessness tamed as his reputation began to grow among Europe's corporate elite.

"Can you swing past the site on the way?" Rayan asked. "Just for a minute." They were so close it would barely count as a detour.

"This is turning into quite the compulsion," Mathias grumbled, but he hit the turn signal and moved into the other lane. "I'll tell you what's changed since yesterday—not a fucking thing. Wait until there's some actual progress."

Rayan grinned. "I like to see the pieces coming together."

Mathias parked across the street from the construction site, and they both got out of the car. Rayan found his gaze drawn first to the sign at the entrance to the site. It wasn't anything special, just the name of the building in simple black type printed on a white board held up by two wooden posts. When Rayan had told Laurent and Asmarina that he'd secured the remaining funding for the build, Asmarina had insisted—despite his protests—that he get naming rights.

Mathias pulled out his pack of smokes. "See? Same as before."

Rayan angled his head, noting the new framework they'd erected since the previous day. Mathias was wrong. Each time Rayan came, he saw incremental progress, the project one tiny step closer to completion.

Once the city had green-lit the proposal, things had moved surprisingly fast. Mathias had told him not to worry about the mayor, and as of yet, they hadn't run into any issues from town hall. The parcel of public land, not far from the existing camp, had sat empty for decades, and when they'd applied for planning approval, the council had granted it without incident—along with each permit that followed.

A brief announcement in the newspaper had been met with surprising positivity, not just from residents of Calais but other surrounding towns as well. It turned out they weren't the only ones wanting to improve the situation for those who continued to flock to Northern France in search of safety. In the wake of the attention, Durand seemed to have changed his tune. He lapped up the praise, taking credit for helping facilitate the build. He'd even held off on demolishing the remainder of the camp in the meantime, so the Jungle persevered, increasingly crowded and dangerous but still a home to many. Rayan didn't give a shit about credit. All he wanted was to see the project realized. And every day, after work, he made the trip from the center or the service office to walk past the site.

"You know it's just a drop in the bucket," Mathias said, lighting the cigarette between his teeth. "This doesn't solve anything."

"I know. But it's a roof over someone's head, temporary as it may be."

"And you're not fazed that it's built with dirty money?"

"I'm not exactly squeaky-clean myself."

Mathias smirked and exhaled a stream of smoke from his nostrils. "Maybe you have learned something."

"That I can use what I have to do better?"

"No. Christ." Mathias's upper lip curled in disgust. "Never hesitate to exploit a weakness. That's the real lesson here."

Rayan laughed.

They stood and watched as several workers loaded a platform with steel beams and attached it to the hook block of a nearby crane. Once it was secure, the men stepped back, and one of them raised his hand to the operator in the cab. The cable went taut, and the platform slowly began to lift off the ground.

"You figure it'll be another six months?" Mathias asked, watching the swinging platform move through the air.

"If there are no delays. Construction's slowed across the city, so they're making the most of the work."

"And the wait-list—has it been finalized?"

"Almost. We don't want to tell families until we're sure they have a place."

"I don't have to guess who'll be at the top of that list."

"It's not preferential treatment," Rayan protested weakly. "Farhan's still waiting on his asylum appeal, and the girls need a stable place to live while they're attending school. They're exactly who we had in mind when we envisioned this place."

Mathias snickered. "Who knows? You could even scale it. The city might just prove accommodating with future projects."

Trust Mathias to see how to build on an opportunity.

The residence was a promising step in the right direction, but there remained a growing need for housing support in both Calais and the surrounding townships. There was potential for this to be bigger still. Rayan had narrowed his focus to good deeds, forgetting that resourcefulness, a dash of friendly intimidation, and a fair amount of tenacity went a long way toward getting results. The meeting of those two strengths—Rayan's desire to help and the skills he'd gained from a life spent gaming the system—was actually rather brilliant. Here they both were, on full display, the conflicting sides of himself merged to create a universal good.

Mathias tapped his ash. "So, you break even yet? Or is the ledger still skewed in one direction?"

"Thought you told me not to think like that."

"Knowing and believing aren't the same thing."

"Considering the murky means by which the funding came about, the ethics of the endeavor are debatable."

"Think of it as a donation from one criminal to another."

"Do we still get to call you that?" Rayan took in the expensive suit, the perfectly slicked-back hair, and the air of authority that radiated from the man. Nothing had changed there. Mathias looked as he had the day they'd first met—yet, at the same time, entirely different. "Careful, Mathias. You're in danger of becoming a decent human being."

Mathias shot him a dirty look. "That's why I've got you to keep me honest."

"You always will," Rayan said with a smile.

The crane hoisted the platform high into the cloudless blue sky, and Rayan's eyes were once again drawn to the sign: Maison Résidence Samira Ayari.

Maybe, just maybe, she would be proud of him—for surviving, for making it here. And if pride was a swing too far, perhaps she could settle on forgiveness—the way he had forgiven her.

Mathias took another pull on his cigarette and squinted up at the half-finished masterpiece bearing Rayan's mother's name. "Take it in, Rayan. This is your legacy."

"No," Rayan replied, turning to the man beside him. "It's ours."

Epilogue

OTTAWA

I 'd like you to run the names again then get the results to legal," Frances said into the phone, swiveling in her chair to look at the rain sliding down the window. From her office on the fifth floor of the RCMP Headquarters Building, she could see out across the Rideau River. "That's right. They'll take it from there."

She hung up and began gathering the printouts for her next meeting. There was a knock at the door.

"Come in," Frances said.

It was Sergeant Ellen Ling, a promising young officer that Frances had selected to work under her when she first transferred divisions. "I have your uniform for the ceremony on Friday, Superintendent."

Technically, Frances was still Inspector until Friday, but she wasn't about to quibble over the details. She shuffled the documents into a folder and got to her feet, tucking the folder under her arm. "Thank you, Sergeant. Just hang it by the door."

But Ling hovered in place, her expression perplexed. "There's just one thing."

"And what's that?"

"With all due respect, Superintendent," Ling said hesitantly. "I don't think it will fit."

They both looked down at Frances's protruding belly, well past remaining hidden behind the starched confines of her scarlet Mountie jacket.

"Right." Sometimes Frances felt if it weren't for the baby getting between her and her shoelaces each morning, she was in danger of forgetting it was there.

"There's a maternity uniform I can request if you'd like," Ling offered. "I wanted to check with you first."

Frances understood the sergeant's caution. She hadn't been overly forthcoming about the pregnancy, waiting until she was clearly showing before

208

mentioning anything at work. She'd been unable to get over the suspicion that it would set her back professionally—a fear that had so far proven unfounded. The agency had been almost irritatingly supportive. *They have a maternity uniform, for Chrissakes.*

Frances nodded. "Let's go with that."

In the end, her long-awaited promotion hadn't come about from her closing a high-profile case but because of her dogged commitment to the job. After returning from Montreal, she'd requested a transfer out of Organized Crime and into the Professional Ethics Office. When a leadership opening came up a year later, Deputy Commissioner Gill had put her forward for the promotion. She'd received the confirmation exactly three weeks before her fortieth birthday and two months before her due date.

Working at the Ethics Office kept her in Ottawa full-time, so she was there for Diana and the kids—for every birthday party and dance recital. It made Frances feel grounded and gave her the space to take stock of what she wanted. And she wasn't sure that still involved cornering criminals in abandoned warehouses. There was plenty of good policing she could do without having to take an axe to her personal life.

As an unintended consequence of being back in the city, she'd often found herself bumping into Ethan. It happened frequently enough that they started joking that maybe the universe was trying to tell them something. He and the vet hadn't worked out, and he'd dropped a few hints about the hypothetical coffee date he had been trying to get Frances to commit to—something planned instead of their impromptu run-ins. Despite her misgivings—she didn't want to fuck things up again—Frances finally relented. Coffee had progressed to work lunches, then movies and dinner, and before she knew it, she was spending several nights a week at his apartment.

Being with Ethan was like finding a missing piece of herself. She was a different person when she was with him, and she liked that version far better than the one without him. Things were easy between them, their shared history filling in all the awkward gaps. It was as though, having been to the brink and back, they'd seen the worst of each other without losing the love, and it frightened her to think how close she'd come to throwing that away.

She was the one who asked if he'd consider moving back in. When Ethan agreed, he said it was only because she needed the furniture. The last time around, she'd been the more ambivalent of the two, dragging her feet when Ethan brought up joint checking accounts and engagement rings. Now Frances knew what they had was worth fighting for.

If she had anyone to thank for that realization, it was Mathias fucking Beauvais. When the Montreal underground had unexpectedly imploded, she'd watched the developments with a mixture of shock and relief. She knew for certain that if Mathias had remained in Canada, he would be the one filling the power vacuum Giovanni Bianchi's assassination had left behind, and she could only imagine what would have come from that. Forced to choose, she regarded Bianchi as the lesser of the two evils.

A part of her wondered if news of the family's plight would compel him to crawl out of the woodwork, yet she'd heard nothing, not even rumors. It seemed the man had well and truly disappeared. For a while, after she'd returned to Ottawa, Frances had made a half-hearted attempt to track Mathias down. She'd felt like Captain Ahab, obsessed with the one that got away. And then, eventually, she'd given that up as well, finally conceding her win.

Once Sergeant Ling left, Frances stepped out of her office and headed down the hall to the conference room, where Inspector Dixon was waiting. They were meeting to discuss the handling of several of her cases while she was away.

"Allen," Dixon announced when she walked into the room. "Must be looking forward to putting your feet up."

"I can see why you're in a rush to have me gone," she retorted, pulling out a chair and taking a seat. "I manage to run circles around you even while growing a tiny human. Me going on leave makes you look better."

Dixon laughed. "You know we're all desperate to have you back."

She and Ethan hadn't exactly planned for it to happen, but they also hadn't done anything to prevent it. She'd already made her peace with the fact that, biologically, kids were not in the cards for her, so it had come as quite a surprise when her body decided otherwise. Ethan was more than thrilled. Shortly after finding out, they'd been lying in bed one morning when he'd gently broached the subject of marriage.

"What if I proposed with the ring around a pacifier?" he teased, tucking a loose strand of hair behind her ear. "I call it double entrapment."

Frances laughed and swatted his hand away. "I can't decide which is more heinous, that or a shotgun wedding."

They decided to wait until after the baby was born. That way, they could all be there, even if the kid was too young to remember. They would have a simple ceremony down at city hall, just their little family of three. Diana, of course, was devastated. Apparently, she'd been planning Frances's wedding since the sixth grade.

It was a girl. But only Frances knew that. Not one to leave anything to chance, she'd insisted on finding out. Ethan had sworn her to secrecy. He'd already informed his boss of his plans to quit after the baby arrived and seemed unnervingly ready for life as a stay-at-home dad. He'd made her late for work twice already by serenading her belly with acoustic covers of his favorite Radiohead songs.

Sometimes his devotion to their unborn daughter made her nervous, not because she wasn't convinced he would be a wonderful father but because it made her question whether she was equipped to be a mother. She'd never been particularly maternal or prone to sweeping emotion. Yet sometimes, when Frances was alone and felt the baby kick, she was struck by something indescribable—scary and beautiful at the same time.

She took that as a good sign. While she was a rookie when it came to most things about motherhood, she'd learned, in her years of police work, that *scary* was something she could handle.

FREE SHORT STORY
A Life Chosen: The Lost Week

It started out as a joke, nothing more than a rumor: someone was going around Montreal pretending to be a member of the family.

This story takes place shortly before the events of Chapter Ten in *A Life Chosen*, Book I of the Montreal series. It covers a week in the life of Mathias and Rayan as they hunt down an imposter passing himself off as a member of the family and find themselves felled by an unexpected foe.

Get your free copy at **sydneyrutherford.com/the-lost-week**

About the Author

Sydney Rutherford is fond of travel, a morally ambiguous protagonist, and the fragility of the human condition. She writes contemporary m/m romance with a penchant for noir, and currently resides in Aotearoa New Zealand.

Find out more about her books at sydneyrutherford.com or sign up to the mailing list for bonus content and upcoming releases.

Thank you for reading. If you enjoyed this book, please leave a review.

www.ingramcontent.com/pod-product-compliance
Lightning Source LLC
Chambersburg PA
CBHW051249250626
47155CB00009B/3221